DYING for DOMINOES

JANE ELZEY

Scorpius Carta
Arkansas

DYING FOR DOMINOES

Copyright © 2020 Jane Elzey.

Scorpius Carta Press
P.O. Box 11, Beaver, AR 72613

First Scorpius Carta Press Digital edition: May 2020
ISBN 978-1-7346428-0-3 Hardback Edition
ISBN 978-1-7346428-1-0 Paperback Edition
ISBN 978-1-7346428-2-7 Ebook Edition

The interior of this book is typeset in Adobe Caslon Pro.

Book and Cover design by Bailey McGinn
www.baileydesignsbooks.com

For Marjorie

"Use all the abundance you possess."

—EUDORA WELTY

CHAPTER ONE

"Five."

"Five."

"Fifteen."

"Twenty-five!" Amy yelled and slapped the domino tile on the table with a loud clack. *Whoo-hoo!* If every game went like this one, no one was going to break her winning streak. Not this year. Maybe she was a bit over-the-top giddy, but she didn't care. Capturing that Tiddlywinks title was worth it, even if it was only a thrift store trophy with bragging rights.

Zelda's hand, poised with the scorekeeper's pen, slowly counted the pips at the end of the tiles in play. Just like Zelda to be painstakingly accurate when the score wasn't hers.

"Twenty-five," Zelda agreed and marked Amy's score.

"Take that to the boneyard," Amy said, playfully driving the dig deeper. "It's your turn, Genna. Count 'em and weep."

"*Cheeeeater*," Genna drawled, stretching the word like saltwater taffy. "You're not winning this game, Miss Amy 'Big Points' Sparks.

I'm taking you to the boneyard. I'm going to—" Genna stopped like an absentminded professor as she studied the domino tiles in her hand. "Dang," she said after a long pause and shook her head. Genna pursed her lips, and the smoke from her cigarette curled around her face before it floated off in a breeze full of wisteria and birdsong.

"No points?" Amy teased, watching Genna's eyes narrow. She knew her tortured look was fake. Genna was almost a good sport. *Almost.* "You can't make *any* points from that pile of bones you're hoarding over there?"

"Next round," Genna promised, pointing at Amy with two manicured fingers that held a cigarette just as long and thin. "Just you wait, my pretty."

"Oh, you don't have enough time in your hourglass, dearie. Unless you've got some hocus-pocus up your sleeve." Which, she could only hope, Genna did not. If anyone could beat her at dominoes it would be Genna, who was a clever player an even better cheater, if she was honest with herself.

"Aren't you on fire today?" Zelda said. "You're as sassy as Julia Sugarbaker after a top-shelf margarita."

"Sugar who?" Rian asked.

Zelda shook her head in disbelief. "Where were you in the eighties, Rian? Don't you remember *Designing Women*? They were all Southern sass, curly perms, and big earrings."

Rian shook her head and Amy settled her shoulders. "As it happens, I know *Suzanne* Sugarbaker. She was a friend in high school."

"I can't believe that," Genna said, pouring herself another glass of wine. "Suzanne didn't exist when you were in high school. If you're as old as I think you are."

"Okay, so I went to high school with the actress who later *played* Suzanne Sugarbaker. And she could have been one of my best friends, except she didn't know I existed. She was a senior prom queen and I was a goofy freshman."

"*Goofy* I might believe," Genna said with a grin. "You know they were all friends with Bill and Hillary." With her lips curved into a plump crimson smile, only the faintest laugh lines formed around Genna's mouth and crayon sky-blue eyes. *Ageless* was how Amy described her. Genna had been forty-nine and holding for more than a decade now. So what was it? Magic? Or the face creams she imported from France? Whatever it was, Genna looked like the youngest member of the foursome rather than the oldest.

"And as for hocus-pocus," Genna continued, "I have more of that in my pinky than you'll ever know." Genna witch-wiggled her fingers at Amy. "And then I've got voodoo, hoodoo, and panache in all the rest," she added, twirling her fingers in the air in a final flourish.

Rian laughed and held up her thumbs. "Is that like Sleepy, Creepy, and Doc?"

Genna ignored the gibe with a huff. "This is a game for stratagem, my friends. It needs ruse and subterfuge—machination, timing, and tempo. It takes prowess . . ." Genna paused to puff her cigarette. "And some good bones. Which I do not have."

"Five hundred dollar words and a five-point score," Zelda said. "I'm not impressed."

Amy laughed brightly. Where would she be without her best friends? In front of the television with a remote and a pint of Ben and Jerry's, most likely. Their dominoes game was the highlight of her week. Their friendship was the closest thing to sisterhood she would ever have. They gathered weekly on the deck at Genna's house when the spring sunshine warmed the air enough to let them outdoors without a coat and gloves. Because smoking wasn't allowed at the Cardboard Cottage, they had all agreed Genna's deck was the best place to let their alter egos shine. Not that they were Dr. Jekylls and Ms. Hydes. They were successful businesswomen, but they did enjoy an excuse to let Sassy, Silly, and Tipsy come out to play.

They gathered under cover of an old wisteria vine that had grown into a twisted, gnarly pergola. Today it was a fragrant purple haze, and dominoes season had just begun.

Amy looked down at the table. The dregs of tapas and wine cluttered the glass surface where the dominoes marked a path like a Mayan tattoo. *Arkansas, the Natural State,* beckoned from the bottom of an ashtray overflowing with Genna's cigarette butts and one fat roach of some of the best bud Rian had ever grown.

Amy fingered the dominoes in front of her like a prized pile of jewels. She loved everything about this game: the sound dominoes made against the table's glass surface, the girls' acerbic banter and bickering over scores, and the final coup when there was one proud winner and three sore losers.

Late afternoon sun fell over her shoulder and flashed on the rhinestones in the dominoes. Blue-and-orange sparks of light glittered off the Swarovski pips in the dominoes set that cost her two hundred bucks.

It was an extravagance she couldn't afford, not since she had just bought the building and begun stocking the store. Every resource—cash and credit—was at its limit. Still, she had to have them. There was no walking away from dominoes with bling. Smiling at the salesclerk, credit card extended, she had given a silent and heartfelt plea to *Juno Moneta,* Roman goddess and ruler of money and minimum payments. Go, *Juno Moneta!*

And today, for the third week in a row, she was winning at dominoes. *Machination, my foot!* Skill and luck and good bones were what it took to win.

Turning her attention to Zelda, she asked, "How are the birthday cruise plans going? Is Zack still going to pay for it? It's okay if he doesn't. We can all pay our way if we don't go anywhere too expensive."

"Nope," Zelda said with more fervor than Amy expected. Zelda karate-chopped the air in front of her. "It's all on his tab. I don't care how broke he says he is. I don't care if we cruise to Mexico or the Mediterranean, but I want to celebrate my five-oh with my best friends, and he's going to pay for it." She chopped the air again to accent each word. "Every. Single. Penny. Whatever it takes. Even if that includes a get-out-of-jail-free lawyer." Zelda cast a knowing look at Rian.

"I know my border crossing didn't go as planned," Rian said. "Can't I ever live that down? I thought *el cabrón* meant captain, as in leader of the guard. Anyway, what's a grand among amigas and thieves?"

"Three grand," Genna corrected. "Your Spanish is awful." Genna took a drag on her cigarette and glanced at Zelda. "Wait, you said Zack says he's broke? That can't be true."

"You're right. If he can afford a Hummer, he can afford our cruise," Zelda replied. "I know he has money stashed somewhere. All I'm saying is he owes me this and I'm not giving in. He needs to put out or get out. That's it." Zelda gave the air one last chop.

"Well, hellfire," Genna added, her eyes darting to Rian and back to Zelda. "It's your birthday, and you should laud the day with divertissement. I'll even write a panegyric to read while we're afloat."

"Oh jeez," Rian muttered. "What's a panegyric?"

"I'm still stuck on divertissement," Amy said. "And it's your turn, Zelda."

"Hellfire," Zelda echoed absently. Her eyes were on the bones cupped in her hand. "I can't talk about it right this minute. I have to count."

"Use your toes," Amy said.

"Use Amy's toes. They match the pips," Rian mused.

"'Sunrise Surprise Tequila,'" she said, wiggling her toes in her sandals.

"That's the name of this color."

"No surprise to tequila." Rian shivered to make her point. "After our last bottle of *Patrón*, Zelda slept in a canoe with a zoo of daddy longlegs. Or so she claimed." Rian eyed Zelda with suspicion. "I, however, don't remember a thing."

"We sent you home in a one-horse open sleigh," Genna said. "The horse's name was Charlie."

"We sent you home in a cab," Amy corrected. "The cab driver's name was Charlie."

"Hush . . ." Zelda warned. "I can't count with y'all making so much noise." Zelda closed French tips around the dominoes, dark head bouncing softly as she counted the dots. Her eyes betrayed her when she saw the play in her hands.

"Ten!" Zelda yelped triumphantly, banging the tile against the glass, and then marked another X on the score sheet. Zelda proudly patted her hair, which was currently the color of a good batch of brownies—and not the kind that Rian made for friends enduring chemo. "Zack's being stubborn and I don't like it," Zelda snapped. "I just need him to go away. Disappear. Vamoose." She snapped her fingers. "Like magic."

"Hoodoo," Genna added.

"Hey, Houdini, work on making this disappear." Rian lit the roach with the grill lighter, raising her eyebrows to keep them from catching fire. She handed it to Zelda, who chuckled and exhaled through pursed lips.

A lull in their conversation drew them into the quiet as the Ozarks dusk draped over them. The sun fell behind a canopy of black walnut trees just starting to flaunt the chartreuse of their late-blooming leaves. Genna lighted the lanterns on the corners of the railing, and the deck sprang into a shadow play of light, dark, and drama. Then, putting a flame to the kindling already set in the chiminea, the fire sprang into existence, spreading its warmth and light into the darkness. With the sun now hiding behind the mountains, the temperature dropped, and they drew their sweaters around them. Rian pulled a ball cap from her pocket and covered her head.

Their eyes sparkled in the flickering light. Shadows made gross caricatures of their movements, their arms long and exaggerated like monsters. Only the clank of the tiles remained the same.

"I am as serious as a heart attack," Zelda said, finally breaking the silence with a clank of her blank five. "I need to get rid of Zack. Vamoose. And y'all need to help me."

Amy's stomach clenched. The hair on the back of her neck prickled. Get rid of him? The silence ticked off the seconds like a chess clock in her head.

Rian slammed the table with a double blank. "You're a hoot! And that's five points."

"Wait? What? Gone as in divorced? Or, gone as in dead?" Amy asked.

"There's nothing better than a dead husband, I've been known to say," Genna offered, poking Rian with the butt of the lighter. "Seeing how I've buried two. God rest their souls."

"Nothing better than a *stiff* husband, I've known you to say more than once," Rian countered.

"Oh, this is good! This could be 'The Viagra Murder'!" Genna drummed her fingers over an imaginary keyboard. "The headline reads: *Stiff, Stiffer, Stiffest. If it lasts more than four hours, consult your medical examiner.*" Genna giggled. Then she laughed harder, drawing everyone's full attention. Then her breath stuck in her throat and then Genna snorted wine out of her nose.

Everyone howled.

"If you were completely serious—" Genna said, catching her breath.

"Which you're not," Amy interrupted. "Zelda is *not* serious."

"We could host a murder mystery party where no one would know who killed him," Genna continued. "We could hold the party at Tiddlywinks and invite the whole town."

"That's wrong on so many levels," Rian said. "I don't even know where to start."

Genna shook her head. "Nah, that won't work. Dead isn't that easy."

Rian rolled her eyes. "I can't believe you just said dead isn't that *sexy*."

"I said, dead isn't *easy*. You need a hearing aid."

"I need another drink," Zelda added.

"We need coffee," Amy argued and quickly left the deck.

The routine was familiar in Genna's kitchen. She leaned against the counter, mesmerized by the drip. The coffee brewed while she stewed. What was Zelda talking about? Divorce? Or something more sinister? Did she want him gone? As in dead and gone? Or just out of her life? She knew the marriage had soured as Zelda often complained that Zack was demanding and secretive.

If Zelda wanted Zack out her life, he had to go. *Vamoose! We'll show you vamoose, Zack Carlisle!*

Amy returned to the table, satisfied with her solidarity, bearing an insulated pot and four mugs like a warrior bringing spoils of war. She found the three of them uncharacteristically quiet. Handing Rian a mug, she silently marveled at her hands. Always so clean for someone who dug in the dirt for a living. Rian leaned back in her chair, cradling the cup in front of her chest, and then turned her gaze toward the horizon of dark mountain peaks, a faraway look in her espresso-brown eyes.

The evening had taken a strange turn, and Amy wanted desperately to recapture the gaiety and lightheartedness of the game. She noticed Zelda's fingers toying with her bracelets, realizing, even in the flickering light, that the stylish collection of bangles covered bruises that had not yet yellowed on top of bruises that had. Zelda lowered her gaze and shuffled the jewelry in place.

"Dead could be easy," Rian said finally, bringing her gaze back to her friends. "It's getting rid of the dead that gets you caught in the end."

"That's because dead bodies weigh a lot," said Genna with confidence.

Know-It-All Genna, who weighed all of 120 pounds in wet jeans.

Rian shook her head, scattering her shoulder-length brown curls. "Bodies don't weigh any more dead than they do alive. They say the soul weighs twenty-one grams, so a body may even be lighter dead.

"If you believe in souls," she added.

Zelda cleared her throat. "Then what do you mean it could be easy?"

"No one gets caught in the killing," Rian continued. "They get caught afterward trying to get rid of the body. Maybe someone finds it rolled up in a carpet. Or dumped in a shallow grave when a coyote drags out a femur."

"You watch too much Crime Time TV." Amy wished they were talking about anything else.

"And you work for Dial-a-Psycho."

She felt her chin jerk in defiance. "I do not. I don't have psychic powers. I have, I have . . ."

"You have too many points in this game," Genna snapped. "Are you using your psychic powers to predict the dots?"

"I'm not psychic."

"What do you call it then?"

"A pain in the butt. Just like you."

Zelda leaned forward and whispered, "How *do you* get rid of a dead body?"

Genna leaned in and whispered, "We put it in a suitcase and drop it overboard on the cruise. I have a big one and it's on wheels."

The corners of Zelda's mouth lifted into a smile then quickly disappeared.

"You're teasing," Amy said, holding Zelda's gaze with her own.

Rian laughed and raised her glass. "Thank goodness we're all just stoned and not that stupid."

She shivered as Zelda's laugh rang loud in the dark, and then suddenly, her dominoes victory felt hollow, like a diseased tree left to rot.

CHAPTER TWO

Amy stood at the door that separated her private life from the rest of Bluff Springs. Bending down to rub Victor's soft tabby coat, she petted him until he purred, tweaked his whiskers, and then opened the door that led from her apartment above the shop. Victor, meaning *the winner of the game* in Latin, was her lucky cat. He spent his days at Tiddlywinks in the sunshine of the front window or draped across the back of the wingback chair, loving every minute of attention he received from Tiddlywinks patrons. He was a beautiful Maine coon tabby, and a great draw to tourists passing by the Tiddlywinks window.

Now dashing down the stairs ahead of her, he waited impatiently, tail snapping as the familiar scent of freshly baked crumpets and cinnamon drew her slowly down the creaking stairs.

When she moved in, she painted the stairs bright blue and strung white Christmas lights along the handrail to light the darkness of a stairwell without windows. Her favorite places in Mexico looked like this. Azure blue paint and twinkling lights made her remember that festival feeling, and, like in Mexico, *el gato* waited at the bottom of the stairs.

Opening the door that led outside, she and Victor stepped out on the sidewalk and passed under the hanging sign of the Cardboard Cottage & Company, all curlicues and painted daisies. From apartment to shop was a twenty-nine-step commute to work, including the stairs. Who could beat that! Still grinning at her victory by a landslide at the domino table—winning streak still unbroken— she hopped over the last two steps of the hopscotch drawn on the sidewalk that led to the main entrance, with Victor now meowing at the door.

As she unlocked the door with the ornate antique key, she entered, feeling pride she had never known before this. For the first time in her life, she was anchored to a place and time. She was part of something good. Really good. Tiddlywinks was a fun business. Her home was right above the shop, and her cat was happy to greet customers all day long. She had best friends—a sisterhood if she could dare say it. Something she had never known growing up as an only child in a family as restless as gypsies. Even better, this little clutch of women carved out their lives in the most eclectic ways that were never dull, never boring.

She patted the ancient oak doorframe as if it, too, were a loyal friend. The Cardboard Cottage & Company was housed in a Victorian-era building that, throughout the many decades, housed tenant couples who had probably argued passionately and then made love. She could feel their history in the echo of the plank floors and in the scent left behind in closets and cupboards.

The feeling wasn't about paranormal residue or pesky ghosts. No, this building made her feel buoyant. From the moment she entered with the sales agent, she knew the building had to be hers. She also knew she couldn't possibly afford such a place as this.

And yet, the pieces had fallen into place like numbers in a sudoku grid.

The banknote had been the biggest, scariest commitment she had ever made. And she couldn't be happier to have taken the step.

Bluff Springs was a magical little tourist town where people came to spend a few days of quiet before returning to their busy lives in the city. Compared to cities she grew up in, Bluff Springs felt like Never-Never Land. It was Never Land. It was a quirky town in the Ozarks of Arkansas, not too far from the Missouri border. Its population barely broke six thousand, a swelling of artists and shopkeepers whose dwellings were wedged into the rock bluffs as ancient as time itself. It was a darling little town that drew people in, much like the *Lost Boys* of Barrie's tale. Grateful it had drawn her in, she wasn't moving anywhere. Not anytime soon.

The day was still early when she opened the interior door to Tiddlywinks Players Club, knowing the other shops in the Cardboard Cottage & Company would be opening soon. The yeasty smells coming from the Crumpets and Cones bakery that also shared the building were already drawing customers to the window display outside.

As she turned on the overhead lights, the room sprang to life. Old polished wood and musty cardboard greeted her. Bookshelves lined the room, and colorful cardboard boxes and tins lined the shelves. Like a library, they spoke of other realms to explore. Like a library, Tiddlywinks Players Club was a place to recapture memories and a place to make them new.

The best part of her shop was watching customers' eyes light up when they spied a game they hadn't played since childhood. It didn't matter whether they were age sixty or twenty-nine, time turned back just a little when they turned the corner into her shop.

It felt good to give strangers a little jolt of joy.

While she dusted the tables with her pheasant feather duster, another gift from Zelda, Victor patrolled the room before he landed in a sunny spot in the window for his morning bath ritual.

As she playfully batted him with the duster, something caught her eye. A man was watching her from across the street—or so it seemed. He was leaning against the building, the dark calico colors of the stone wall nearly camouflaging his thin frame. He turned his head slightly, and the sun reflected from his glasses. Even though she didn't recognize him, she raised her hand in greeting and then stopped as he turned curtly and walked away.

She moved from the window and finished dusting then caught a whiff of her best friend before she heard the *clop-clop* of her Jimmy Choo mules on the hardwood floor.

"*Yoo-hoo,*" Zelda called as she passed the open door of Tiddlywinks, heading for her shop. Amy followed the scent down the hall. Spice, amber, and sandalwood—deep, dark, and exotic—trailed through the air.

Zelda's shop, Zsa Zsa Galore Décor, wasn't much more than a cubbyhole. The room had been a butler's pantry in its first lifetime. Now it was a bright collage of shabby chic and upscale collectibles for the happy homemaker not on a budget. People loved Zelda's cozy style and seemed willing to pay almost any price for it.

An interior designer by schooling and a housewife by trade, Zelda was quickly turning her tiny shop into a lucrative business. It had been Zelda's idea to turn each of the main rooms of the building into retail space for lease. Credit where credit was due. It was Zelda's idea and Genna's business plan that made it possible to secure the banknote. On top of that, Zelda claimed her cubbyhole spot, named a generous rent price, and set up shop. Zelda was generous to a fault, and those were the best kind of friends to have.

Standing in the hallway, she watched as Zelda pulled a wagon filled with bright pillows into the hall to prop open the door, where a hand-lettered script greeted the customers:

I like a mannish man who knows how to treat a woman—not just a man with muscles. –Zsa Zsa Gabor

Paraphrased for the sake of space, for sure, but the sign fit Zelda, who had been married four times, herself.

"Don't tell me you don't have a hangover," Zelda said to Amy when she looked up from her task.

"I won't, then. You know two aspirin before bedtime does the trick."

"Ha!" Zelda put a hand to her temple. Her dark hair flipped slightly below a rounded chin that fit perfectly with a generous smile and deep-set green eyes. "Let's not do that again."

"*Right*," she agreed with sarcasm. "We *never* overindulge on game night."

Zelda plumped the pillows again before arranging them just so.

"It was a great game. And victory was mine yet again."

"Oh, don't gloat," Zelda warned. "We had enough of that last night, too."

The jangle of the bell on the main door caught her ear, and she looked up as a group of tourists made their way to Crumpets and Cones, the delicious smells likely dragging them in by their salivary glands. The last of the group entering the Cardboard Cottage lagged, coming in with a bit of odd hesitancy before turning away from the bakery and entering Tiddlywinks instead.

"Gotta go," she said as the visitor disappeared through the door of Tiddlywinks. "Good morning!" she called cheerfully as she entered. A man was standing at the glass curio case, his back turned to her. Turning at her words, he nodded a greeting. She stopped mid-step. The hair on her arms tingled as if pulled by a magnet. This was the same man she had noticed watching from across the street.

As a small community, most residents knew each other by sight if not by name in Bluff Springs. She didn't know his face.

"Is there something specific you're looking for?" she asked, her tone terser than she wanted.

He didn't respond.

"We have games from every era. We have new games, used games, even vintage games," she explained, trying to brighten her tone, then motioned to the curio cabinet. "We also have collector's items. As you can see, we have a few rare games from antiquity."

The glass cabinet, a curio dug out of Zelda's basement, had a glass front and a hefty lock. Its shelves held a modest collection of items for collectors who wanted games when pieces were made of ivory or bone, glass, or marble. There wasn't a huge calling for these higher-ticket items, but they were worth the investment when they sold.

The man scrutinized the case and then turned to look at her. His sharp nose balanced thin wire-rimmed glasses. He was tall and wiry in his frame, too. His gray trousers and white button-down shirt were wrinkled and looked at least a decade out of date. When he peered at her curtly from behind his glasses, his eyes seemed to land on the burn scar that ran along her hairline, then he glanced away.

Her skin prickled. Everything about this man made her uneasy.

She stepped forward and put on her best shopkeeper smile. "What can I help you with today?"

The man worked at pulling a smile into place. "I need a gift for my nephew," he said finally. His tone was sharp, his voice a nasal tone as if his glasses pinched his nose. "Something a nine-year-old would find . . ." He paused. "Suitable."

"A video game, perhaps?" she said, motioning to a collection of them with a step in that direction.

"No," he said abruptly. "Something more useful—educational, perhaps . . ."

"Will he be playing with friends or something more solitary?"

His hesitation spoke volumes. Scanning the shelves for possibilities, she felt his presence behind her.

"Ah-ha!" Pulling a box from the shelf and setting it on the table nearby, she watched his expression as she dusted off the box.

"This is a Gilbert Chemistry Experiment Lab Kit. Maybe you recognize it? It's from the 1950s." Her mood shifted. Even she was uplifted by its playful magic.

She ran her hand across the cover, brushing across the detailed lithographic image of a mid-century dad and son earnestly engaged in an experiment. The kitchen dinette where they sat in the picture was covered with tools and beakers that spoke of a 1950s idea of the future. Lifting the latch that secured the bright orange metal case, she opened it as if it were a sacred tome.

The case revealed three compartments. Reaching out, she touched the glass jars set in a cardboard cutout frame before stepping back to give him room to explore the box for himself.

"This is what any nine-year-old would covet," she said with assurance. "There are twenty jars in all. Each is labeled with whatever chemicals are needed to expand a young boy's mind, if not blow up his mother's kitchen," she said and chuckled out loud at the thought. "Everything from magic tricks to crime detection. Just what a lonely boy needs."

His continued silence made her question her choice. Usually, she homed in on the right game for the right person. Usually, people were excited when they made a find like this. As excited as kids at Christmas.

He reached out and touched the jars, and the gesture had more tenderness than she expected. She hit the mark after all! Wasn't she the Vanna White ready to reveal the hidden letters.

"This is quite special. As you can see, this side of the kit holds the test tubes and the test tube holder. And this other side has all the tools and instructions." She read from the box, "Everything needed for a glass-blowing experiment, fingerprint crime detection, and chromatography for analyzing chemicals with color.

"Here are the instructions, still intact." She held the booklet out to him, surprised when his eyebrows rose as he accepted it.

"It's copyrighted in 1956."

"Where did this come from?" he demanded.

She flinched then forced a smile. He wasn't going to spoil her day, odd duck that he was.

"I buy much of my inventory from estate auctions. Why do you ask?"

He touched the case again but didn't answer.

"I'm guessing you recognize this as a Gilbert kit. As in A. C. Gilbert. He started the Mysto Manufacturing Company in the early 1900s." Accepting the booklet from his outstretched hand, she replaced it in the box. "Gilbert was a magician, and his best friend was John Petrie. I think you'll recognize that name, too."

He nodded.

"Together they created toys that appealed to the curiosity and fantasies of boys of this age and era. Back when boys wore cowboy boots and girls danced ballet."

She folded the panels and replaced the latch. "Although there were millions made, they are hard to find now. Especially in this condition."

"How much?" he barked.

"One seventy-five," she replied without hesitation.

The man jerked his hand away from the box. And then, as if he had no other choice, he lifted his worn leather wallet from his pocket.

Bingo. She did have a knack for knowing people and their games. She smiled and rang up the sale, noticing that his eyes swept over the locked curio cabinet yet again.

"Can I show you something from this case? Has something caught your eye?"

He glanced at her and then the case.

"No. Nothing."

Though anxious for him to leave, her curiosity was piqued.

"Are you visiting family in town?"

"No." He pulled the package from her proffered hands.

"Just passing through?"

He pushed his frames up his slender nose, smudging the glass with his fingers.

"Yes. You could say that."

"Ah, just my lucky day, then." She smiled warmly. "Fair luck and fond memories," she called as he exited her shop, bag in hand, without another word.

CHAPTER THREE

It was almost lunchtime when Rian O'Deis slipped in to open her shop in the Cardboard Cottage & Company. Amy looked up as Rian passed by Tiddlywinks's door.

"Better late than never," she called, but Rian seemed not to hear.

Directly opposite Zelda's pantry, the Pot Shed was the bastardized leftovers of the original kitchen, with one east-facing wall window and three rough brick walls whitewashed at some point in history. The glass panes of the window were so old they distorted the view almost like a Toulouse-Lautrec cocktail of absinthe and champagne.

Ablaze in light and color, the store was fragrant with culinary, herbal, and medicinal plants warming in the sun. A large wooden potting trough filled with potting soil emanated its earthy scent. Surrounding the trough were brightly colored pots stacked on the floor beneath the ceiling fan that squeaked along with the Royal Philharmonic Orchestra playing softly in the background.

Save the Bees popped from the front of Rian's goldenrod yellow shirt, tucked neatly into belted Levi jeans. Yellow laces in her black high-top sneakers matched her shirt.

Amy poked her head in the doorway, one foot in and one eye watching her shop entrance.

Rian stood with her hands on her hips.

"What are you doing?" Amy asked.

"I can't remember."

"Ah, a senior moment."

"Precisely," Rian answered. "I'm wounded from last night's domino game. Wounded and sore. You bested us with your double fives and slayed me with your pimento cheese."

Amy smiled. Yup. Bested, boasted, *and* slayed.

"What are *you* doing?" Rian asked. "Besides looking like the cat who ate the rat. Or is it the cheese? Jeez, my brain is wounded."

"It's a canary. The cat ate the canary. And I came to ask for your help. I need you to hold the ladder while *I* get a box off the top shelf."

"What you want is to hold the ladder while I get something off the top shelf."

They both looked up as a woman entered the Cottage in a soft rustle of skirt and canvas shoes. Thin and pale, her head was covered with a silk batik scarf, her blue eyes sunken into dark circles.

"Becky," Amy greeted her softly, reaching to hug her gently. Her bones felt fragile beneath her pink cotton shirt. "It's good to see you."

"Likewise." Her smile stretched across a face still beautiful despite illness. "It's good to be out and about." She knew why Becky was there.

"I can't stay but a minute," Becky said to Rian. "Harold dropped me off at your doorstep. He'll be back and fretting if I stay too long."

Rian nodded and pulled a shortbread tin from her canvas bag. Wrapped with a bright yellow handkerchief, the four ends were tied in a knot in the center, making a soft cloth handle. A prayer card for Saint Peregrine hung from the knot by a piece of jute twine.

"Baked fresh this morning," Rian said, putting the tin in Becky's hands.

"Thank you. Bless you. It makes a world of difference, you know."

Becky left a single bill on the counter as she left the room and then was gone with the same soft swoosh of cotton.

Amy glanced at the bill. Benjamin Franklin glanced back.

"Now I remember what I was going to tell you. Genna said she's on her way in. I just saw her at the bank. She's all atwitter about some magazine that wants to do a story on the Cardboard Cottage women of Bluff Springs."

At that very moment, Genna burst through the front door and sent the bells jangling again.

"Gawd," she said, marching to where Amy and Rian stood in the hall. "The traffic! It took me four loops around the block to find a parking spot. I had to park in the loading zone, and I only have fifteen minutes before the traffic cop writes me a ticket. He's always looking to make trouble for me."

"Breathe," said Rian.

"You breathe," Genna snapped. "I've got things to say!"

Genna tossed her head, swinging strands of a long silver ponytail fastened at the nape of her neck. Genna was as tall and thin as a reed at the water's edge but unlike anything she had ever seen wild in the woods. Genna didn't flaunt the old money and bright promise she came from. Even though it shone through anyway like Sunday silver pulled from its velvet-lined box. Amy envied Genna's confidence. She would love to have a bit more of that herself, even if Genna was a bit too stubborn if you got in her way.

Genna hugged Amy and they walked back toward Tiddlywinks. "I have the most amazing news . . ."

The door jangled again. Zack Carlisle moved past them. "Where is she?" he demanded, stomping all the way to Zsa Zsa Galore's.

Amy watched from the door of Tiddlywinks as Zelda stepped from the doorway of her shop, her hands on her plump, curvy hips.

"Where is she, *who*? *She* has a name, you *fool*."

Zack rushed toward her, and Zelda took a step back from him. He reached out and grabbed her shoulders, and Amy held her breath. Zack pulled Zelda into a hug.

"My wife," he said. "That's her name." He held Zelda at arm's length, smiled at her, and then turned to smile at the audience standing in the hallway behind him. It wasn't a large hallway, long or wide, and sound traveled easily through the wood walls. No need to strain to hear from where she stood.

"Zelda, I need to get some papers out of the safety deposit box. I can't find the key. Do you have it?" His voice escalated with the accusation. "Did you hide it?"

Zelda stepped back and his arms dropped to his sides. They were standing at the wagon outside her shop door, a family of shoppers squeezing by them, hoping to escape the now-crowded hallway and the discomfort of eavesdropping on a family squabble. Zack didn't even seem to notice them now.

Zelda picked up a bright pink pillow and held it to her chest, her hands nervously massaging the silk material. "Why do you need to get into that box? What are you doing? What are you after?"

Zack's shoulders tensed and he took a step toward her. "It's cell tower business. Nothing that concerns you. I can promise you that."

"I don't know where the key is," Zelda said quietly, her eyes trained on his. "I haven't been in that box since we added your name as a titleholder. Can't we do this later? In private?"

His face flushed with anger. "No!" he hollered. "Where is that key? I know you're hiding it from me! I know you are!"

"I am not. Why would I?"

Amy heard the fear and frustration in Zelda's voice. She had found it easy to see why Zelda was first drawn to this man with his dark hair and eyes the color of estate-aged bourbon. Even when they first met, he reminded her of the cad on the cover of a bodice ripper romance she read that winter when there was nothing to do but wait for the snow to melt. As that story unfolded, the shy but simmering teacher on vacation in Prague fell for the man whose heart seemed as gray as his gaze. Amy had fallen in love with the bandit long before the heroine did, all the while knowing he was danger with a capital D.

Zack was a capital D.

Amy stepped forward, her hands balled into fists at her side. "*Stop it!*" Her breath felt hot and angry. "Our customers don't need to listen to this. Neither do we."

Zack grabbed the pillow Zelda was holding and flung it against the wall. Then, turning abruptly, he strode past Rian and Genna, then past the customers in line at Crumpets and Cones. Just as he reached the front door, he turned to Amy.

"Mind your own business, *bitch*."

Zelda's face flushed and her eyes filled with tears. Retrieving the pillow from the floor, she plumped it back into place, turned on her heels, and returned to the interior of her shop. Zack stood on the sidewalk outside, looking as if he wasn't sure which way to go. A beefy hand reached out and clasped Zack's shoulder in a not-so-gentle grip, and she recognized Sammie's boyfriend, Beau. She couldn't hear what was being said, but judging by the angry red seeping up Zack's neck and face, Beau wasn't asking for the time.

Good for Beau. Zack needed to be dropped a peg or three.

Inside Tiddlywinks, a group of tourists was just starting a game at one of the tables. Once satisfied they were content, she slipped back down the hall.

Genna had her arms around Zelda and rolled her eyes at Amy.

"Are you okay?"

"Yes," Zelda mumbled, her voice thick with tears. "No. No, I'm not okay. I'm tired of this. And it's getting worse. He's so . . ."

"He's so angry," Amy interrupted.

"And aggressive," Genna added.

Zelda groaned. "He's a beast. And I'm stuck with him. I don't know what to do."

Genna hugged her friend. "This will make you feel better. Almost as good as a new pair of shoes. I pulled strings with the editor at *Belles & Bloom* magazine. They are going to run a feature story on us. On the Cardboard Cottage & Company, and how we've turned an old building into a thriving women's business co-op."

Amy cleared her throat but let the comment go. There was no *I* in the word *team*. They all played a part in the Cardboard Cottage & Company success.

"Here's how it works," Genna added, her voice rising with excitement. "They'll set up a photoshoot in all of your shops after closing. The lighting will be ideal. Just think of it! Pages of glossy photos. Maybe we can get Sammie to share her Irish family recipe for crumpets or something."

"This is wonderful news!" Amy said, beaming at Genna. "We can plan an open house and—"

"Here's the thing. They'll be here Wednesday."

"This Wednesday? But today's Monday!"

"Oh, my," Zelda said as her hands flew to her hair. "That's not much time to get ready. I need a haircut and a pedicure and a new pair of shoes."

"They aren't going to take pictures of your toes, Zelda, and your hair is impeccable as always. Look, my dears, this is an opportunity we can't let pass us by. Who knows when they will have another opening. This one only came about because a writer bailed on a feature planned for this upcoming issue.

"I will write the story, of course," Genna continued. "Who else is as qualified to write about four sexy fifty-year-old women who turned a ho-hum building into a booming business co-op?"

"*Booming* may be a bit of a stretch," Amy argued. "I'm making the mortgage on this place and a little profit to put in the bank, but if anything happened to any of us, I would be up the proverbial creek."

"And I'm not yet fifty," Zelda said stubbornly. "So don't say I am."

Amy and Genna laughed. Zelda might go kicking and screaming into her fifties. Amy was right there behind her, but Genna might stay in her fifties for at least another twenty years.

Genna flipped her silver ponytail with a quick flick of her wrist. "It will be perfect, you'll see. Don't you worry 'bout a thing. Not a thing. Actually," Genna added with a glance toward the door, "I'm a little worried I have a ticket on my car. Ciao," she added and left them grinning ear to ear.

Don't you worry about a thing! Humming the Stevie Wonder song, the rest of the afternoon flew by, and she let the day's drama fade with it. How exciting! Free publicity for the Cardboard Cottage & Company could be a big boost to business. It's what she needed to get her finances back on track. She was still humming when she locked the door and climbed the stairs, Victor in her arms, to the quiet of her apartment.

CHAPTER FOUR

Amy lurched awake. Panic crashed over her and left her wet with sweat. Though expecting the swirl of emergency lights to blaze across her eyes, she discovered the night was still thick around her. Lying still, eyes closed, she anticipated the sirens to resume their ear-splitting wail.

Silence surrounded her as she listened in the dark. Only the gentle hum of the refrigerator and her own quickened breath were sounds she recognized on this side of the dream.

Forcing her eyes open, the faint green glow of the bedside clock and the night-light in the bathroom were the only lights in the room. There was nothing flashing. No blasting sirens outside.

It was just a dream.

Her warm breath brushed her arm as she sighed with relief and realized her arms were crossed tightly at her chest. She let go, let her shoulders relax. Her fists uncurled, opening to let her fingers drag slowly to her side.

Just a dream. Relief flooded over her in a new wave.

Pushing at the images caught in her mind, she felt the dream still circling on the edge of her wakefulness. With eyes closed, she saw the lights from an emergency vehicle flash across a plaid shirt and a dark head of tousled hair. Despite the red glow of the lights from the ambulance, the face was pale with death.

She knew that face.

The feeling spread, unwelcome. A foreboding crept from her center like a cold, intrusive hand, drawing her even further from her sleep, beckoning her with silent fingers as if it held something secret in its grasp. She shivered involuntarily. This secret she didn't want to know.

She knew that face. It was Zack Carlisle.

And this Zack Carlisle was dead.

It couldn't be true. Too much ice cream before bed. Too much talk about husbands and bodies. Too much.

Vamoose!

Amy dragged herself from her bed and stumbled to the bathroom. Splashing cold water in her face, it slapped her awake like a hostile hand.

In the dim light of the bathroom mirror, she looked at herself, her nose inches from the glass. Freckles, now faded with age, were scattered across her nose and cheeks. They shared a familiar space with a slightly lopsided smile. Her hazel-brown eyes shone eerily bright even in the darkness of the mirror.

What had she just seen?

A face pale with death.

Was it real?

She patted her hair. On a good day, her curls spiraled out from her head like something crazy unless she belted them down. After tossing in her sleep, they had gone wild. Tugging at the copper-colored curls, she knotted them at her neck.

Still looking in the mirror, her fingers traced the burn scar on her forehead that ran just below her hairline. It didn't hurt anymore. It was just a scar. But scars didn't always heal on the inside the same way they did on skin. She brushed a stray curl from her cheek.

"Tele*pathetic*," she hissed at her reflection.

She didn't have special sight, even though she wanted to. She didn't have gifts that foretold the future, even though she had hoped they would emerge over time. A secret family gene passed down, skipping a generation now and then, had obviously skipped hers. She had intuition like any woman and vivid dreams that sometimes seemed to come true. But she wasn't gifted in that way.

She splashed her face once more, determined to ignore the sick feeling of dread that rose within her. Yes, sometimes the dreams did come true.

Reaching for the stone that hung from her neck, she fingered the Celtic knot inlaid with peridot and tiny diamond, yearning for the familiar texture of warm stone and cool silver along with the ache of remembering someone long gone.

She rubbed the stone. Peace flooded over her.

Grandmother. They would always be connected by an invisible thread.

Victor purred when she pulled him to her and snuggled back beneath her lavender-scented sheets. His sleepy, questioning eyes blinked and then closed, his mittens kneading the folds of the duvet bunched around her neck.

The veil of night was beginning to thin through the curtains now. Dawn was not too far ahead. Cinnamon drifted up from the bakery kitchen below, and closing her eyes, she hoped for a little more sleep.

The sirens woke her yet again. This time they were real.

CHAPTER FIVE

After throwing back the covers, Amy ran to the window over-looking the street. Two patrol cars were pulled to the curb, lights splattering the morning calm. Her heart lurched. Grabbing her robe from the hook behind the bathroom door then throwing it around her, she ran down the stairs, hoping, wishing, praying for anything other than a dead Zack Carlisle.

The front door of the Cardboard Cottage & Company stood open to the morning air, and glass shards lay scattered on the sidewalk.

"Watch yourself," one of the officers said, pointing to the ground.

She looked down at her bare feet, still white from winter, bright painted toes poised to step on broken glass.

"What happened?"

"Break-in," he said simply. "This is your place, right? Amy Sparks?"

Amy nodded. "Anybody hurt?"

He shook his head. "Not that I can see. Maybe the fool who broke the glass," he added under his breath. "Go get some shoes on," he ordered. "You can't go inside without shoes. You'll cut your feet."

As she ran upstairs, her mind filled with questions. Who would do such a cruel thing? What were they after? What did they get? The same questions looped through her mind as she raced back down the stairs, now in jeans, a T-shirt, and sneakers, her hair again pulled tight at the back of her neck.

"We've already secured the property, Ms. Sparks. It's safe to go inside. Although I don't think you're going to like what you see."

They entered over the crush of glass. The front door of Tiddlywinks was now a gaping hole that once held beautiful, antique stained glass. Shards lay scattered over the dark wood floor of the hallway and the interior of the shop.

When she flipped the light switch, her breath caught in her throat.

The shelves, once so organized and welcoming, were a disheveled mess. Boxes were dumped to the floor, boards and game pieces were strewn like leaves in a fall wind. Puzzle pieces lay scattered across the room as if someone had swept an arm across the table in a broad swipe of anger. Or revenge. Her heart pounded as she struggled to comprehend the cruel mind behind the rage. Her eyes filled with tears.

The curio cabinet door hung open. Glass glittered against the black lining on the shelves. Empty velvet told her there were pieces missing. Confused anguish filled her.

"Why?" she asked. "Who? When?"

"I don't know why or who," the officer said softly, "but when is pretty clear." He glanced at the notebook in his hand, an old-fashioned metal spiral with a stub of a pencil jammed into it from the top. "Sammie Walsh at the bakery called in at six fifteen. How come you don't have an alarm?"

"I didn't think I needed one." She rubbed the tears from her cheeks. "Is Sammie okay?"

Sammie used an outside door to the bakery kitchen on the other side of the building. The backdoor led to an alley where the trash pickup and deliveries were made. Sammie parked her car right outside the door, so she wouldn't have seen the damage until she came to the front of the bakery. She wouldn't have noticed the glass on the ground until she readied her shop to open.

"Is she still here? I hope she wasn't in the kitchen when this happened. She usually gets here before five."

The officer shrugged. "I didn't see anyone. My guess is that this happened in the dark of night. Cowards don't do this kind of thing in the light."

"Cowards?" Amy asked.

"Burglars. Thieves. Punks. They don't do their dirty business where people can see them and know them for who they are."

Amy nodded absently then crunched her way to the shelves. Tears streamed down her face in hot, heavy drops.

This wasn't burglary. These weren't punks. This was revenge.

Zack Carlisle's parting comment came to her mind.

Mind your own business, bitch.

"Come on," the officer said and put a warm hand on her shoulder.

It was a welcomed touch. A gesture of this kind was common in a small town, compassion that so many people in big cities never knew could be shared, even among strangers.

"Nothing you can do here now. I'll drive you to the station where you can make your report. You'll need to take inventory later to determine what's missing. And we'll keep an officer here to prevent any further theft. You have insurance?"

Amy nodded. "But not enough."

"You can never have enough insurance. I know that for a fact. My wife sells the stuff, and I can tell you I'm insured to the hilt."

Smiling weakly, she accepted his arm, grateful to have his warm support. Then, glancing back at the bakery, she felt for Sammie, too. The doors to Crumpets and Cones were closed and the bakery was dark. This would have frightened Sammie more than most. Conversations over tea had given her but an inkling of the violence Sammie knew firsthand as a youth. Though a brave woman bold enough to leave Ireland and start a new life here, she had lived under the strain of fury that pitted neighbor against neighbor. That reality would always haunt Sammie. Ireland may have called it *the troubles*, but it was a civil war. For Sammie, violence on the doorstep of her bakery would have been too close to home. Amy's heart ached with that knowledge, and she hoped Sammie had Beau's strong arms around her now.

CHAPTER SIX

"This is horrible." Zelda pushed her bangs from her eyes as she stood at the door of Tiddlywinks surveying the damage. "Who would do such a horrendous thing?"

Amy couldn't respond. How could she accuse her best friend's husband without accusing her best friend at the same time? Of course, the timing could have been a coincidence. There was no proof or evidence to point a finger at Zack, or at anyone for that matter. It wasn't that Bluff Springs was crime-free. It wasn't a crime-heavy town, either, but it did have its share of break-ins and burglaries.

By the time Zelda arrived, Amy had already taken pictures of the scene, then began to pick up the pieces strewn on the floor. Making slow but steady progress, she stacked items to be repaired in one pile and those that were a lost cause in another. She wouldn't trash them just yet. Maybe they could be upcycled into something clever. No idea as to what that was at the moment, but she and Zelda could get creative later.

The closed sign still on the front door of Crumpets and Cones was expected. Sammie had left a message by phone that she was taking time off. That, too, was a benefit of small-town living. Shopkeepers and restauranteurs with family emergencies and such often had to close their business for a few days under those circumstances. Not everyone had staff to pick up the slack.

"I'm so, so sorry," Zelda said. "What can I do to help?"

Amy accepted Zelda's warm embrace. "The good news is that I am insured, and I think it really looks worse than it is. My insurance will help replace what's ruined, and most of the games can be replaced. Not the antique ones, though. Those may be a complete loss. It's going to take some time and energy to hunt them all down again."

Rian appeared behind Zelda. "We're here to help. Tell me what to do."

"I want your help," Amy said, "and I appreciate your willingness, but I don't know what to ask you to do. I feel lost."

"We can sweep up the glass. We can help tidy the shelves."

"Aren't you going to open your shops?"

Rian stuffed her fingers in the top pocket of her jeans. "I'm okay if we close the Cardboard Cottage until we get this sorted out," she said. "What about you?" Rian asked, turning to Zelda.

"I'm okay with that. We're in this together. Lock, stock, and barrel."

Lock, stock, and barrel. She liked the sound of that. Tiddlywinks was in a state of chaos, which put them all in a state of chaos. More mess than loss, with the exception of the antique marbles that were missing from the curio cabinet. Amy thought again of the strange man with an interest in the cabinet. Maybe Zack wasn't the guilty culprit. Now she was glad she hadn't spoken any blame to Zelda, even if it was on the tip of her tongue.

They spent the morning bringing Tiddlywinks to a point of order that she could live with for the time being. While making her list of items to replace when the insurance funds arrived, she looked up as Ben, Rian's on-again-off-again boyfriend, arrived carrying a load of building supplies. Ben was a cop a couple of counties over, and his presence made her realize that Rian was more invested in that relationship than any of them knew.

Ben nailed plywood to the open doorframes at the front door of the Cottage and at Tiddlywinks Players Club. Zelda, armed with paint and brushes, painted *Closed for Repairs* on the wood and added colorful daisies and curlicues that matched the Cardboard Cottage & Company sign.

"You really need an alarm," Ben said. "And a security camera."

"On my list," she said as the lock went in place. "Let's call it a day. And thank you. All of you. I don't know where I'd be without you."

"Well if I were you, I would be in Little Rock with me and Genna," Zelda offered, unknowingly smearing paint on her cheek as she swept bangs from her eyes. "She's going stained glass hunting down near Little Rock. She's going to look for a replacement for your door."

"Wow!" Amy said. "Genna didn't waste any time."

"She was going anyway. You know how Genna is about her stained glass collection. But now, we can go with her."

"You go," Amy said. "I'm not feeling like a road trip. Genna can take pictures of anything that catches her eye. I'll give her the dimensions of the door."

Zelda glanced at Rian.

"Thanks, but we've got plans," Rian said with a side glance at Ben.

"I bet you do," Amy said and watched as Ben's face colored.

CHAPTER SEVEN

Amy tossed under her lavender-scented sheets until they coiled around her like a python wrapping its prey. She felt the wind in her face as if she were flying in the breeze. Horse and rider sailed through the mud, rider pressed tightly against the flanks of a horse with wild and determined eyes.

"Bonaparte," a voice said in her head.

She sat up and turned on the light.

If she had her days straight, there were only a few days left in the racing schedule at the Hot Springs racetrack before the Arkansas Derby. Maybe Bonaparte was running in one of them.

Pulling a dog-eared diary from the bedside drawer, she smoothed the purple paisley cover, smelling faintly of lavender. The book matched the color of the walls. The walls matched the drapes. The drapes matched the sheets and the pinstripe nightshirt she wore to bed. These were now clammy as if she had ridden the horse through the mud herself.

She scribbled an entry, and then glancing at the bedside clock, she saw it was just after midnight. Reaching now for *Psychic Studies for the Intuitive* from the bedside shelf, one of the many that promised to decipher dreams and visions of the tele*pathetic*, she pulled the bookmark from the page and began to read herself back to sleep.

The phone jarred her to the present.

"Hello?"

"Help me!" Zelda squealed.

Her eyes widened in the dark.

"He—he—he's dead! They found him in the parking garage!" The words barely came through the receiver above Zelda's sobs.

Dread soured in her stomach. "Zelda? Is that you?"

"At the hotel. With my favorite champagne!"

"Zelda, what are you saying? Where are you?"

"Zack is dead!"

Amy let go of the breath she was holding, heart pumping fast as Zelda's words hurled into her ear. She exhaled audibly.

Zack Carlisle was dead.

"Where are you?"

"I—I'm staying at the Bennfield Hotel. In Hot Springs."

"What? What are you doing down there?"

Zelda drew a stuttering breath, her words choked by emotion.

"Zack called and said for me and Genna to meet him here. He—he said we could play the ponies. I thought he was going to g-g-give me money for our cruise tickets. I thought that's what he was after in the safety box."

"Zack is dead?" She couldn't believe it was true.

Zelda drew another stuttering breath. "Cops are everywhere," she wailed, "and Genna's already left! I can't reach her."

"Are you still at the hotel?"

"I'm at the police station."

"The police station! Are you being arrested?"

"No! Come . . . help me!"

The conversation stopped as Zelda's sobs overtook her.

"Get them to take you back to the hotel and just stay there," Amy pressed. "Don't talk to anyone else. I'll be there as fast as possible. I'm leaving right now."

As she dialed with one hand, she grabbed necessities with the other and then, stuffing them into her overnight bag, she cursed into the phone as the call went to Genna's voice mail. She left a message and then dialed Rian only to leave the same.

Where were they? Why weren't they answering their phones?

She glanced at the clock. Twelve forty. Of course, they wouldn't answer a late-night call.

Amy maneuvered her car skillfully through the dark mountain road and then floored the Miata when the wheels hit the interstate on-ramp, pushing the car until the speedometer reached eighty-five. The drive to Hot Springs would take her more than three hours at a safe speed from here. She knew she needed to make it in less. Gripping the wheel, she willed the miles to fly past and the cops and the deer to stay safely out of sight and off the road.

Her doubts had to stay safely submerged, too. And yet, suspicions, like the boulders in the river they kayaked in the summer, were ever-present and dangerous. Those sleepers, the rocks unseen just under the surface, would toss you into the cold current if you didn't keep a close eye on the river. No, she hadn't kept a close eye, and now her suspicions were surfacing with bone-jarring fear.

In six years of friendship, the four friends had talked about many things. But never murder. Not until last week. Last week it was just a drunken joke. What woman didn't want a crappy husband dead and gone at some low point in her marriage?

Dead as in dead husband. Dead as in stiff husband. Dead as in too close to the truth.

Amy bit her lip. Her gut tightened. How else was it possible that

Zelda had wished Zack gone, and now he was?

Zelda wanted him dead. Was that what happened? They would do anything for each other. Rian, Genna, Zelda, herself. That was true. But murder? The word tumbled in her head.

Had they taken friendship that far?

No. She couldn't believe that. How could she believe that? How could she betray her best friends with such a thought?

"No," she said out loud to the darkness. "I can't believe it. I won't believe it."

She shook her head, and tears she didn't realize were there fell down her face, and yet she couldn't shake the doubts from her mind, which rode with her for another hundred miles.

CHAPTER EIGHT

The hotel room was eerily quiet. Amy's voice seemed to echo off the walls of the old hotel. This was their favorite place to stay during horse racing season and lazy spa getaways when all four of them could find the time. Today it felt dark and dirty. She arrived before dawn, her stomach in knots and her hands aching from their grip on the wheel.

Zelda was now snoring softly in the adjoining bedroom, and she, now whispering into the phone, knew Rian was straining to hear.

"The cops say it was a hit-and-run accident. But with a strange twist. According to the cop I talked to, the impact wasn't what killed him—something about probable velocity and rate of speed in a parking garage. I didn't understand what she was talking about. Police mumbo jumbo."

She cupped her hand around the phone. "What killed him was the champagne bottle he was holding. The bottle broke when he hit the ground and a shard of glass pierced his neck." She paused. Rian was silent. The room seemed to hum in the quiet.

"He bled to death."

"Hail Mary," Rian said.

"*Nach a Mool.* This cop said even if the EMTs arrived earlier, they couldn't have saved him. He bled to death within minutes. It was *Veuve Clicquot,*" she added.

"What?"

"The champagne. It was *Veuve Clicquot.*"

Zelda's favorite. Rian sighed into the phone.

"They identified him from his wallet. So, it's clear he wasn't robbed. He still had his credit cards and a wad of cash in his pocket."

"What else did he have on him?" Rian asked.

Amy reached for the envelope the police had given Zelda. "His cell phone," she said, dumping the contents on the bed beside her. "There's a ring of keys. I don't know what this is. Maybe it's part of a check that's been torn up. I can't tell."

"Is that all?"

"There's a receipt for a purchase at Victoria's Secret. And another for the champagne. No bag of pot if that's what you're asking. If there was one, I'm guessing it was seized by the police. There's a single key on a round cardboard ring. It's marked L91."

"I need that key," Rian said.

"Why?"

"It doesn't matter."

"What do you mean? What is that key to?"

Suspicion rose in her again, like sleeper rocks in the river. Did she really want to know? Or would knowing the answer make her feel guilty of a little more than curiosity and gossip?

"Never mind. It doesn't make any difference. Where's Zelda now?"

"Right here. Sleeping. What's this key for, Rian?"

She could hear Rian's mental wheels turning. "Amy, it's really nothing of importance. Just put it in your pocket, and I'll get it later. Okay?"

"Okay," she agreed, but she wasn't satisfied. She wasn't willing to push it, either.

Rian exhaled into the phone. "Where was Zelda when—when it happened?"

Amy took a deep breath and began to recount the story she had pieced together. "Zelda told me she was asleep at the time. Then she claimed she couldn't find him. I don't know what she meant by that. I couldn't tell if she was having trouble remembering, or if she was changing her mind about where she was. I think the police woke her up late, and she and Genna were at the bar for quite a while. Zack never showed up even though he paid the bill in advance when he made the reservation. Before I could ask any more questions about what the police said, she started sobbing. So I gave her a pill. Maybe tomorrow she will make more sense. Honestly, I don't know if she remembers. Maybe she doesn't want to remember."

Silence filled the distance between the two friends. Sitting on the bed in the darkened hotel room, she watched the shreds of dusty light showing through the gap in the yellow brocade curtain that covered the heavy leaded glass window. Street noise from the busy avenue below filtered up to the third-story window.

"The authorities are scanning security cameras for the hit-and-run car."

"Oh, no," Rian said. "Genna's car!"

"What about it?"

"Her Mercedes will be on the video footage."

"Why would that matter?"

Rian was silent. "I think her tags are expired."

"That's a lie, Rian, what is going on?"

"Genna hit a deer on the way home last night. It did some damage to her car."

"Genna hit another deer? She's like a magnet with those things!

But, I don't understand. Why does that matter?"

"It's just going to complicate things, that's all," Rian said. "Really bad timing."

Her eyes widened. Thoughts tumbled. "What are you saying? Do you think she hit—"

"I've got to go," Rian interrupted. "Things to do," she added before the phone went dead.

Lowering the phone from her ear, Amy suddenly felt exhausted. Her warm bed and cozy cat felt like ancient history. In some ways it was. She closed her eyes and wished she could wake up from this reality the way she woke up from her dreams.

Was this coincidence that they had been talking about dead bodies over dominoes, and now they had one?

Zelda had made a birthday wish that came true.

The quiet of the hotel room wrapped around her, and she was transported in time and memory. She was sitting in front of a fortune-teller, one of many she had visited over the years. This one had warned her about making wishes. She was in Cassadaga, an old town in Florida where seers, séancers, and spell enchanters made a living working their craft. She and her college buddies drove over to have their palms read and fortunes told. Her friends wanted to know about their future husbands and how many children they would have. But she didn't get what she paid to hear. The woman grabbed her hand tightly in her own and pulled Amy's attention in with piercing black eyes. She smelled of stale coffee and cough drops. Her voice was like gravel.

"You must never make a wish you do not want to come true, for this power is in your hands," the crone told her. "Nothing gives the *Moirae* more pleasure than to spin and stitch and snip the threads of the hubris of humanity!"

The woman dropped her hand and laughed.

Was she confiding something sacrosanct into Amy's ear? Was she predicting this? Amy thought the fortune-teller was teasing her. She wanted to be able to see the future, the same way the witch did. With her own eyes, or in the eyes of her dreams. Her innermost wish.

Tele*pathetic*.

The memory troubled her now as much as it had then.

A story by W. Somerset Maugham came to mind. It was an eerie tale about a merchant and his servant. Maybe the horse in her dream wasn't Bonaparte. It could be the pale horse of Death racing toward its next victim. Maybe Zack drove to his own Samarra, as the servant did in the story, where Death struck him down.

She slipped into the adjacent bedroom and looked quietly at Zelda, who was still sleeping soundly. The faded bruises on her arms were exposed above the sheets. In a rush, she realized this abuse had been happening for a while. There was no doubt it had been happening long before Zelda finally confided her own deeply held secret. Amy's heart ached with the pang of guilt. No matter how long it had been happening, it was that much too long. Worse, it had gone unnoticed by her friends. Friends who swore to be allies through thick and thin.

Some friend she was.

And now it may be a little too late. Why hadn't Zelda asked for help?

Amy shuddered. She *had* asked for help. Zelda asked them to help her get rid of Zack. She said, *I need to get rid of Zack. Vamoose. And y'all need to help me.*

And now Zack was dead.

Maybe this was what the witch had foreseen so many years ago. Maybe this was the hubris she predicted.

Maybe her dreams were starting to come true.

Except, she didn't see a hit-and-run killer behind the wheel in her dreams. She saw a horse on the track. She heard sirens and saw a death mask.

Her imagination took off like a horse from the starting gate. What if Zelda went to the parking garage to meet Zack? What if they argued and she got in the Hummer to drive off? What if he stepped in front of it and she hit him by accident? Maybe it wasn't an accident. Maybe she hit him with the car and left him there to die. Stood over him and watched him bleed.

Perhaps Zelda didn't know he was dying, didn't see the glass shard in his neck.

And Genna? Had Genna really hit a deer as she claimed? Maybe it was Genna who bumped Zack with her Mercedes. But why? The thought struck her hard, like a punch to the gut. Genna and Zelda could have made this murderous plan on their way to Hot Springs. They could have conspired to put Zack out of Zelda's life. *Vamoose!*

Amy shook her head. Unbelievable! How could she have such thoughts about her friends?

She crossed to the bathroom and, sitting in the dark, perched on the side of the antique tub, drinking deeply from a cup of tap water. The tiny black-and-white tiles of the floor seemed to swim at her feet.

And then she saw the shoes.

Zelda's favorite Jimmy Choos were in the tub, a thin line of red leaking into the drain. She stared at them for a long time before she picked them up. Turning them over, she saw that only the slightest trace of rusty red remained in the treads in the soles. Most of it had been washed free and now ran somewhere out of sight in the Hot Springs sewer.

Out of sight but not out of mind.

She didn't need to think about it. Tossing the shoes into the trashcan, she yanked out the liner, then twisted it closed. She let the shower run long after the red stain was gone.

Retracing her steps to the bedroom, she paused only for a moment to gather the hotel key. She walked out of the hotel and several blocks before turning into an alley, tossing the bag into a dumpster. The shoes hit the bottom with a thud of permanence. It was a thud of satisfaction. No one else needed to know what she had just done, not even Zelda. Whatever secret lingered on the soles of those shoes, it would now stay hidden.

CHAPTER NINE

Amy stood in the doorway behind Zelda at her home in Bluff Springs.

"Who was that?" she asked.

"I don't know," Zelda said. "Never seen her in my life."

The kitchen counter behind them overflowed with covered dishes brought over by friends and neighbors who had stopped by to offer condolences. She accepted the dish from Zelda's outstretched hands and added it to the collection on the counter.

Food was a peace offering. An effort to console. She knew that. She also knew it was a good excuse to find out the sordid details, the little particulars that had not been included in the newspaper. The word about Zack's death had taken to the streets of their little town like a fire in the wind. The news of Zack's death had broken the headlines as one would expect in such a close-knit town.

Local dies in a hit-and-run.

The effort of their peers was sincere, but none of it was wanted.

Not by Zelda.

Amy yanked the phone cord from the wall, drew the curtains, and made Zelda a stiff drink. She didn't know what else to do.

They arrived home mid-afternoon. She drove the Hummer and Zelda drove Amy's Miata.

The Hot Springs authorities concluded the Hummer was not involved in the accident, with the interior swept clean and evidence collected. Receipts from a gas station, mall boutique, and liquor store told the story of Zack's last errands. Nothing seemed out of place. Zack kept a clean car. There was no evidence stuck to the Hummer's grill, no cracked windshield, nothing to place suspicion on anyone.

Red tape and protocol with the funeral home had taken more energy than Amy had to give it, but she refused to leave Zelda alone. She herded Zelda through it all like a protective mother hen. Like a sister. It was all she could offer.

Now back in Bluff Springs, Amy should have felt relief, but she didn't. She had gone home briefly to check on Victor and his food and water supply. While the closed-for-repairs sign was still up at the Cardboard Cottage & Company, the cash register wouldn't be ringing up any sales, although bills were still piling up. Lots of things were piling up. She couldn't get the bits and pieces out of her head. Zelda's shoes. Genna's busted grill. Time and place. Wishes and dreams.

The authorities said a reckless driver would soon come forward and confess. She didn't know what to think about that. A reckless driver full of rage.

Amy eyed Zelda now, silent behind the dark lenses of her oversized Fendi shades.

"Not again!" she bellowed as the doorbell rang. Amy opened the door and her mouth, ready to pounce on the unsuspecting well-wisher.

The officer smiled in greeting. "Mrs. Carlisle, I'm sorry to impose at this time considering your loss, but there are a few questions that have come up regarding your husband's death."

"I'm not Mrs. Carlisle," Amy said curtly. "She's resting. Now is not a good time."

She heard Zelda rise from the chair behind her.

"I'm delivering a message from the Hot Springs criminal investigation team. They need to revisit Mrs. Carlisle's statement," he said rather stiffly as if he were following a script from the procedure manual. "They've made arrangements here at the local police department. I presume that it will be acceptable. We also need to talk to, uh . . ." He glanced at his notebook. "Amy Sparks, Genna Gregory, and Rian O'Deis? O'Dees?"

"It's pronounced oh-day," Amy replied.

"They would like to speak with Rian Oh-day," he said with emphasis, his tone suddenly gruff.

"But why?" Zelda pushed her way past Amy. "Why do you need to talk to them?"

The officer answered her with silence. He reached into his pocket, pulled out a business card, and handed it to Zelda. "I'm sure it's just routine," he said. "If you could tell them to be there tomorrow at 9 a.m.?"

He turned away just as Amy slammed the door.

CHAPTER TEN

The Miata bounced over the gravel road to Rian's homestead. She turned her face to the sun flooding the car, its top down, every inch bathed in the brilliant spring sunshine. Cotton ball clouds puffed through a radiant sapphire blue sky, and the pungent, sweet smell of honeysuckle wafted from the roadside.

She didn't come out here often, but when she did, she felt like a pioneering woman. Rian's home was a small log cabin with white chinking and a covered porch with two rocking chairs facing the mountains to the west. It was rustic, the way most old Ozark homesteads were. A family heirloom, the cabin was left by Rian's grandparents who milled the logs from the land.

Amy parked at the toolshed and got out.

Lucky guess. Rian's truck and her Fiat were parked on the grass in front of the house, but she wasn't on the porch. Scanning the grounds, she spotted both Rian and Genna.

The pond was at the end of a gentle slope. The dock jutted out into the water about twenty feet. It was an Ozarks postcard kind of view.

The kind Norman Rockwell would paint if he ever had reason to visit. She laughed to herself thinking of a calendar of the four of them painted with rosy cheeks and naïve smiles. A poker game would be perfect. He'd paint Genna with a cigarette in her mouth as she tried to slide an ace out of her sleeve, sleight-of-hand. Rian would be feeding the dog under the table, and Zelda would be staring at her cards in deep contemplation. If Rockwell was kind, and he would be, she would be beaming ear to ear at the royal flush in her hand.

"Speak of the devil," Genna called as Amy strode across the grass toward them.

"Gee, thanks. I guess I won't take that to heart."

Rian and Genna were perched on the dock, their legs swinging over the lake. Except for their age, they looked like teenagers at summer camp. She kicked off her sandals and stood on the warm planks, letting the sun dapple her feet.

"We were just talking about you and Zelda," Genna said. "Were your ears burning?"

"My everything is burning," Amy said. "It's a top down kind of day." She plopped down on the dock beside Rian.

Genna pulled a pack of cigarettes from the neck of her Ralph Lauren boots that were standing empty beside her. Rian pulled up the trap moored to the piling and fished out a can of beer.

"Thanks," Amy said again. The can was spring-water cold. She popped the lid and took a sip. "Perfect. I needed that!"

"What brings you out my way?" Rian asked.

"The police showed up at Zelda's door today. We've all been summoned to the station downtown tomorrow. I couldn't reach either of you by phone, so here I am. A messenger in the flesh."

"I bet this is about that deer," Genna said. "I called my insurance company and they asked if I filed a report with the police. They sounded like they didn't believe me."

Amy wasn't sure she believed it herself. And yet it made as much sense as the rest of it.

Genna flicked her ash. "It's the truth. They can take it or leave it."

"You don't have any proof," Rian said. "Except for that spot of dried blood I saw on your bumper and a big fat dent."

"That's what happens when you hit a deer."

And a body. Amy squirmed with the thought. She drank deeply, hoping no one else would see that thought in her eyes.

"So they want to talk to us," Rian said. "What about?"

"He didn't say. He just asked for us to show up."

"Well isn't that a boot to the britches," Rian said. "What do you have to say about the accident?"

"Me?" Genna asked. Rian was looking straight at her. "Not much to say. I hit a deer that ran in front of me."

"I meant the *other* accident," Rian said wryly.

"I don't know anything about that," Genna claimed. "I don't know why they would ask me questions about that. I was on my way home."

"What if it wasn't an accident?" Amy ventured. "I got a feeling it wasn't just a hit-and-run."

Genna blew smoke into the air where it hung heavily over the dock. She waved it away with her hand. "Your Spidey sense telling you that?"

Amy bristled at the tone and the cheeky look Genna gave her.

"Look, I left Zelda in the bar at the Bennfield Hotel. She was one martini short of drunk and pissed at Zack for being late."

"Zack was late?" Zelda had told her that, too.

Genna nodded. "He told Zelda he would meet her there by six thirty."

"You didn't see him when you left the hotel?" Rian asked.

"No."

"Did you see anybody you know?"

"No."

"Did anybody see you?"

"What are you getting at? Did anyone see you, Rian? Didn't you say you met Zack down south that day?"

Rian twisted a sprig of hair between her fingers and tugged.

"I met him outside of Hot Springs," she answered after a pause long enough to make Amy wonder if Rian was going to answer at all. "I wasn't planning on going that far south with my deliveries, but it was a pretty day for a drive in the Fiat. We met down near one of the cell towers."

Rian took a sip of her beer and swung her legs in the water.

"He showed up. I gave him what he wanted, and he went on down the road. He said he had business there before he went on to Hot Springs to meet Zelda. Said they were going to play the ponies. That was the last time I saw him."

"What time was that? If I may ask."

"You can ask," she said, looking sideways at Amy, a grin on her lips.

"Okay," Amy said. "I get it. You're not going to put yourself in the picture."

"And here's another thing I'm not going to do."

"Not going to do what?" Genna asked. "Pay your taxes? Buy new shoes?"

"I'm not going to the police station." Rian shoved her hand into her jeans pocket as if anchoring her decision. "I don't want to be anywhere near cops asking questions I don't plan to answer. Maybe you don't want to answer questions, either, Genna. In case somebody gets the wrong idea in their heads about your dimpled bumper."

Rian pulled out a joint she had tucked in a book of matches in her shirt pocket.

"Where is Genna's car?" Amy asked.

"We took it to my detail guy to fix it quick like a fox," Rian said, passing the joint to Genna. "He's good that way. No one will ever know it was wrecked."

Why was Rian being so James Bond with Genna's car? Clandestine, even. Did she think there was a connection between the Mercedes and Zack's death? If so, Rian was trying to put some distance between Genna, the Mercedes, and the hotel parking garage in Hot Springs.

Amy had done the same thing with Zelda's shoes.

The lake and its quiet pulled her in as they settled into silence. She plunged her toes in the cold water.

"Brrr . . ." She yanked her feet out and then settled them back in. The water was clear even though the mud bottom made it look dark at first glance. It was too cold to swim in yet, even if she was brave enough to slide in. Warm sun and the cold beer made her content, like Victor in the windowsill at home. She closed her eyes and leaned against the dock post.

"You know my granddaddy used to stock this lake with bass and bluegill," Rian said. "I bet there's fish in there as big as Nessie. They raised what they butchered and grew what they ate. Right here on this homestead for more than sixty years."

Amy opened her eyes and turned her face to the water. It was a beautiful spread.

"What's happening with you and Officer Handsome?" Genna asked.

"Nothing."

"You know Ben wants to be with you."

"And you know that's none of your business."

"Ouch," Amy said. "That's a touchy subject."

"Well, what's wrong with him?" Genna pushed. "Nasty feet, stubby fingers? Why don't you want to be with him?"

"Seriously? He's a cop. I grow pot. We're like Dave Starsky and Jane Goodall."

Genna chuckled. "Don't flatter yourself."

Rian grinned back. "How about Belle Starr and Dudley Do-Right?"

She pointed a finger at Rian. "I'd say you're getting closer."

"Exactly. That's why I'm keeping my distance."

Amy giggled. She had only met Ben a few times, but he didn't have that tough cop air. When he showed up to help with Tiddlywinks after the break-in, she saw why Rian liked him so much. Theirs was definitely an odd pairing, though, if she thought about it. No wonder Rian kept him a semi-secret, even from her friends.

Amy giggled again. The dragonflies buzzed over the lake like toy airplanes landing, fueling, and taking off again. A chorus of nature serenaded them with shoreline song, and the peepers peeped unseen from the river reeds. She felt the beat. The bullfrogs added their noisy baseline like syncopated jazz.

"Arkansas means *south wind* in the language of the Quapaw tribe," Amy said dreamily. "They lived here a gazillion years ago, you know. The French Jesuits called them *Oo-gaq-pa*. Another tribe called them *Ar-ka-na-se*. Then the white men showed up. They wrote down what they heard. And now they call us *Arkansawyers*."

Genna chuckled. "That reminds me of playing that game 'Telephone' as kids. By the time the whispers made it around the circle, the comment was a bit lewd and always funny."

"Hmm," Rian hummed.

"Sad about Zack," Amy said.

"Crying shame," Rian added.

Genna drew her bare feet from the cold water, wrapping her arms around her knees. "We missed a perfect photo op for the Cardboard Cottage & Company, and now we've got another dead husband. What a mess."

Another dead husband? Maybe Genna was talking about her deceased. *God rest their souls.* They both died of natural causes, albeit a bit prematurely.

"You know we're going to have to answer to Zelda sooner or later," Genna said.

"Later," Rian snipped.

"We can't collect on the insurance until we do."

"They know. They're watching. Someone is always watching."

"Your paranoia is showing, Rian. Don't you think we'll get our money?"

"Your greed is showing, Genna."

"It's a legitimate claim. Zack died in an accident, didn't he?"

Amy's head buzzed. "What are you talking about? What insurance? What claim?"

Genna exhaled the last drag from her cigarette and stuffed the butt into the empty beer can. The smoke curled out of the opening like a chimney and then fizzled out in the wet dregs.

"Well, that's a cat out of the bag," Rian said. "That's not at all how I thought that should've been played."

"What is going on?" Amy asked. Her head was starting to ache. Was there anything that appeared on the surface the same as it was below?

"Genna and I have a financial interest in Zack's cell tower business."

"It started out as a very simple arrangement," Genna said. "Zelda didn't know about it. Unless Zack told her. He wanted to keep it quiet for the time being."

"But why?"

"I'm not sure," Rian said. "And now I regret that. I regret the whole thing. Zack was one scary, shady dude."

Genna turned to face Rian. "Now what are you talking about?"

Rian was silent, her gaze on her hands in her lap. Amy looked at Genna and then back at Rian. Like watching a silent ping-pong match between fortitude and grit. Tenacity and defiance. Guilt and blame.

"Look," Genna said, "if there's something you need to tell me, now is a good time to do so."

Amy heard the anger. Genna was dauntless when she was angry. Her stomach fluttered, and a sense of panic took flight. If anyone could battle it out with Genna and win, it would be Rian. Whether it was physical or not.

She certainly wasn't going to get in that fray. Still, Rian was silent.

"Rian!" Genna exclaimed. "You better spill it and spill it now."

Rian sighed, and Amy felt the resignation in that breath. It was as if she let go of a lot more than the stale air she was holding.

"Zack was pressuring me for a share of Granny's business, and I didn't know how to stop him. I think there were some good old boys down in Hot Springs who didn't take kindly to Zack stepping into their territory, which is what I think he was planning to do. I'm not sure about all that now, because, well, I shouldn't have believed anything he told me. But somebody was looking for Zack's weed connection. I am that connection. And he was brash enough to bring them right to my front door."

"Oh," Amy whispered, familiar with Rian's code word for her pot trade. Granny's sweaters were the green goods sold in Rian's undercover business. "That *is* scary."

"Like sleep-with-your-gun scary," Rian admitted. "It got all tangled up. And I really wanted to untangle it before . . ." Rian's voice trailed away and fell silent.

"Before what?" Amy asked finally, her voice barely above a whisper.

"Before I lost it all. Everything I've worked so hard for. It's not about the money. It never was."

Amy's head was spinning. She couldn't believe she didn't know about any of this. Not even an inkling. She had happily skipped her way to the Cardboard Cottage every day thinking they were a merry little band of women making a lighthearted living. Maybe they did have secrets. Everyone had secrets. But theirs were silly, simple, and safe. Like what they did in the privacy of their domino game. Or how much wine they smuggled to Arkansas disguised as Omaha Steaks. Or where they hid each other's keys when they had a bit much to drink and a cab was in order. Simple things. Safe things. Not drug dealers and dead husbands.

She didn't know about Rian and Genna being in cahoots with Zack. That was a secret so deep not even Zelda knew. She hadn't known about the insurance money. She hadn't known about the Hot Springs thugs. She was out of the loop of all these goings-on going on right under her roof. All of it right under her nose. Secrets and lies, among close friends literally in each other's business every day. She didn't know whether to be angry or hurt or jealous of being left out of the loop like some outsider.

Genna had been silent, and Amy couldn't tell what was looping through her head by the expression on her face. Her eyes were focused on Rian and nothing else, it seemed, her crimson lips pursed into a thin line.

"Why didn't you tell me this?" Genna asked finally. Her voice was tender.

Rian shrugged. "The less you know about my sordid details, the better. I didn't want to drag any of you into this." Rian shifted her weight from one cheek to the other on the hard dock planks. "I love making people feel better. People like Becky. All those people sick on chemo and pharmaceuticals that cure one organ and kill another. I didn't study botany in college to work in a lab making poison and GMOs.

"Growing pot—there's no time clock. No boss. No propaganda.

Just ordinary civil disobedience. Just like our ancestors who fought against tyranny. You may not know this, but the first draft of the Constitution was written on paper made from hemp. Jefferson and Washington both grew cannabis on their farms. It was part of their everyday lifestyle. Funny how we haven't moved on very far."

The mood shifted. The flutter abated inside Amy, and they were again just friends on a dock in the quiet countryside. She could feel Rian's desperation—it was so tangible, like an ache from a sore muscle. Like an ache from a broken heart full of grief and loss.

"Well, did you know that Thomas Jefferson was also an avid backgammon player? He played to relax while writing the Constitution. Probably with a little special help." She grinned at Rian. "But you're not a dope grower, Rian. You're a medicine woman. You grow medicinal herbs and make tinctures and cookies and . . ."

"And dope," Rian interrupted. "I grow pot. And that's still illegal. Not that I have all that much regard for the law. Ben excluded," she added with a grin. Rian flicked the paper end of the roach into the lake and then turned to face her friends.

"I know that's a lot to take in, but we're in the middle of some nasty business here. Zack is dead. Genna has some lame story about hitting a deer. We have an insurance policy about to pay out significant money. If anybody looks too closely, we look guilty. Zelda wanted him gone. And now he is.

"Any which way we turn, we've got our fingers in this sticky pie. We have to put as much space as we can between him and us. And I don't need anybody connecting Zack's death with my little cannabis patch in the mountains. I'd rather let the whole business die on the vine right along with him. Zack was a nuisance, and his death has benefited us all."

Rian turned to face Genna. "Tell us what really happened in Hot Springs. We need to know."

Genna was silent for a long moment. Amy could tell she was corralling her thoughts and how they fit the picture.

"We arrived at the Bennfield Hotel at happy hour. Zelda went to the front desk to check in and get the key. I had a dry martini with three jumbo olives—just like she likes it—waiting for her when she joined me at the bar. The reservation was made and paid for by Zack. Sneaky creep," she added. "He was definitely up to something."

"Did you see Zack's Hummer in the parking garage when you got there?"

"I didn't see the Hummer. But we were early, and Zelda wasn't expecting him until after six."

Genna paused as if remembering. Amy hung on every word.

"I was watching the TV above the bar. The local news was on, but the sound was down too low to hear it, so I was looking at the faces and wondering what they were saying. It's a game I play with myself sometimes," she added.

"Then I saw the news crew was in Blue Mountain with a swarm of protestors in front of a church."

Rian perked up. "Blue Mountain? That's one of the land leases we just bought."

"Yep. Wicked Creek Road. That's why it caught my eye. The town water tower was in the background. They use the initials *WC* on the tower. Cracked me up. Don't they know what a water closet is? Not far removed from an outhouse!"

"They were protesting?" Rian asked. "I thought that lease was already signed, sealed, and delivered. That's what Zack told me."

"I'm guessing something went awry. As I said, I couldn't hear what they were saying, but there were two protest lines, with picket signs, and some really angry eyes. One of them was a man whose face was florid. I mean absolutely vermillion. I remember thinking he was the little engine that could and did and was about to drop from exhaustion.

"But he didn't. I think he just spit his anger at the reporter's microphone." She paused for a moment. "There was this lady right behind him. Looked kind of like Carvey's Church Lady on Saturday Night Live. She had eyes like daggers aimed at the back of his head. There was a fat man in a tan suit. I thought, tacky color for a politician. I don't know why I thought he was a politician. I didn't recognize him. I thought I knew all of them."

"Did you recognize anyone?" Rian asked.

"Nope. And then they flashed on the picket signs." Genna laughed. "One of them said, 'Thank you, Jesus, for bringing moble 2 our town!' Spelled m-o-b-l-e!"

"And the opposition?" Rian prodded.

Genna laughed again. "There was an old farmer dude in overalls and a John Deere cap with a sign that said, 'Dial tone is the Devil.' Imagine that. It's funny now, but it made me mad then. How in heaven's name do they come up with this stuff? I don't understand why people believe God's paying attention to the dial tone on their phone. The world is rife of evil. Real evil. Who cares whether you talk on a cell phone or a can with a string? Picket something that matters. Global warming. Human trafficking. Government waste. Get off your pious butts and do something that makes a difference! Or go home and be quiet," she added with a flourish of her hands.

"Sheesh. I guess I got off track."

Amy was always surprised by Genna's passion. Genna could stand aloof one minute and then roll up sleeves and dig in the next. She had seen her in action many times.

"There was also the American Beekeeping Federation Convention in Hot Springs. The reporter was yammering her way around the expo booths and then he was joined on camera by the Arkansas Honey Bee Queen. She had a yellow-and-black sash across some serious cleavage. All blonde hair, long legs, boobs.

"And then I went outside for a smoke. Zelda came with me. We had to dodge the housekeeping cones and wet paint signs."

"And still no Zack?" Amy asked.

Genna shook her head. "I paid the bill and I left her there. She was pissed and ready to skin him alive when she saw him. Well—not really. That's a manner of speech."

"And then you hit the deer," Amy said.

"Yep," Genna drawled. "What a mess."

Yes, a mess. And yet, there were some pieces to the puzzle falling into place in the back of her mind. Rian's words echoed in her thoughts: *If anybody looks too closely, we look guilty. Zelda wanted him gone. And now he is.*

Wishes and dreams.

CHAPTER ELEVEN

Amy glanced at her friends seated next to her. They were lined up in hard metal chairs, looking stiff and uncomfortable. She clutched her hands to her stomach to still the queasy rumbling. The smell of microwave popcorn and Lean Cuisine meals lingering in the stale air didn't help. She checked her watch. Twenty minutes had passed like a day in eternity, in insufferable silence. No one seemed to notice they were there. No one seemed to care.

Zelda was escorted somewhere down the hall after they arrived, and they hadn't seen her since.

Rian rose and leaned against the wall opposite the chairs. She stood with her feet crossed, one toe to the ground, while her eyes seemed locked on the line where dirty beige walls met the gray linoleum tiles. Her fingers were shoved into her jeans pocket. The other hand twirled a brown curl. Sunglasses poked from the pocket of her scotch plaid shirt, with the sleeves rolled up to her forearm in precise wide cuffs.

Amy's eyes lit with surprise when she saw Rian drive up, especially after her declaration about being questioned. Rian must have had a change of mind. Or a change in tactic. She wasn't sure which, and she wasn't going to ask—not here, anyway.

Amy glanced at Genna. She was sitting in the chair like a plank of southern pine. Her mouth was pressed into a tight line of Lancôme's Rose Contre-Tremps. Her matching manicured fingers were drumming the chair arms without making a sound.

Genna's white linen tunic and matching pants seemed out of place in the stark police station. As if dressed to impress, her pricey pink coral beads hung in layers from her neck. Pale pink faux snake ballet flats were planted flat on the floor, ankles touching.

Almost six feet at sixty, Genna commanded attention by the way she entered a room. A twinge of envy sliced through Amy as she looked at her friend. Even seated in the police station, waiting for who knew what, Genna was all confidence and composure. She was a woman who knew how to get her way and didn't have an ounce of regret for the ways and means of how it was done. Genna uncrossed her ankles, and her signature perfume with its subtle notes of purpose and prosperity drifted toward Amy. A clock ticked above a dusty plastic tree. The air conditioner droned on and off, sucking the breath from the building and then blowing it back in.

A woman in uniform appeared from behind a heavy steel door.

"Amy Sparks? This way." She looked up and their eyes met.

The muscles in her legs tensed, but she followed obediently, her sandals slapping against the floor as if keeping time. At the door, she paused and glanced behind her. Genna and Rian were being led to similar rooms nearby.

A bead of sweat trickled between her breasts as she entered the room. It was bright and bare except for a table and three chairs. It still smelled of popcorn and aftershave.

"We appreciate your coming," the woman said. Her words were polite enough, but they seemed empty of feeling.

"Are we in trouble? Have we done something wrong?"

"That depends on your definition of wrong." The woman smiled briefly. "We're all guilty of something. Sit," she ordered.

Amy shuddered as the cold chair bottom met hers. Wary now, she studied the woman sitting in front of her. Her eyes were black-brown and too small for her face, and her hair was pulled back tight and slick above a shiny forehead that held the telltale tan of a ball cap like maybe she played softball or golf in her spare time. The short sleeves of her white shirt hung loosely, and her belt bunched at the waistband. She had lost weight recently.

She pursed her lips. This was just a detective doing her job, nothing more. There was nothing to be frightened of. She was a woman who put on her pants the same way they all did.

The detective shifted her gaze to the manila folder open in front of her. Amy swallowed hard. More sweat beaded between her breasts.

"I understand you are friends with Mrs. Carlisle. How long have you known her?"

"About six years."

"How would you describe the nature of her relationship with her husband? Her deceased husband," she corrected flatly.

Her shoulders jerked as if she had been shoved.

The detective raised an eyebrow.

Her chest tightened. Another drop of sweat trickled from beneath her bra. She was not going to crumble beneath that gaze and those eyebrows that looked as if they had never been plucked. She inhaled deeply through her nose and then exhaled through her mouth.

Be calm. Be the calm you want to be.

Her jaw relaxed. She squeezed her trembling hands in the deep of her lap and looked at the detective with a steady gaze.

"I'd say they behave the way any married couple behaves."

"Which means what?"

"Which means they have good days and bad days."

"What would cause a bad day?"

She shrugged. "An argument."

"Do you know what they argued about?"

"Money. Chores. Things Zack wouldn't do that Zelda wanted him to, and vice versa."

"These were heated arguments? Were they physical? Abusive?"

Her eyes widened. Did the detective notice? She had to keep her feelings off her sleeve. She had to keep emotions in check. She wouldn't speak about Zack's violent nature. She wouldn't betray her friend in that way.

"They were just loud. Maybe some hurtful words."

"You must be very close to Zelda Carlisle to know those details. A close confidant, even."

Amy nodded and then regretted it. Sweat trickled beneath her shirt.

"Is Zelda Carlisle the kind of person who would kill her husband?"

"No!" she barked, her head shaking with determination. "Never! She's kind and generous. And she loves Zack. She loved Zack," she repeated firmly. "I know she did."

"Even when he was abusive?" the detective asked.

She answered with silence.

The detective pulled a photo from the file and placed it in front of her on the table. A dark-haired man in a red madras shirt and a pair of khaki shorts was sprawled on a dirty concrete floor. She winced. Her stomach lurched.

The shirt and pants were the same ones she had helped Zelda pick out for a gift last Christmas. Dark hair curled at the back of Zack's head, which was turned to show his profile. A dark stain pooled around him and bloomed from his neck like a limp parachute that had not done its job.

She closed her eyes against the image, but it was still there. Nausea rocked her. She had never seen a dead body. Not outside of her dreams.

Amy stared at the table, the photo in the periphery of her vision. She couldn't keep her eyes on the photo, but she couldn't keep her eyes away from it.

The detective placed another picture next to it. There were other cars in the stalls at the parking garage, but here they were shown mostly from the license tag down. The focus of the photo was a line of tire marks that led from the top of the garage runway. The detective pulled the third photo from the folder. The garage exit sign above a door was the focus of this one, taken just outside the edges of where he lay.

The detective tapped the photo of the sign and Amy's eyes followed. "Carlisle was walking toward the stairs in the parking garage when he was struck down. A vehicle would have had to swerve out of its lane to strike him."

Amy looked up, a thousand questions running through her head, none of them willing to be spoken.

Tapping the photo of the cars and the tire tracks, the detective said, "Let's say the average speed in a parking garage is less than five miles an hour, if that. If someone got struck at that speed, the force would knock them down, most likely. But the car that made these tracks was going much faster. Faster, because it needed to. Because the driver wanted to hit Carlisle. Wanted to knock him down. Wanted to kill him."

Amy could feel her face drain of color.

"Tell me about Genna Gregory's car being involved in an accident that night."

Amy shifted uncomfortably in the chair, now painfully aware of the sweat between her breasts. She hoped there was no stain darkening the front of her T-shirt.

"Genna? An accident?"

"She claims she hit a deer. Were you not aware of the fact?"

Her mind raced.

"If Genna said she hit a deer on the way to Hot Springs, she hit a deer. She had no reason to lie about that."

"'*On the way to Hot Springs*,' you said. And you believe her?"

"Of course I do."

"I see." The woman made a note on the folder.

"I saw it!" The words were out of her mouth before she knew it.

"Saw what?"

"I saw the deer on the side of the road! Genna showed me the picture. And I saw her car, too. There was deer fur on the bumper."

Did the detective believe her? Did she believe herself? Why had she said such a stupid thing? There was no picture. And maybe there was no deer. She didn't know. Not really. What *did* she believe? Was Genna telling the truth? Or was she covering up for something far more horrible?

She bit at her lip, then swallowed. Sweat trickled beneath her shirt. "It happens all the time, you know. Arkansas has one of the highest deer collision statistics. Did you know that? Of course, you did, you're a cop. I know that because I read about it in an insurance study. I don't know why. It just caught my attention."

The floodgates opened to let every fact she knew tumble down the spillway. There was no obstacle powerful enough to make it stop.

"There are over two million car accidents because of deer. Not just in Arkansas, of course, but everywhere. Except in Hawaii, because they don't have many deer. October and November are the worst months because the deer are rutting. I know it's not October.

It's spring, but that doesn't mean the deer aren't still out jumping in front of cars." Amy finally stuttered into silence.

She stared at the woman in front of her. Was that a smile of amusement?

The detective pulled yet another photo from the file and laid it on top. It was a picture of Genna and Zelda in the Mercedes. The car was entering the parking garage of the Bennfield Hotel.

"You'll notice," the detective said, "there is no damage to this car at their arrival."

Suddenly she was aware that everything she had said was recorded. That every word would come back to haunt her. Every word would be questioned until her story was as full of holes as the colander in the sink—noodles, like lies, knotted by boiling water.

The thought loomed heavy with the realization. Dominoes on Genna's deck had turned deadly. And she was smack dab in the middle of it.

Rian's words came back to her. *If anybody looks too closely, we look guilty.*

She felt guilty even though she knew her hands were clean.

"What is the nature of Rian O'Deis's employment?"

Amy tugged at her bra. "She runs the Pot Shed at the Cardboard Cottage & Company." Her voice sounded faint and far away in her own ears.

"Funny name."

"She sells potted herbs."

"And this is what she does for a living?"

"She also buys and sells vintage cars."

"That's an interesting occupation. A bit unusual for a woman."

Amy frowned at the rudeness of the accusation. First Zelda, then Genna, and now she needed to defend Rian, too. If the police knew or suspected what else Rian did for a living, they could try to trap her into an admission they would all regret.

"The car thing is kind of a hobby. But it's perfect for someone like Rian. And she is good at it."

The floodgates opened again.

"People give Rian their wish list, and she finds the perfect vintage car for them. She found Genna that gorgeous old Mercedes, and Zelda has owned several vintage cars because she likes to drive something different every year. And the Hummer Zack drives— drove," she corrected herself, and then fell silent. The water over the dam finally ran dry. What had she admitted to in that ramble? She hadn't played it like twenty-one questions, with yes and no answers, as she had planned. She had spilled the details that Rian would never have let out.

"Speaking of the Hummer, why does O'Deis have a lien against the vehicle for forty-five thousand dollars?"

"I, I wouldn't know. I don't know anything about that."

"I see." The detective made another note in the folder.

See? What exactly did she *see*? Why *did* Rian have a lien against the Hummer? It must be part of that tangled mess Rain mentioned. Is that how she had made an investment in Zack's business?

L91! She had forgotten to ask Rian about the key. She had forgotten to give the key to Rian.

"Were you not aware of the arrangement between Rian O'Deis, Genna Gregory, and Zack Carlisle?"

"Arrangement?"

"They own the lion's share of Mr. Carlisle's company."

"The lion's share?"

The words felt like a slap in the face. Her cheeks grew red and heated as if they'd been struck with a harsh hand. Nausea churned her stomach into fire. The lion's share. Not an investment. Rian and Genna hadn't just made an investment in Zack's company. They owned it!

They didn't tell her that. They didn't tell Zelda. Anger rose in the back of her throat like too much late-night wine. Her heart sank with a heavy pang.

Betrayal. The ache of how betrayal felt raked through her now. She knew that feeling, a raging fire that burned friendships to the ground. She drove 1,200 miles to hide from that rage six years ago. Humiliated and heartbroken, she fled her hometown, a tank full of lies she had been told fueling every mile of her escape.

She swallowed her anger, fighting against the emotion. She wouldn't let it overtake her now. She wouldn't let it ruin *this* friendship. That was then and this was now. There had to be a reasonable explanation here. There had to be. And she would find it. If she ever got out of this stark room and out from under the detective's hard gaze and never-ending questions, she would hunt it down. She would demand the truth.

The detective was watching her closely, brows furrowed, eyes bright.

"You didn't know of their business relationship?" she asked.

Amy shook her head. It was easier that way. Safer to stay mum.

"Then you wouldn't know anything about the insurance policy?" The woman paged through the folder. "Proceeds of two hundred and fifty thousand dollars. Each. That's quite a bit of money."

Amy didn't respond. Yes, that was a lot of money. Yes, they had kept this a secret. Yes, there was much more going on at the domino table on Genna's back deck. But murder?

Yes.

The answer struck her hard, like a bat to a ball. It was right in front of her. Right there all along. They had conspired to a common end. Zack's end, and the impenetrable cold, hard floor of death. And they had conspired without her. They had made their plans and carried them out without her ever knowing.

No! This couldn't be the truth.

"I understand you were the first to arrive at Mrs. Carlisle's aid on the evening of the accident," the detective was saying.

She blinked as if it would push her thoughts back, or the fears that tumbled along with them.

"How was Mrs. Carlisle's demeanor the next day?"

Had they killed him? Had they planned it? The question echoed in her head, hollow like the way a hawk call echoes across the hills and hollers.

"What?"

"I asked about Mrs. Carlisle's demeanor that day."

"She was distraught. She was as any wife would be if her husband died that way." Amy looked up, tears pooling at her lashes.

"Did you notice anything unusual at the time?"

"Unusual?" She saw Zelda's shoes in the bathtub. She heard the *thud* of the bag as it disappeared in the dumpster. She heard the sirens wail in her head as she awakened from her dream.

"No," she said quietly.

"Thank you for your information," the woman said suddenly as she scraped the chair back from the table and rose. She smiled briefly but, again, without feeling. "This is all we need," she added and opened the door to Amy's freedom.

Amy rose on unsteady knees. She entered the room feeling nervous. She was leaving in despair.

There were too many secrets hidden under the bones of her fancy dominoes with their crystal pips. Too many bones indeed.

* * *

Rian waited in the empty room. She pulled lint dregs from her shirtsleeves and faded Levis. She pulled a pocketknife from her jeans pocket to clean her nails, putting it away after she realized she was probably being watched. This was her favorite pocketknife, the one her father had carried. The antler handle was worn smooth and dark from his touch. She would fight anyone who tried to take it from her. She crossed her arms across her chest and lounged back in the chair, her eyes closed, her sneakers crossed at her ankles under the table. To anyone watching, she hoped she looked like she was taking a nap, but her mind was busy retracing the steps of that day.

The day Zack was killed.

Rian had driven the dusty road until she saw the base of the cell tower. Zack had given her the address, and she knew it was one of the tower sites the company leased. Rian had pulled into the driveway and stopped. The cell tower rose from a patch of mowed land shaved from the top of a mountain. A good three hundred yards from the tower, under a canopy of mimosa tree shade, sat an old mobile home. At one time it was the Cadillac of manufactured housing, but in the bright light, it was dull and neglected.

She geared the Fiat into reverse but sat a moment, looking at the sad sight. On either side of the rusty steps, five-gallon paint buckets had once held something tall and flowering. They were now dry dusty stalks, camouflaging the underbelly of the mobile home. Sun-bleached yard ornaments sat forlornly and forgotten in the brown brambles. Not far from the driveway, at the base of a tree, a single homemade wooden cross marked a plot along with a wreath of faded plastic flowers.

She eyed the John Deere tractor parked under the carport, noticing the bright green was a startling contrast to the drabness of its surroundings. A blue-and-white pickup truck, a Ford F-150, was parked beside the tractor with the cab pointed out. It had that square look of a mideighties model. The one just before Ford changed the design of America's favorite pickup by rounding out the corners and expanding the cab into a place a man could go to worship. This was a working man's truck, and she noticed the white side panels were immaculate.

The truck had seen its day on the farm, but she could tell it belonged to someone who knew how to treat a vehicle.

She couldn't say that about Zack.

Rian backed out of the driveway and turned the Fiat so she was facing out under an oak tree hanging over the road. She was far enough back from the county road that she couldn't be seen by passersby, and far enough from the homesite to go unnoticed by the owner, who would probably question who she was and why she was there.

She had patted the dash of her Fiat 1500, five-speed—her favorite car ever. It was a jewel she plucked from an auction one day when she had a fist full of cash. The Fiat was the same make and model Gina Lollobrigida zipped around in during wartime Italy.

Zack drove like someone who knew the dirt road by habit, gunning the Hummer around the bend, spinning in the dirt before lurching to a stop in front of her Fiat. A cloud of dust had settled over everything, including her.

"Jerk," she said. No wonder Zelda wanted him gone. She handed him the bag of bud and the key to L91. Their conversation was brief. He was cocky as usual. She watched as he drove down the road and turned into the driveway at the cell tower site.

Rian opened her eyes. The door opened with a heavy metal clank, drawing her from her thoughts and memories. Her eyes followed a woman as she sat down opposite. They both smiled, but Rian didn't mean it and she didn't think the officer did, either.

"What's this all about?" Rian asked.

"Just a little routine police business," the woman answered. She splayed her hands out in front of her, covering the folder and the pages inside. "How long have you known Zack Carlisle?"

"A while."

"How long is that?"

Rian shrugged. "Five years give or take."

"How did you meet him?"

"I don't remember."

"Don't remember or don't want to share?"

Rian looked the woman in the eye, dark eyes that didn't give away much. "I don't remember."

"How long have you known Zelda Carlisle?"

"A long time."

"Ms. O'Deis, can you be more specific, please?"

"August 1992."

The detective scribbled in her notes.

"What was your relationship with Mr. Carlisle?"

Rian steepled her fingers to her chest. "What is it you want to know?"

"I want to know about you and Zack Carlisle."

"He was my friend's husband."

"Nothing more?"

"We weren't screwing around if that's what you mean."

"You had no other business with Zack Carlisle?"

"None to speak of." None she *would* speak of. It was her business to know the answer to that.

"What is the nature of your partnership, then?"

Rian blinked to hide her surprise. She didn't see that trap before it sprung. She wasn't about to let it close in around her. "I must have misunderstood your question," she said.

The two stared at each other. The silence was brief but thorough. Rian laid her hands on the table in front of her, her fingers splayed open. "What is it that you want to know?" she asked finally.

"Tell me about this partnership."

Rian leaned against the chair back and crossed her ankles. "I invested in his company because he needed cash. I had some cash to invest. It was a simple business opportunity."

"For you and Ms. Gregory?"

"I can't speak for Genna." She *wouldn't* speak for Genna. Genna's point of view might confuse matters a bit, but she'd have to let that ride itself out.

"Where did the cash come from?"

Rian's gaze was steady, pointed, intense. "Why does that matter?"

The detective smiled. Rian didn't smile back.

"I understand you sell used cars?"

"I sell vintage cars."

"What's the difference?"

"Usually about ten or fifteen grand. Vintage cars have a higher price tag and better clientele."

"Zack Carlisle's vehicle—did he purchase it from you?"

"Yes."

"Is it vintage?"

"It's more a collector's item. A 1992 gloss green Hummer is not so easy to find."

"Why is that?"

"Ninety-two was the first year they made civilian Hummers—only made a few hundred of them. Only made two in gloss green."

"Where did you find it?"

Rian cocked her head. "Now, that's a trade secret. I have sources."

The detective shook her head slowly. "Where did you find it?" she repeated. Her tone had turned terse.

"I bought it from a military collector in Delaware," she said finally.

"Why the lien?"

Rian raised an eyebrow. The detective had caught her again unaware, a trap set and left hidden. She had to be careful. Someone had been doing their homework. "Ah, the lien," she said, her tone light. "It was because Zack was short of the selling price, and I didn't want to sell it to him for less. We made a compromise.

If he sells it, I get my money off the top."

"And now?"

Rian shrugged and let out a sigh. "The lien is still good."

"Are you aware that Genna Gregory's car was in an accident the night of Mr. Carlisle's death?"

Rian nodded. "Coincidence. Nothing more than that."

"But she didn't report it to the authorities."

"We were all a little distracted that day. She reported it to her insurance company."

"Is that something we can verify?"

"*Can* you? I don't know. I guess that depends on you and the insurance company."

The detective nodded curtly and focused on Rian with a dark-eyed stare. "Now about this corporate insurance policy."

The two women looked at each other with determination. Neither spoke. Rian let the silence grow. The detective spoke first.

"I understand the insurance proceeds at Mr. Carlisle's death will be payable to you and Genna Gregory equally. Five hundred thousand dollars is a lot of money."

Rian didn't speak.

"Why won't you answer?"

"You didn't ask me a question."

The officer leaned back and stretched her arms to her sides and then above her head before landing them akimbo behind her neck, lacing her fingers shut. She coughed and let it rumble into light laughter.

"It would be best if you would be more forthcoming, Rian O'Deis. We can continue to play cat and mouse if you like. I can be here all day if we need to be. If you have nothing to hide about this relationship, or the money, or his death, now is the time for you to speak up."

Rian leaned forward on her elbows. "Detective," she said quietly.

She kept her voice flat and smooth as if she were encouraging a hungry dog to let go of a bone. "You and I both know that under these circumstances things appear somewhat suspicious. But I assure you, our goal was just about being smart in business. Zack Carlisle climbed cell towers for a living. The risk of an accident was high from the get-go, and he was the only one of the three of us who knew anything about this business. That insurance policy was meant to insure our investment, which it has. I agree this circumstance is unfortunate—a man is dead. But there's no rationale for making a mountain out of our molehill, and no evidence that we had anything to do with his death. We're just two women who wanted to protect the investment of our life savings."

Rian leaned back and steepled her fingers, her elbows resting lightly on the arms of the chair. "Now, if we were men, you wouldn't be questioning our motives or our methods. Don't you think that's true?"

It surprised Rian when the detective nodded. It thrilled her, too, but she kept the elation from showing. Sometimes stating the obvious helped avoid what wasn't.

The woman shuffled the papers, stacked them back into the file, then pulled out a photograph of Zack Carlisle dead. It struck Rian as cheap, a sandbag attempt to pluck tears from a dry creek bed. She hated Zack Carlisle. She wished he'd disappear—just as Zelda wanted him to. She wasn't sad about his death, but she would share none of this with the detective. Or with anyone. These were feelings she would keep to herself.

"Did you see Zack Carlisle the day he was killed?" the detective asked.

Rian dabbed at the corner of her eye at a fake tear. "I did not."

"Where were you?"

"At home. On my farm."

"Can anyone vouch for that?"

"Just the chickens in the yard," she said. "I live alone."

* * *

Genna tapped her fingers on the tabletop in the empty room. The rhythm was a comfort somehow. She squirmed in her seat then crossed and uncrossed her legs. She chewed and spat out an entire pack of gum, as gauche as that was. She cleaned out her purse and left the crumpled tissues and gum wrappers in a neat pile on the corner of the desk.

She had been waiting for more than forty minutes. It was more than an hour since her last cigarette, and she was ready to bite someone's head off and serve it up for lunch.

She knew they were watching her from somewhere behind the scenes and that her impatience might be misunderstood.

She thought about lighting a cigarette anyway when the door opened and a man about her age walked in. He was short for a man by her way of thinking. He was overweight, balding, and dressed in beige. Terrible color for a man of any age. He introduced himself as one of the Hot Springs detectives on the case of Zack Carlisle's death.

He threw down a picture of her car before she could gauge his temperament and seductively plan her moves, so she knew matters were headed from bad to worse. The photo was of her car entering the Bennfield Hotel garage.

"Oh for crying out loud," she mumbled.

The image was a black-and-white and grainy as old leather, but Genna recognized her 1983 Mercedes 300D. In color, the Mercedes was a perfect shade of red. Amy had tried to nickname it "Big Apple" after her favorite OPI nail polish color, but she had put the kibosh on that.

"Your friends say you hit a deer on your way to Hot Springs that night." He pounced at the photo with a pudgy finger. "We know that's a lie. There's no damage showing in this photo, time stamped at 5:15 p.m."

He grinned like the Cheshire cat in Lewis Carroll's strange land, and Genna saw the gray, coffee-stained teeth of someone who didn't have a good relationship with a dentist. She ran her tongue over her own white pearls that were indeed semi-precious. She had the dentist bill to prove it.

He swung the chair around and straddled the hard, gray seat. "So did you hit a deer on the way to Hot Springs or on the way back to Bluff Springs?" His voice boomed in the sparse room. Genna could smell coffee and cigarettes on his breath. It made her jones for a smoke even more.

"Why, yes I did, Detective," she said sweetly, fighting fire with peach blossom honey. "My friends have the event confused. After all, they weren't there. It happened *after* I left the hotel."

"Damn convenient," he barked.

"For whom, may I ask? Certainly not for me or the deer."

"Don't play smart with me, Ms. Gregory. The law doesn't appreciate a smart-mouth no matter how pretty they may be."

Genna winced.

"Let me get this straight. You hit a deer on the way home, and now your car is sitting in your driveway as pretty as can be. No dents, no nothing. What was so important about getting it fixed in such short order? What was so critical that it couldn't wait a few more days?"

Genna blew her breath audibly through her nose. She sounded like a horse about to stomp over the finish line in fourth place. She pawed at the desktop with her manicured fingertips.

"Well, if you must know," she said, speaking as if to a petulant child, "I have a significant engagement in Little Rock with a senator next week. I needed it repaired quickly."

"You could have rented a car," he said.

Genna didn't respond. She wasn't about to be baited by his point of view.

"Funny though," he said, his voice now calm, his words slowed to a drawl, "we can't find any records for the repair. Nobody in town seems to know a thing about it. Not a single body shop in the area claims to have worked on a red 1983 Mercedes four-door."

He shrugged his shoulders. "So, you have a fairy godmother or something? Somebody who waves a magic wand and turns your busted carriage back into a princess ride?"

"I prefer queen to princess," Genna said snidely under her breath, knowing her attitude might engage a consequence. "Here's what I can do," she said bravely, a new tactic in mind. "I don't recall the name of the establishment because he's a friend of a friend, a shade tree mechanic who lives out somewhere deep in the hollers. If you let me out for a brief break, I'll get his name and number, and you can go ask him yourself."

She wasn't confident she could cover her words. Rian would never give up the name and whereabouts of her friend's garage, and she didn't remember a fraction of the twists and turns they took to get there. But if she didn't get to a cigarette in the next thirty seconds, she was going to die trying.

She perched a perfectly drawn eyebrow at the detective. "Agreed?"

The detective threw his head back and laughed, shaking the girth at his belt. Suddenly he leaned forward and smacked the table with his fist.

"There's an awful lot of tomfoolery going on with you ladies," he said, his face threatening as it turned an angry shade of purple. "None of your stories seem to match up. Why don't you just tell me what happened that night? Maybe Zelda Carlisle was behind the wheel of your Mercedes with a little too much alcohol and pent-up anger?

Maybe she just meant to bump him to give him a little scare."

Genna pursed her lips. "That's not at all what happened," she said hotly. "I never saw Zack. Zelda and I were at the lobby bar together until I left. Until then, I never left Zelda's side. Not for one single minute."

"Not even to smoke? Hey, I'm a smoker, too. I know what that feels like."

"We went out to the portico but Zelda came with me. They had just painted the concrete floor, and they had part of it roped off so we couldn't sit down. I smoked, and Zelda paced. Then we went back inside."

The detective nodded, and a cumbersome silence fell over the room.

"I need to tell you, Genna Gregory, that we've been doing our homework since this . . . accident. Frankly, we're starting to think this was no ordinary hit-and-run. We've been asking ourselves how it is that all of you had reason to be in Hot Springs that night."

Before Genna could utter a word in her defense, he formed a fist with one hand.

"*Boom!*" he shouted and smacked his fist in his hand. Genna jumped in her seat. "Then you're not in Hot Springs and Carlisle's dead.

"And then *boom!* A deer jumps out in front of you and crumples your grill right where a man's knees would be. Coincidence?" He shook his head slowly. "Hard for me to believe."

He wiped his hand across his forehead now blistered with sweat. "Around here, we call that *opportunity*. And now with Zack Carlisle gone, you get a nice little chunk of cabbage to add to your bank account." He grinned. "We call that *motive*.

"And boom," he said, this time not so loud. His fist was silent on the table. "Your car is free of any evidence that could connect you or your Mercedes to the crime. And that," he said, rising from his chair, "is a well-laid plan of *murder*."

Genna's eyes widened in surprise and then turned to flint. "Oh, no, you don't," she said, jumping up from her chair. She pointed a thin, brightly manicured finger at his face and hissed, "You won't slog me down some sociopathic-trodden path, you overblown frog. Zack Carlisle brought this down on himself, and you're not going to back us into a corner. Not while I'm around." Genna spun around and grabbed her purse then bustled toward the door, long legs striding with indignation.

"I guess we are done here, Ms. Gregory," he said to her back, a furtive smile playing on his lips as she swung the door open. "Stay in touch, won't you?"

* * *

Zelda shivered. She was colder than she could remember ever being, even colder than when she fell into a pond and was hauled out through the shards of sharp gray ice. She was lucky that day. Her family was nearby when she fell through a soft spot on the pond's surface—they heard the crack of ice and her call for help.

Her fingers felt numb beneath her thighs, where she held them to still the trembling as much as to keep them warm. Startled, she opened her eyes. She was all alone in this gray place. The detective was gone, and she was lying on a cot, a green wool blanket covering her bare arms and legs.

The timbre of voices leached through the walls, and she could hear the rise and fall of emotion, the hum of other noises, too. Although unable to discern the words or the people who spoke them, she could imagine who they were. She could imagine what they were talking about.

Zelda and Zack. And what they thought she had done to him.

Pulling the blanket tighter around her shoulders, she struggled to piece it together. She remembered being led to a room and left shivering for a while before a big, balding man introduced himself as a Hot Springs detective and sat down. Heavy eyebrows arched like two dark caterpillars balanced above his eyes, as if ready to roll off at any moment. He had little hair anywhere else on his head, and the contrast was amusing. She had stifled a smile.

He opened a file to recap the details, which she had given in Hot Springs the morning after Zack's death. He read from the folder without emotion like a court reporter reading testimony back to the jury. But she didn't need to be reminded. She remembered that day clearly.

The police had driven her to the morgue where she identified her husband. Even as she nodded her response, the gray, lifeless body didn't look like the Zack Carlisle she knew. He looked like a mannequin made up for Halloween. Funny what comes to mind in such circumstances, she had thought at the time.

While she was standing beside the body, her father's voice rushed to her mind like a warm embrace.

Hey Z, what did the dead raccoon say in his will? Leave it to Beaver!

His hearty laugh filled her memory, a genuine guffaw that followed a joke even after telling the same one a dozen times. And then, standing by the man who had once been her husband, Zelda smiled. She glanced up at the policeman beside her, but it was too late. He had seen her smile.

"Do you still stand by your statement?" The detective in front of her had pointed a stubby finger at the page. He had stopped reading and glared at her over the rims of his glasses as if he were studying a caged animal. She had felt like one.

"I do." The words made her ache. Those were the very words that got her into more trouble than anything else.

I do.

After three marriages that ended in divorce messier than a spring tornado, she had sworn there would be no more. Zack would be her final "till death do us part." How cruel those words seemed to her now.

"Once upon a time . . ." the detective said as if he were starting a children's story, "this looked like an accidental hit-and-run, a quirky accident without much rhyme or reason. But when no one came forward to confess—which they usually do when their conscience keeps them up at night—we started to look at this from a different angle. And then we saw a few things that didn't match up."

Staring at him, straining to listen, she had struggled to stay above the noise in her head.

"Mr. Carlisle—your late husband—was walking on the left side of the parking garage toward the stairs when he was struck down. That means whoever hit him swerved out of their lane to strike him."

She wanted to cover her ears.

"He was carrying a couple of bags. One held an expensive bottle of champagne. I guess he thought he was going to be celebrating. Maybe he turned around when he heard a car racing up behind him. Maybe he loosened his grip on the other bags and tightened his grip on the champagne. Maybe he pulled the bag to his chest the way a running back would hug the ball."

Why did he tell her this? The ache rose from her belly. Her ears filled with a soft, whining hum.

"It could be that he recognized the person bearing down on him. Maybe he thought it was a joke, a prank that would end with the bumper inches from his knees. But it didn't happen that way, did it?

"No," he had answered himself as the hum in her ears grew louder.

"No, indeed. And that's how an accidental hit-and-run becomes a homicide. Nothing else explains the tire marks at the start of the skid, where the driver punched the gas before she hit her target. That's no accident. And no stranger would run a man down that way," the detective said pointedly.

"This was rage," he added quietly. The hum in her ears reached a deafening pitch. "This was the rage of a wife who wanted her husband dead."

Wanted her husband dead. It was all she heard before the room went dark.

Zelda shifted under the blankets, remembering. She heard the door open, heavy steps drawing close, and then the balding head appeared over her, his charcoal breath once again fouling the air.

"Wh-what happened?" she murmured.

"You fainted right out of your chair."

CHAPTER TWELVE

Amy sat at the long library table and let her eyes sweep over the room, taking in the details and mentally making a list of chores yet to do. With the doors to both the Cardboard Cottage & Company and Tiddlywinks soon to be repaired, she hoped their idyllic world also would soon return. Genna had persuaded a stained glass artist she knew to put the project on the top of her list. In the artist's capable hands, the glass would be matched as near perfect as possible. The door would be pricey, but she trusted her insurance would cover the cost.

The Cardboard Cottage as a whole was still closed, including the bakery, going on more than two weeks now. She was riddled with angst about the money not coming in, but she agreed with Genna and Rian that the shops should stay closed out of deference to Zelda and the circumstance that surrounded her.

Even so, she wanted to keep working at it, even if behind the scenes. She couldn't just lock up and leave it. Order was being restored. What could be saved from the trash bin was patched and put back on the shelf. Estate sales notices were piling up on her calendar, and so was her excitement to shop them. Hunting treasures at sales and auctions was exciting.

Insurance would cover everything, minus her deductible. Even a loss-of-income check was on its way, and it was more than enough to cover the mortgage payment. Thank goodness she had listened to the advice of her insurance agent. The policeman's wife had been right about that, too. You can never have too much insurance.

She walked to the back of the shop and opened a door that led to a large storage room. Musty, stale air greeted her, and she propped the door open to let in a little breeze. Along with getting Tiddlywinks back on its feet, she had decided to put any leftover proceeds from the insurance payment toward the creation of an escape room. It would be a perfect match for Tiddlywinks, and escape rooms were gaining in popularity in tourist towns.

She paced the floor, counting her steps. It was about twelve feet square, just the right size for a small group of players. Lock, Stock, and Barrel was one of the names pinging her interest. She liked the way that sounded. Rock, Paper, Scissors was a contender, too. Both had appeal, but she hadn't decided on which name to use, if either. If it wasn't for what was going on around them, she would be giddy with the possibilities that lay before her.

She wasn't proud to admit it, even to herself, but she felt more grief about the demise of the games she lost than she felt for the demise of her friend's husband.

The antique Sulphide marbles stolen from the locked curio case had not resurfaced. She hadn't really expected them to be recovered, although she was a bit surprised they hadn't been found in Zack's pocket. The police didn't yet have any leads about the break-in, and there was never any evidence to point the finger at Zack. Not that it mattered. Not now. But the timing of the break-in was too coincidental, too close to Zack's outburst for her to draw any other conclusion. Was she being unkind to think he wrecked her shop as revenge? Probably. Zack had been angry because she defended Zelda. Because she always took Zelda's side. Because she thought Zelda could do far better than him, and he knew she felt that way.

But of all the things to steal from the shop, the old marbles were the least valuable. If he wanted something to pawn for money, there were other items in the case that fit that bill better. He wouldn't have known their worth, so she could only surmise he smashed the glass and grabbed the first thing he could.

The whole incident bothered her though. Even if the marbles were precious, they didn't seem worth the effort. The damage to the shop didn't fit the theft. And the theft didn't fit the damage to the shop. It was a puzzle all its own.

Amy walked back through the shop, turned off the lights, and pulled the plywood closed where it hung on the hinges Ben had added, along with a padlock and clasp. She glanced at the darkened bakery window as she passed under the eaves. The *Sorry, No Crumpets Today* sign hung lopsided from a string in the window. She missed the smells of cinnamon and yeast. She missed Sammie's Irish tea and cream. She missed Sammie. She hoped she would take this time for an overdue vacation, and more, she hoped she would return when their shops were ready to reopen. There was a chance Sammie might choose to move on.

She climbed the stairs to her apartment and let herself in.

Sitting on the edge of her bed with her head in her hands and a cat on her lap, she knew Victor was content. She was not. Her head was full of questions.

It was clear the investigation into Zack's death had turned from an unfortunate accident in a parking garage to something else entirely. Murder. Manslaughter. Something more than an accidental hit-and-run. The police interrogation had left her feeling vulnerable and betrayed.

Genna had recapped her interview, recounting her outburst at the detective as if she were playing charades. Zelda told them she fainted. Rian had shared nothing.

Something horrible had happened in that parking garage. Somehow, she had to find out what. Somehow, she had to find out who. And she needed to do that before they all landed in jail. It was bound to happen. It was just a matter of when.

The more she thought about it, the more troubled she felt. Someone would soon be arrested for Zack Carlisle's death. Zelda had to be the first in line. And yet, if she looked at it from the detectives' points of view, all four of them were suspects. Although she wasn't anywhere near Zack on that fateful night, she had no proof otherwise. For that matter, neither did the others. No one could vouch for her whereabouts any more than she could vouch for theirs.

Was Zelda so angry with Zack that she stepped on the gas with murderous intent? Had they argued? Had sanity and reason been taken over by rage fueling her anger and bravado? It was possible.

She hated herself for thinking it.

Was Genna's Mercedes involved? That would make sense why Genna said she hit a deer. She would say it to cover for Zelda. Genna always left the keys in the console of the Mercedes. It was a habit none of them could make her break. Zelda *could* have gone looking for Zack and found him. Then *bam. Bump!* Dead.

Shaking her head didn't help shake the picture out of her mind. It only disturbed Victor and he rose, circled her lap, and then settled himself once more.

Genna might have encountered Zack on her way out of the garage. That seemed more likely given the timing. But would Genna kill for the insurance money? Somehow it didn't seem likely.

And yet, money *was* a motive, and there was a lot of money riding on Zack's accidental death.

What if all three of them had set that plan in motion and drew Zack to his death?

A lump formed at the base of her throat and she swallowed it down. She touched the burn scar on her forehead. It happened so very long ago. And yet, she wondered if she would ever be able to leave it behind. She wanted to. She wanted to leave it in the past and let it go.

She wanted to let go of her fear of being left out. Excluded. Teased for being a frizzy redhead, or plump, or for the freckles that grew more plentiful in the sun. That, too, was a long time ago. A childhood ago. Still, those were the emotional buttons this memory pushed.

She fingered the peridot and diamond at her neck.

She hadn't been teased by these friends. Not here and now. But she had been left out. Excluded. The pang touched her, even though the thought of what they did was evil beyond her imagination.

Moving into the kitchen, she filled the espresso pot and set it on the stove. At the window, waiting for the sound of steam behind her, she gazed at the scene below, at the bright green in the leaves, at the little creek, at the water tumbling over the jagged rocks.

Her world changed for the better when she wandered into Bluff Springs. Now she was the proud owner of the Cardboard Cottage & Company and its successful resident shops. She had three friends who felt like sisters.

It could disappear in a puff of smoke.

If she believed that, the police believed it. And if the police believed it, they were looking for proof. Unless she got there first.

"Unless I get there first," she repeated out loud to no one, but Victor came to investigate anyway. He rubbed his head against her legs, swirled through them, and butted her shins. She reached down and stroked his back from the top of his head to the tip of his tail in one smooth stroke. He chirped a meow and lifted his head for more.

She had to do something. She had lied so easily about seeing Genna's wrecked car. She had lied about seeing the deer. A big fat lie by Amy Sparks, thank you very much. And now she didn't know what the real truth was and who was telling it.

She had to know who killed Zack Carlisle. And yet she was afraid to know. But if she was going to get at the truth, she'd have to do a little digging. And by digging, that meant snooping in other people's business. The thought was both thrilling and terrifying.

She would follow in Zack's footsteps the day he died.

She would find a way to follow him through his day until he met his end.

She wouldn't let Zelda know what she was about to do. Like a spark of genius, the plan took hold. She dialed the Golden Moon Retreat, and with a familiar plea to Juno Moneta, she booked the top spa package.

Zelda would never refuse a day at the spa.

CHAPTER THIRTEEN

"Yo! Zelda! You missed points," Genna said, pointing to the tiles just played. "We're trying to let you win, in case you haven't noticed."

"My heart's not in the game today," Zelda said quietly. There were dark circles under her eyes. Amy noticed that one of her fingernails were bitten to the quick. Zelda had begged off the last two games, but Genna had insisted they play today.

"Your loss is my gain," Genna said, scoring ten points from the mistake.

The dominoes splayed on the table like simple stitchwork. Amy poured another round of wine—a Pinot Grigio they bought at a San Joaquin Valley wine tasting and had four cases shipped home disguised as Omaha Steaks. Arkansas was dry in many counties. Shipping wine was as illegal as what Rian sold from the trunk of her car, although the antiquated laws were beginning to change.

Before the Cardboard Cottage & Company, the foursome took a trip together every year. Now, as shop owners, they closed the

Cardboard Cottage & Company for two weeks in the winter when tourism was sketchy at its best and nonexistent when the weather took an icy turn.

The California wine country had been their destination last year. Memphis and the Jack Daniel's distillery were part of their adventure the year before. Scotland was still down the road.

Amy glanced from one to the next. None of them seemed exuberant tonight, as if their trip to the police station had left them saddle sore, like a bumpy ride over terrain they didn't want to cover.

"Remember when we were at that cute little boutique winery, and Zelda got so drunk she backed into a tray of wineglasses?" Amy asked. She hoped to brighten the mood.

Zelda huffed. "Thanks for the reminder. *I remember* when you got carsick on the train and threw up in your new three-hundred-dollar Coach bag. Tit for tat."

"Don't forget what happened on the Jack Daniel's tour," Rian said, grinning at Genna. "I can't wait to see how well you behave on our scotch tour of Scotland if we ever get that far on our bucket list."

Genna nodded and lit a cigarette. "You promised to take me even if I'm an urn of ashes by then."

"I did," Rian said. "I promised."

"Where *are* we going next? I love our road trips," Amy said. "It's good Karma. C-a-r-m-a. Get it?"

Rian rolled her eyes.

"Where are we going next?" Genna asked. "I'm ready for a getaway."

"Actually, I have a request for a seventies Cadillac. Convertible. Preferably brown. And I have a lead down near New Orleans."

"Oh, yes," Amy said. "We could do New Orleans." Wherever they went, they would have a good time. The back seat would hold a basket of road food and wine and a little more wine in case they got lost in a dry county. After all, thirst was a terrible thing, according to Winston

Churchill and four good friends who enjoyed their libations.

Rian's vintage car trade made for a great excuse to travel. They never went for long, or far, but over the years they had taken road trips in vintage Thunderbirds and lightning-fast GTOs. She could just see them in a brown Cadillac, top down, tall sexy fins swimming down the road like a mermaid in water.

They were on their way to buy a Jaguar in Kansas City when a tornado touched down. They were only an hour over the Arkansas-Missouri border when the dark clouds overtook them. She would never forget that trip. None of them would ever forget it. They spent two days underground in an abandoned storm shelter. Two days with a basket of picnic foods and wine, and a friendship that deepened with every passing hour.

Amy reached for a nibble from the tapas plate. As the winner of the last game, she had provided the olive tapenade full of garlic and olive oil to spread on focaccia bread. Her courage was now boosted by the wine.

"I've been thinking about the four of us. I've been thinking about how close we are. I don't know what I would do if we were not together like this. I don't even want to think about something happening to keep us apart. And I would do anything for any of you. For any reason."

Rian raised an eyebrow. "Anything?"

"I'd do anything to keep us out of jail."

Genna burped. "That's ominous-sounding."

"Your burps are always ominous," Rian shot back. "Like the creature from the black lagoon."

Genna made a pinched face. "Some cultures not only consider belching a necessity but a compliment to the chef, as well. So Amy," she said, turning from Rian to Amy, "my compliments. But why would any of us go to jail?"

Amy wanted the right words in her mouth before she spoke. It would be so easy to upset the applecart already leaning on three wheels. "I got the impression the police don't believe it was an accident," she said finally. "They think we all had something to do with it. And then I was thinking, too, that it was odd we were talking about it, and then it happened."

"What is this *it* you keep referring to?" Genna demanded.

"Zelda said she wanted him gone. And now he is. And maybe if we stop keeping secrets from each other, we can get out of this mess before we all land in jail for murder."

"What are you yammering about?" Genna said louder than necessary.

"I know what she's getting at," Zelda said quietly. Zelda's eyes were on the dominoes in her hand, but it was apparent she wasn't seeing them. "She believes I killed Zack."

"No, I . . ."

"Then what do you think?" Zelda's tone was sharper than she had ever heard her be.

"She thinks you ran him over with my Mercedes," Genna added. "She thinks we dreamed up that story about hitting a buck."

Amy's anger flared at the accusations. "I want to know why you were all in Hot Springs and why I wasn't. I want to know what was going on behind my back!"

"I was never *in Hot Springs*," Rian hissed. "I was *outside* Hot Springs. I was out in the boondocks waiting for Zack to show up so he'd have weed for the weekend."

"What's eating you, Gilbert Grape?" Genna nudged Rian's arm and then touched the sleeve of her purple-and-green plaid shirt. "No one's accusing you of anything but bad taste."

"They confiscated all of that anyway," Zelda interrupted. "That's one personal effect they didn't give back to me." She looked at Rian and said, "You were the last person to see him."

"Me? Wait a minute. The last time I saw Zack, he was alive."

"And how could you prove that?" Zelda asked pointedly. "If someone wanted to know."

Rian stared at Zelda with dark eyes. Her tone was sharp. "You'll have to take my word for it."

Genna interjected, "And I was on the phone with Rian. That was right after I hit the deer."

"What?" Rian turned to Genna in surprise.

"You remember. We talked about that, uh—oh, I don't remember what we talked about. But we talked about it, whatever it was."

Rian was quiet for a moment, her dark eyes scanning Genna's.

"We talked about baseball," Genna added with a smirk. "Your favorite subject."

"And what time was that? Should anybody ask," Amy added.

"Oh, for pity's sake," Genna yelped. "I don't know what time it was! It was whatever time we need it to be. I may have been a little tipsy. Plus, I don't like baseball, so I wasn't listening. And, I don't like all those deer that keep jumping out in front of my Mercedes!

"Amy, listen to me," Genna continued, her face flushed. "None of us had a reason to run Zack over. Zip. Nada. Nil. That's the story, no matter who is doing the telling. Or who is doing the asking. Not one of us had a motive nor opportunity to kill Zack. Even if that fat, stinky old copper thinks we did! Got it?"

"Except for me." Zelda's voice was barely audible. "I doubled Zack's life insurance policy six months ago. He thought it was a good idea."

"Why did you do that?" Amy asked.

"Protection against the odds. Zack was a horrible husband."

"Holy cow."

Capital *D*. A horrible husband and a horrible human being who someone wanted to kill. Someone wanted to put Zack out of their misery. And did. "*Nach a Mool.*"

Rian turned to face Amy. "Why do you always say that? You're not Jewish."

"I was raised by Jewish people from New Jersey."

"I thought you were from Florida."

"Florida is dominated by Jewish people from New Jersey."

"You were raised Jewish? This is news to me," said Genna.

"I spent a lot of time at my best friend's house."

"She was Jewish?"

"Her maid was Jewish."

"What does that mean anyway?" Rian asked. "Snatch a mule? Knock a mule?"

"*Nach a Mool.* It's Yiddish. It means 'and so on and so on.' Kind of like yada, yada, yada."

"I don't get it."

"Of course you don't. You're Catholic."

"Hail Mary," Rian said and gently flicked a ladybug off her bare arm. She watched as it flew into her wineglass, grimaced, and fished it out with her fingertips. "This is getting messy."

Amy agreed. "We have to stick together on this. The police are asking questions and we look guilty."

"Guilty of not scoring points with these bones," Genna said sharply. "And it's your turn!"

Her smile felt empty. They were going around in circles. One minute it was certain they were in the clear, and the next minute the tracks got muddy. Didn't she trust them? Didn't they trust her?

The thought made her heart ache. Why couldn't she just let it go?

Because there were too many secrets. Secrets getting uncovered leaving more secrets hidden. Because if they just left circumstances to chance, they might all wind up in jail for a crime of murder. She had a plan, and tomorrow, she would put it into action.

CHAPTER FOURTEEN

The day dawned sunny and full of possibilities. Pacing the floor with excitement and a twinge of guilt for the underhanded thing she was about to do, she waited until it was near time for Zelda to leave for the spa. Her appointment was at ten, and she had an hour's drive. Zelda had, of course, tried to talk her into coming for a shared spa day. She had begged off with an excuse that seemed to satisfy Zelda without much effort. She sensed that Zelda was looking forward to some private time, under the warm capable hands of her favorite masseuse and a facial that would put her right with the world. Or as much right as could be achieved under the circumstances. While the gift was a distraction to get her out of the house, it was a good distraction, and Zelda deserved every spa-scented moment of it.

After pulling on a black shirt and sweatpants, she laughed at herself in the mirror, looking like a thief about to burgle a museum. No need to be dramatic. She changed into her favorite carpenter-style jeans and a T-shirt. Both were far better suited for incognito in a nice neighborhood in the middle of the day. She belted her hair into a tight knot, stuck a screwdriver and a nail file in her pants pocket, and set out for her caper.

Within minutes she was parked behind the clubhouse at the end of Zelda's street. Right on time, Zelda pulled out and turned west.

She slipped into the back yard and retrieved the key from the top of the electrical box. The house was quiet, and the shades were still drawn.

The envelope with Zack's pocket items was on the desk in a spare room he used for his office. She unwound the string and peeked inside to find a wallet, keys, and an old-fashioned flip phone in a leather case. She opened the wallet and thumbed through the bills, all twenties.

She opened the cell phone, but the screen was black.

"Dead," she said under her breath. She would have to charge it before she could access Zack's calls. She ruffled the papers on the desk for the charger, opened the drawers, and scattered the contents with her fingers.

She spied the phone charger in the wall socket near a side table and plugged the phone in.

Now eyeing the file cabinet, she pulled at the drawers. All but one were unlocked. That one was the one drawer she needed to see.

After fishing out the keys from the envelope, she tried each one without success and then shoved them into her pocket. Now more than ever determined to get at the contents of the locked drawer, she stabbed at it with the nail file and then the screwdriver, making a mess of the paint around the lock. Apparently, only a key or a true thief could open it. She had neither.

There were two rings of keys in the desk drawer. There were loose keys scattered among the papers. Several had round cardboard tags attached. G94. L16. She remembered L91 and Rian's interest in it. She had forgotten to ask about it yet again.

She tried the keys one by one.

Finally, the lock opened. The key was marked Z01.

Disappointment filled her. The drawer was empty except for a few folders pushed to the front of the drawer by its metal follower block. A small box was shoved against the back. Pulling the manila folders to her lap, she sat down to read. There were files, documents, insurance forms, and leases for cell tower sites with such legalese that although she read and then reread them, they still didn't make sense. One folder had a page of ruled paper with a list of names written by hand. Some were crossed out, others had a check mark beside them, and three of the names were marked with hand-drawn stars. She didn't recognize any of the names.

She pulled the final folder out and opened it. Bingo. Newspaper clippings from Arkansas, Mississippi, and Louisiana crammed the folder in disarray. She scanned through them quickly, studying the photos more closely, but didn't recognize any of the people in the photos or their names. She grabbed one of the articles and began to read.

It was about Zachary Taylor. Not Zachary Taylor, the twelfth president of the United States. This was a Zachary who had a different past. One that had to have changed before he became Zelda's Zack Carlisle.

She stifled a whistle. Zack wasn't who he claimed to be. Not if he had different names in every state.

Amy jumped when Zack's cell phone rang.

Should she answer it? The thought was swift. She let it ring, hoping it would capture the number and record any message the caller might leave. It could be a clue.

Now intrigued, she read the newspaper articles in detail. They were an odd collection of strange stories, but now that she realized Zack was a man of many names, it was easier to read between the lines. Zachary Taylor, ZC Dupoint, Zack Carlisle—they were all the same man who left a trail of angry people behind him wherever he went.

He was mentioned in real estate deals that went belly-up. He was blamed by those who were burned as the cause and culprit in his scams. He was named in lawsuits for promises gone bad. There were stories about cell towers and cell tower leases, and how investments could be secured for a high rate of return. There were obituaries for people she didn't know. One was a story about a bereaved husband who lost his wife and dog to cancer and blamed the cell tower that sat on his land. There was a news clipping about bird deaths, another about bee deaths, and a beekeeping farm that bankrupted when their commercial colonies mysteriously died. Mysteriously, it claimed, right after a cell tower was erected nearby.

The last page in the folder was a flyer claiming that cell towers caused brain tumors because of the radiation being emitted.

Amy laughed out loud. Zack had kept it.

Zelda had borrowed Zack's Hummer to get redbud trees at an end-of-the-season sale. She had dragged Amy along. Zelda purchased several trees, but when they rang up at $6.66 apiece, Amy insisted she add three angel wing begonias to her purchase. The *angels* would make it right.

"Never mess with the Fates," Amy told Zelda as they loaded the trees in the car. It might be a silly superstition, like crossing your fingers or knocking wood, but it didn't hurt to be safe.

The flyer was on the windshield when Amy and Zelda got back to the Hummer in the parking lot. Neither one of them questioned why someone would leave it there, nor did they notice if the message was meant for them alone or shared with everyone parked at Walmart that day.

"Cell phones and cell phone towers are going to fry our brains into crispy pork rinds," Amy read to Zelda out loud. They were on their way home via the fun route, as they called it—through the liquor store drive-through, down the back bumpy roads so they could smoke the roach they found in Zack's ashtray, and then finally through the Dairy Queen drive-through for chocolate ice cream cones.

They left the flyer in Zack's front seat.

A smile crept across her lips. Zack had kept it. He must have wondered if it were true.

Something pinged in her head and she looked at the paper again, noticing a corner was missing, as if someone had snatched it from a corkboard, or another person's hands. Opening the envelope of Zack's pocket items, she pulled out the scrap of paper she had noticed earlier. The corners weren't a match.

Disappointed, she put the scrap back in the envelope and sat back against the worn cushion of the chair.

Suddenly she felt at odds with her surroundings. She was nosing around in someone else's business, a dead someone's business, in a house that wasn't hers. These files and clippings belonged to a man now deceased, whose widow was her best friend. Guilt flooded her. Zelda would be angry if she found Amy thumbing through her husband's private affairs. Would she feel betrayed, even if Amy was trying to help?

Did Zelda know about these files, or was this yet another aspect of Zack's life that Zelda shut out of her awareness? It was odd that he kept these newspaper clippings. Maybe he had remorse for people he harmed. Or maybe was he collecting them like a scrapbook of little trophies he kept locked up.

Zack was a con man. The realization was powerful in her mind. It loomed like a beacon on the top of one of his towers.

A con man. And he had taken Zelda as his fool.

Maybe Zelda learned the truth about his past after she married him. Or maybe she didn't know still. And what could she do about it any of it, if she had?

Was that why she wanted Zack out of her life? They all thought he was rude and abusive. Now she knew there was even more to his despicable nature.

She reached for the locked box in the back of the drawer. None of the keys fit. The contents, at least for now, would go unknown.

A notebook calendar in the envelope took her to the day of his death. Zack lived a busy life until the end. She stuck the notebook in her pocket and moved on to the cell phone, now charged enough to use.

Her belly grumbled. Grumbled again a few minutes later. What would be the harm? Zelda would never notice a sandwich missing.

She rummaged around the fridge and found a package of bologna. Leaning against the counter, she rolled up and wolfed down three slices. She grabbed a jar of pickles and ate two spears. With surprise, she noticed the clock above the sink told her she had been there for three hours. It was a good thing Zelda was away for the day.

She turned when she heard feet shuffling outside the front door, not ten feet from where she stood at the sink. Her heart banged in her chest. Zelda was back early from the spa! How would she explain what she was doing in the house? How would she get out of that little lie?

Amy was poised for a quick flight when the doorbell rang.

Zelda wouldn't ring the doorbell.

Amy crept to the hallway and padded silently to the door. The bell rang again, and then the intruder knocked.

She peeked into the peephole.

There were two uniformed officers on the step outside.

"Zelda Carlisle," a male voice said from the stoop. "Mrs. Carlisle!"

Were they there to make an arrest? They must have found some evidence that convinced them of Zelda's guilt. And maybe there were police at Rian's house and Genna's door at this very minute, too. Even at her apartment.

Her mind sharpened into focus like the lens that zoomed in on the faces outside. She needed to make a decision right now. Right here. She either needed to give in to her friend's unimaginable guilt and then find and destroy any evidence that could prove that guilt, or she had to find the real killer, because it didn't seem as if the police were interested in looking any farther than Zelda's front door.

Could she convince herself one way or the other? Could she do whatever she needed to do? Wrong or right. Moral or not.

It's what family does.

If Zelda had mowed Zack down in the parking garage, she had good reason. She could get a good lawyer. She could show defense. She could . . .

The bell rang again.

"Mrs. Carlisle," the voice said again. Then silence.

She heard the shuffle of feet. In the peephole, she saw the two policemen retreating down the walk.

But they would be back. She knew they would be.

Amy retreated to the hallway, hidden from the windows. She stood silently, her heart pounding. She crept back to the peephole. The police were gone.

She tidied the room, closed the door behind her, and made her way back to her car.

Safely back at her own apartment, she knew what she had to do. She was already in too deep. She had tossed out the shoes. She had lied. If she was going to be a loyal friend, her loyalty would have to start now.

She needed a plan. She would start at the end of Zack's day and work backward. But the parking garage of the Bennfield Hotel was the last place she wanted to be.

With access to the inner workings of Zack's world—his voice mail messages, contacts, and calendar of his whereabouts—she could follow in his footsteps. She felt like a stalker predicting her prey's next move, but she pushed aside the feeling and moved on with her task.

Deciphering the entries in the calendar was more difficult than she thought. While she could read the dates and times of his scheduled events, the diary entries were in a personal shorthand, a code language only he would understand. For each entry, there was a letter—a first name, she assumed—followed by a three-character post, like G94 or P42. She had no idea if they were roads, or addresses, or lockers at the Greyhound bus station.

L91 belonged here, too.

What did it open?

She tried to play the voice messages. When it asked for the password, she tried the last four digits of the phone number, which she'd looked at in the phone's settings earlier. It didn't work, so she hung up and thought for a moment. She didn't know Zack well, but she couldn't imagine him thinking up a number difficult to remember. She called voice mail again, this time trying the four digits in their address. With a bit of luck, that worked, and the lady on the other end listed the date and time of the first message.

"You son of a bitch," a man yelled into the phone. "You told me my apple trees would be safe from your backhoe. I even staked out where to go. You *asshole*," the man yelled on, "your idiot drove right through the orchard we planted last year. You're going to pay for this, Carlisle. You're going to pay for my trees or else—"

The message ended abruptly. Whether a bad connection or an accidental call drop, she didn't know for sure. But the next message played after the voice time stamped it.

It was a woman's voice, but no one Amy recognized.

"Mr. Carlisle," the woman intoned. Her voice was cold and exacting, like a schoolteacher scolding him for drawing outside the lines. "This is Margarite Schaffer from Blue Mountain. We will be expecting you at our church's board hearing next Tuesday at six. Sharp. We are prepared to hear your proposal on why the church should consider the cell tower project with your company."

There was a brief silence. "I am—we are," the woman corrected, "aware that your proposal includes several promises that appeal to our board's financial interests. I trust those promises will be kept if we approve to move forward?"

Again, there was a brief silence as if she were expecting him to respond.

"I would encourage you to come prepared. There are strong opinions on either side." The message ended without a farewell, just an audible click from the phone on the other end.

Amy played the next message.

"Carlisle," a gruff voice said, "don't be messing with our game plan, buddy. You make the case like we talked about and everything will be just fine. I guarantee the votes will go in your favor. If you haven't already heard from that Schaffer woman, you can be expecting her call. Don't be fooled," the man warned. "She's not an ally. And she's got more pull than you think. She owns that church. I'm going to be out of town for a few days. Have to hop over to Hot Springs. Let's meet up if you need an advance to get the job done. But get it done."

Click.

Amy tapped *play* on the next message and finally recognized a voice.

"Just got your message." It was Rian. "Granny's going visiting today. Call me back."

There was a message from Zelda that said she'd call him back later, and several missed calls, including three more from Zelda, and a call where no message was left at all. The numbers were listed on the phone, except for one. The last caller's information was blocked.

Would the police have already tracked down these callers to interview them about Zack's death? She didn't know, but she had to find out.

If she called each person and pretended to be Zack's secretary, maybe they would volunteer information without her having to ask too many questions. She wasn't quite sure what questions to ask.

She would have to wait until morning, though. It was too late in the day to do that now.

"Okay, so let's put these pieces together like shrewd Miss Marple might," she said to Victor, who joined her on the couch and pushed his way onto her lap. She had no idea how Miss Marple would do it, even though she had read her fair share of Agatha Christie mysteries. It looked so simple on the page. It was a confusing riot of a mess in real life.

"I'll just call and say there's been a change in scheduling." Victor was listening to every word. "And that Mr. Carlisle isn't available. That's not a lie. I'll ask what I can do to assist them. Maybe I can tell from their reaction what to do next."

Victor bumped her hand with his head.

"We know Zack stopped at the liquor store to buy a bottle of champagne," she said to the cat. He also stopped at a Victoria's Secret. The police returned the bag of garments to Zelda. She had tossed them in the trash. The receipt for the purchase was probably inside the shopping bag.

Amy suddenly felt foolish. What did she know about solving a crime? That was police work. She wasn't trained to hunt down clues or make sense of what she discovered when she found it. She couldn't even make sense of her dreams.

But she had to keep her best friend out of jail. Or all of them out of jail.

Her friends were not cold-blooded killers. Or hot-blooded killers.

Or killers of any kind.

"Stay focused," she told Victor. "Stay focused and think. What else do we know?"

She drew in a quick breath. "Ha! We know he met Rian to pick up Granny's sweaters. And he was alive then. Zack Carlisle was alive then."

Victor jumped off her lap when the phone rang.

"Let's take a walk," Zelda said. Her voice was quivering into the phone.

"You're home early," Amy said. "And you hate exercise as much as you hate liver. What's wrong?"

Zelda exhaled into the phone. "Someone has been in my house. Things are not how I left them."

Amy's heart raced. What had she missed? Her mind traveled through time. What had she left behind?

"Zack's cell phone and keys are gone from his office. I know I left them in that envelope on his desk, the one the police gave me. I was going to put everything in his file cabinet, until . . ." her voice faded away. "The envelope is still there, but not his phone, not his keys. Someone has been here," she repeated.

Amy heard Zelda's fear seeping through the phone like a thick, cold fog. She could put her friend at ease with a simple admission. She opened her mouth, but the words wouldn't come.

"The drawers to Zack's file cabinet were open, too," Zelda added. "The drawers are empty."

"What? The files are all gone?"

She hadn't taken the files. Someone followed in her footsteps. But who? And when? The skin prickled on the back of her neck. Someone must have been watching the house when she slipped in the backdoor with the key. Someone was watching when she slipped out of the house!

Zack's killer? Had Zack's killer been there all along? Was he watching and waiting for—for what? The thought made her shiver.

No wonder Zelda was scared.

"Have you seen Genna or Rian?" Zelda asked. "Neither is answering the phone."

"Not today. Why?"

"I just thought maybe they stopped by the house while I was gone. Do you know if anyone was here while I was at the spa?"

"No," Amy lied. She had been there. The police had been there.

"Should I call the police? It might be important."

"Yes," Amy agreed. "There might be fingerprints or something that could lead them to an arrest . . ." Amy faltered. "Wait, no!"

It would be her fingerprints they found. She hadn't taken the files, but she had fumbled her way through the file cabinet with bare and sweaty hands.

"Let's wait until we talk to Genna and Rian, just in case."

Zelda was silent. Amy wondered what thoughts were going through her mind but couldn't ask. She was a heartbeat away from spilling her secret. How could she tell Zelda the police had come for her without showing her hand?

If Zack's killer had followed her and taken those files for protection, then any fingerprints left behind would be substantial evidence. That would be good. Except her prints would be known, too, especially now that they had her fingerprints on file. They had all agreed to have their fingerprints taken to remove them from any suspicion. Or so they had been told. They had agreed after their interviews. Rian had simply refused.

How would Amy explain her foraging in those drawers to Zelda? Or to the police?

No matter which way she turned her thoughts, she felt trapped by the unknown. This might be their chance to uncover a suspect in Zack's murder. Or it might put the four of them more rooted in the muck.

"*Nach a Mool,*" Amy said under her breath.

"I need to get out of this house," Zelda said. "I don't feel safe. I feel watched. Like someone is waiting to pounce. Come get me and let's take a drive."

"I can't get away right now. I just can't," she said. There was no way she could face Zelda and keep her guilt bottled up. "I'm sorry, but I just can't," she repeated.

It felt like the only truth she had told in quite some time.

CHAPTER FIFTEEN

Amy laughed so hard she almost peed herself. This was fun. Like Thelma and Louise when they set off on their adventure, except she was in Zack's Hummer and no one sat beside her. Instead, Dire Straits was turned up loud. The Bose stereo surrounded the cab with its primo sound, and she could picture Mark Knopfler on stage in a smoky bourbon bar.

"Money for Nothing" may have made the band famous, but it was Knopfler's great guitar and rock-blues vocals that made her dream of another time, a younger time. Music blasting, hands on the wheel beating time, she was twenty-five again and fearless. The Hummer sped down the highway, the GPS guiding her miles, and bluesy rock and roll spurring her on.

A couple of clicks on the Internet told her what she needed to know about the Hummer's GPS system. The addresses of the destinations Zack visited were listed, and all she had to do was figure out to which destinations he traveled that day. It was easier than she thought. In short order, she had a list of where he most likely traveled on that final day. She keyed in the destinations with the idea to follow in his tracks every mile, turn, and stop.

"I can't find the keys," Zelda said when Amy called to see if she could borrow the Hummer to run errands her Miata couldn't handle. It was not an unusual request.

"I'll come to help you look," Amy suggested, knowing where to find them—in her jeans pocket. She hadn't meant to take them from Zack's office, but she had put them in her pocket without thinking and discovered them later.

She had been on the road for an hour when the GPS voice ordered her to take the next exit, right. After crossing the Arkansas River, the GPS had her turn east again. The road ran alongside the river and then turned due south toward Paris. There wasn't much to the town that called itself the Gateway to Mount Magazine, the highest point in Arkansas. From the top of the mountain, one could see a circle view of the Arkansas River, the city of Paris, and the Ouachita Mountains. In the shadow sat Blue Mountain Lake, where the rumors claimed the fish were bigger than the beavers.

Turning onto the highway, she continued west. Another mile down the road turned back north. No wonder it took him all day. East, west, north. This was a winding country. The road was narrow and dusty, throwing up the gold dust of a dry late spring, and the trees were thick with dust on either side of the road. That meant she wasn't the only one who had traveled the road lately. She drove for a couple of miles before she turned a bend in the road and saw the concrete pad and the tower. She wasn't sure what she expected to find, but it wasn't this.

There was no one around, nothing to do, no one to see. What did Zack do when he was here? Check a gauge? Monitor radioactivity? She had no idea.

Amy parked the Hummer in front of the little trailer set about a hundred yards from the base of the tower. It looked like one of the FEMA trailers that had made their way to Arkansas after the hurricane floods down in New Orleans. She climbed the makeshift wooden stairs that led to the door and noticed L91 stenciled above the door with black paint.

L91!

Amy tried the doorknob. It was locked.

She peeked under the floor mat just in case, but there was only a family of roly-poly bugs enjoying the damp shade.

Black plastic covered the glass in the door and kept her from seeing anything inside. She climbed back down the stairs and circled the trailer on foot. There were two windows on either side, both too high off the ground to reach, but they appeared to be covered by the same plastic.

Frowning, she stared at the dark windows. And then, a slow smile spread across her freckled cheeks. She was wearing the same jeans she wore when she drove to Hot Springs. She slid her fingers into her back pocket. The key met her fingertips. The cardboard tag was washed into wadded bits, but the key and jump ring were still there.

She pulled out the key and, tentatively, her hands shaking more than she wanted them to, slid the key to the lock and opened the door.

Her eyes widened. She blinked at the light.

"Oh, my!" she said with a sigh of surprise. She stepped inside and closed the door.

The interior of the trailer held long tables filled with five-gallon buckets full of pot plants all growing under artificial light. She stepped forward and stared. Surprise. Amazement. Stupor. They all ran through her mind in the seconds it took to comprehend what she was seeing. L91 was a pot-growing site. Under cover of the lonely cell tower, where no one might suspect, Zack was growing dope. Is that what all the cardboard tags led to?

Rian knew about L91. Rian was involved in this.

But Rian would never agree to something like this. Rian was a purist. She was pious about pot.

And yet, Rian knew about L91.

And now, so did she. She backed out of the trailer and locked the door.

A rustle in the bushes startled her. Jumping down the stairs, she hopped into the Hummer, slamming the door shut. A family of deer stepped out of the trees to the side of the trailer, tugging on the wild daylilies at the edge of the clearing.

Even though her heart was pounding, she laughed out loud at her fear, hands gripping the wheel. That was a close call. Too many deer in Arkansas. Capital *D*.

She turned back toward Paris and the next destination on the list, but she could feel her disappointment riding along with her. Whatever she had expected to find there, it sure wasn't that. If L91 was a growing shed, the others were likely to be the same. Did Rian know about all of them? Was this the mess she was talking about? Or was this a new direction she was taking her botanicals?

And how did this fit into Zack's death? Rian had met Zack on the road that day. Probably somewhere not too far from here. Rian admitted to that. What else would she admit to when forced to tell the truth, the whole truth, and nothing but?

Amy looked in the rearview mirror, noticing a blue pickup truck with an old farmer behind the wheel, riding too close to her tail. She glanced at the face in the rearview mirror. The face was set and hard, angry, and impatient with her driving. There was no place for her to pull off the narrow road and let him pass on this highway on the edge of the Ouachita National Forest. She kept her eyes on the road, glancing now and again into the rearview mirror. He rode right on her tail until a turn out gave her a place to safely pull off the road and let him past. The truck sped on ahead.

Pulling back onto the road, she drove on.

When she started this morning, she had the confidence she could make a big loop and cover all the stops Zack might have made that day, plus a visit to Blue Mountain and later the apple orchard guy. Now she knew better. As the crow flies, they weren't far from each other or far from here. She wasn't a crow. Back roads and backtracking would make that an all-day mission, and she still had to return home before nightfall.

She went through the phone call in her mind.

Jetson Gregory didn't mention anything about the police when she called and pretended to be Zack's new secretary. A heavy silence followed the introduction, and without being face-to-face, she couldn't tell whether he was confused or cagey. Did he know Zack was dead? She couldn't tell that either, and she didn't know how to ask without tipping her hand. In the end she asked about his apple orchard-- the only clue she had — and that set him off on a tirade of foul language and spite. Listening to him bellow about the damage, she could hear there was no love lost between Jetson and Zack. There was no love lost between Zack and anyone, it seemed.

As he recounted the story with fire under his collar, the construction of the cell tower site in his apple orchard had come to a halt when he barred the way of the backhoe with his body and his pickup truck. The backhoe operator had stalked off in a huff, leaving the backhoe running, which meant the tab was still running on his dime. He was vehement as he retold the story.

The road the backhoe was supposed to take was at the farthest end of his orchard, but not very clearly marked. That was something Zack was supposed to have taken care of.

Zack didn't.

Instead, the machine plowed through Jetson's apple trees, and she imagined the machine going through the trees as if plucking toothpicks from a bowl.

Before he could stop it, the backhoe had destroyed a good quarter of his orchard and twenty beehives, along with the wife's prize-winning rose garden.

He blamed Zack for the damage and he was holding a grudge. Was that enough to run Zack down and leave him for dead? Had he run him over like the apple trees?

"Had he been to Hot Springs recently?" she had asked.

"What business is that of yours?" he snapped in response.

His rudeness took her by surprise, but she had to keep him talking. "I wondered if you were able to keep your appointment with him?"

"Appointment?" he sounded confused.

"At the Bennfield Hotel?"

He scoffed into the phone. "Lady, we're done, here. My lawyers are on that lease contract like white on rice. I'm going to own this cell tower when all is said and done."

No, she couldn't mark Jetson Gregory off the list just yet.

The church lady from Blue Mountain was also on her call list—the voice that dripped ice. She was still like a winter chill when Amy spoke to her, and she didn't seem surprised that Zack Carlisle had not attended her church board meeting. She ended their conversation with a click.

The third caller never picked up, and Amy didn't bother to leave a message.

Tired and weary of driving, she perked up when the robotic voice of the GPS called her attention to a zigzag in the road. Slowing to the speed limit, she followed the directions coming from the device. From the hard pavement, she turned onto a dirt road marked County Road 214 and drove in the dust until she saw the base of another cell tower.

The tower was in the center of a patch of land that looked like someone shaved off the top of the mountain. For some reason, it reminded her of Sam, the sad bald eagle on the Muppets, majestic yet glum. Amy slowed as she approached the dusty driveway that led to a mobile home not far from the tower. The name on the mailbox said "Crawley," and something sizzled in her head. The name seemed familiar.

The driveway led to a dirty white trailer with a set of metal steps outside the door. Someone had made planters from old paint buckets and then left them to wither and die. The homestead had a forlorn look to it, and suddenly she felt miles away from safe.

Slowly she drove up the driveway that ended at a metal carport with an old blue truck parked beside what looked like a brand-new John Deere tractor. The truck looked familiar, too.

Don't they all? Old work trucks looked like old men, hunkered down and weathered.

The curtain in the door window shifted.

Pulling in a little more than halfway up the drive, she stopped a moment before she got out. Hillbilly protocol and all. The curtain's swing let her know they knew she was there. Engine running, gear still in drive, she waited for them to make the first move.

When the door opened and the man stepped out on the step, she knew she was in the wrong place at the wrong time. He lifted a shotgun to his shoulder in one smooth move and sighted the gun in her direction.

He moved down the steps slowly, the gun still at his shoulder. Her heart beat against her chest while her hands gripped the wheel.

There was hostility in his stance, in the set of his jaw, in the grip on his gun.

She wasn't welcome. That was clear.

She turned off the music and listened to the logic of her thoughts.

This was one of Zack's cell tower sites. And she was in Zack's Hummer. The thought struck her. This man thought Zack was behind the wheel of this Hummer. And everything about his stance said that Zack wasn't welcome here, either.

How could she reveal herself from behind the tinted windows? She needed to let him know who she was. If she opened the car door, he might shoot her in the leg. If she rolled down her window, he might shoot her in the head. If she moved closer, she'd only put herself closer to the range of the gun.

In her indecision, she gripped the wheel with both hands.

The Hummer. She was in a Hummer. It was impervious to the gunshot, wasn't it?

The thought was so pure it made her laugh. That's why Zack had a Hummer. It made him feel safe. Behind the dark glass of this tank of a vehicle, he felt protected against whatever bad business he was up to.

The thought boosted her bravery. She lifted her foot off the brake, and the Hummer rolled forward a few feet. The gun barrel followed.

She wasn't brave enough—or stupid enough—to face a gun. Gearing the Hummer into reverse, she pressed on the gas. The discharge from the gun echoed against the mountain behind her, and she heard the *ting, ting, ting* as the buckshot met its mark. She slammed the pedal to the floor and sent a cloud of dust into the driveway.

The old man ran into the yard and fired another round. Instinctively she ducked, turned the wheel hard, and jammed the gear into drive. As she floored the gas, she spun in the dry dirt and the Hummer careened from the drive, almost clipping a homemade grave marker as she spun from the driveway and out on the road. The car held steady as she flew around the curves and bucked over the potholes in a flurry of road soot. Her hands were white-knuckled and gripping the steering wheel like a lifeline in a flood.

Now turning onto the main road, her speed as fast as she dared, she drove sixteen miles and across the Garland County line before she felt safe enough to stop. Her chest ached as if she had held her breath every mile.

The sign above the bar said Cooley's Bar & Package. That had been on Zack's destination list, too. It's where he bought the champagne for his and Zelda's weekend celebration.

Now seated in the coolness of the bar, she was eager to douse her fear and drench her panic with something cold and foamy. Reaching for the beer, her hands shook around the sweating chill of the mug.

If this was the kind of reception Zack faced on his cell tower route, she had to rethink her plan, because this plan was more dangerous than she had ever imagined it might be. How stupid could she be! She was on the trail of a killer. Not on a pleasure cruise. Of course it was dangerous.

Proof she hadn't thought this through. Proof she hadn't really made a plan that fit this. Instead, she had just driven off on a mission.

Should she go to the police? And say what?

Not that she could say she was nosing around in a dead man's business. Or reveal she had tossed out evidence and lied to the cops. Nor could she share that she broke into her best friend's house and burgled for clues. Or even report a man for protecting his property from a stranger, or defending himself against someone he knew and didn't like. She didn't recall seeing a "No Trespassing" sign, but she had been trespassing just the same.

How was she going to explain the gunshot dings to Zelda?

Amy blew into the beer head, gulped down a third of the mug, and felt the alcohol's calming buzz. Adrenaline waned, and suddenly she realized that she was empty, hungry, and a long way from home. Reality hit. She was as far away from the comforts of home and a warm bed as she could be. How foolish to think she could cover Zack's trail and be back in time for dinner.

Glancing up at the bartender, she smiled. He was leaning against the cooler with his arms crossed over his barreled chest and a vintage

Razorback shirt. She hadn't given him much more than eye contact and a request for his cheapest beer since plopping down on the one barstool that gave her a view of the door. He was looking at her, a question in his watered-down blue eyes. His face had been quite handsome years ago, before age and the sunless din of a bar took its toll. A heavy graying beard disguised his mouth and chin. A Charlie Daniels hat sat on his head.

"Want another one?" he asked, walking the few steps toward her and her empty mug. She nodded.

"This is a perfectly drawn mug of the worst beer in the universe," she said as he set the beer in front of her. "I hate Old Style."

"Darling, I got it all. Name your brew."

The sign above the bar said, *No Credit. Don't Ask.*

Amy pushed four quarters across the bar, separating them from a short stack of small coins at her elbow. "What will a buck buy?"

"Old Style," he said with a grin, the weight of his whiskers rising on his cheeks.

She groaned and rolled her eyes.

"That's all you got, sugar?"

Amy nodded. "I have no cash."

The bartender chuckled and shook his head. "Like I never heard that one before," he said with amused sarcasm.

"No, really. I left my wallet in Bluff Springs. All I have with me is a credit card and some change I took from the ashtray." In her mind's eye, she saw her wallet resting beside the keyboard of her computer at home, where she had checked her credit card balances with disappointing results. She grabbed the one card with enough credit to fill up the Hummer's gas tank, but her wallet, with cash and a driver's license, was still where she left it.

Here she was, flirting with disaster. Driving a dead man's car as a murder suspect without a lick of identification and no money.

"Bluff Springs, huh? I haven't been there in a while."

"Same old place. Hasn't changed much since you were there, I'm sure."

"Still got that big rock looks like Jesus?"

"Yep. Still got Rocky top Jesus."

"Still got crooked streets?"

"Yep. But no stoplights. Not a single one. And I'm moving out if they ever put one in."

They both laughed, and Amy felt her discomfort subside. She reached into her pocket and fingered the wooden casino coin snuggled deep in the seam. She pulled it out and fingered the worn wood, darkened by sweat and skin oils. She dropped it on the bar in front of her.

If you're lucky and you know it share this coin was engraved on one side, a casino logo on the other.

The bartender picked it up and chuckled. "I like being lucky," he said and winked. "This one's on me." He pulled her mug from the coaster. "What's your pleasure?"

Smiling, she said, "Stella."

He whistled softly. "That's a long way uptown from Old Style."

"That's what we drank in college because it was dollar cheap and everywhere. Old Style, I mean," she said, her fingers now twirling the tall Weizen glass he set before her.

"And you drank too much one night, right?"

"Not exactly."

The bartender faded away to the other end of the bar, filling orders from other patrons. She watched the fluidity of his motions, a well-rehearsed dance as he popped, poured, blended, and stirred. The bar was crowded. Not surprising, since it seemed to be the closest pub in a county that had been dry since the prohibition like more than half of Arkansas.

A commercial on the radio for a new bar in Hot Springs ended, and old school Jimi Hendrix filled the room. A man at the end of the bar was grooving with the music, his stringy black ponytail bobbing with the beat, his eyes closed. The bartender drifted back in her direction.

"Buy me another, and I'll tell you the story." She smiled her best, most flirtatious smile.

"I've always been a sucker for a redhead," he said with a wink, dancing away to fill drink orders. He returned with another Stella.

"In this bar I went to a lot, we used to have an Old Style beer contest every year." The alcohol was loosening her tongue. "You know, like a wet T-shirt contest but without the water. It was a costume and talent contest. And the winner got pizza and a twenty-dollar tab."

The bartender nodded in encouragement.

She twirled the glass, drank, and set it back down.

"It was called The Shanty. It was a little bar wedged between the shore and A1A in Daytona Beach. What I remember most about that bar was that it stunk like old beer, B-O, and Hawaiian Tropic." She laughed at the memory. "The floors were never swept clean of the sand that got tracked in by thirsty surfers and the chicks in string bikinis who wanted to wax their boards. You know what I mean."

His eyes lit up when he laughed.

"Idiot that I am, I thought I could win the Old Style crown by tapping out 'In-A-Gadda-Da-Vida' by Iron Butterfly."

"Holy shit! That's seventeen minutes long."

She nodded. He knew his music.

"I was dressed like Columbia in the Rocky Horror Picture Show, tap shoes and all. Cute little short shorts."

The bartender grinned with anticipation.

"I was tipsy already, and I slipped about three minutes into it. Went into a split on that dirty floor." She glanced down at the floor beneath her barstool and winced.

"Nasty floor," she said, shaking her head, then lifted the glass in a toast. "I didn't win the Miss Old Style crown, either. I did get some sympathy, but it wasn't near enough to take the sting out of the humiliation."

He chuckled and opened another beer. "Bought and paid for," he said as he set the bottle in front of her. She smiled at his generosity.

"I was in a beard contest once," he said with a grin, his fingers stroking the gray threads under his chin. "Didn't win that, either." His smile was full of charm. "I think that means we have something in common."

He drifted away again, and Amy looked around the bar. A couple sat at a table near the far end, making love with their eyes, their knees intertwined in a not-so-subtle wrap under the table.

Even from this distance, she saw the woman's hair was bottle-blonde, and her smile was all bright white and perfection. Her cleavage, which was much too deep to be real, spilled out of her tank top. A matching black skirt rode seductively up her thighs, and Amy narrowed her eyes to focus on a tattoo there. It was either an angel with wings or a bumblebee.

It had to be a bumblebee. A dotted tattoo trail marked the flight of the bee leading the way to her nether regions some might call the honey pot.

What was she thinking? She sighed and shook her head. Three beers on an empty stomach and she was buzzed.

Her thoughts shifted to Zelda. She met her man in a bar, too. Zack adored Zelda, or at least he appeared to, at first, but expensive gifts and good looks didn't make or break a marriage. Betrayal broke a marriage. Death broke a marriage.

Till death do us part.

Zelda had gotten her wish. *Vamoose.*

The blonde with the tattoo noticed Amy's attention and narrowed her eyes. Turning slightly to look out the front window where the Hummer was parked, she looked back at Amy and smiled with bared teeth.

Amy turned away quickly. The smile wasn't intended to be kind.

The woman must have recognized the Hummer. She must know Zack if she knew his car. Out of the corner of her eye she watched her, questions bubbling forward.

Did Zack have a lover on the side?

Maybe Zelda suspected Zack was cheating on her. Amy glanced back at the bartender, now cramming bottles into a cooler of ice. She motioned with her head in the woman's direction, a question in her eyes.

"Wild as a bedbug," he said in a whisper, leaning across the bar. "Which is where she spends a lot of her time. She's the Honey Bee Queen—lah-dee-dah—and this place is her hive. Her granddaddy owns it. Don't go looking at her man," he warned, "or she'll sting you dead."

Amy smiled. Honey Bee Queen. Not all that different from Miss Old Style. She glanced briefly at the woman before returning her attention to the bartender.

"What's the story about that cranky old guy over off 214? The one living in that sad little trailer under the cell tower?"

"We've got more than a few sad little trailers around here," he answered. "And more than our share of cell towers."

He sounded bitter.

"You must be talking about old man Crawley over in Yell County."

She knew she recognized that name. That was the name on the mailbox. That was the name in one of the articles in Zack's office.

"He does have a sad story," he said, nodding. "He comes in here every once in a while. Came in here a lot right after his wife died. I haven't seen him much lately. His old dog would sit in the back of his truck all day.

"I always felt sorry for that mutt. That dog waited in the hot, in the cold. It didn't matter. I guess he jumped out when he had to mark the bushes, but I never saw him do it. Crawley always parked the cab facing out. The dog would sit and stare at him in through that window." He slapped a threadbare bar rag in the direction of the front of the bar. "I took him out a burger a couple of times."

"How did his wife die?"

"Cancer."

She shook her head in sympathy.

"Dog, too. About three months after the wife died. Penny, I think. The wife's name was Penny."

"Sad."

"Brain tumor."

Amy was still shaking her head. It *was* sad. A man loses his wife and dog at the same time. That would be a hard grief to shake.

"If you take Crawley's word for it, it was that cell tower his trailer sits under that gave them both cancer. That's all he talked about until he got stewed on bourbon. Evan Williams. Neat. That's what he drank."

He mopped at the bar with the rag. "Somebody brought a flyer in here one day about how cell towers were giving people brain cancer and killing all the bees." He nodded with the rim of his hat in the direction of the woman in the black skirt. "Most likely responsible for that flyer, I bet," he said. "Crawley's been trying to sell his land, I hear. No one's buying."

"Why put up the tower in the first place?"

"Money, I guess. I hear those leases pay a tidy sum every month. Money for nothing, you know?"

She matched his smile. Her favorite song.

So that's why he was bitter toward Zack. He blamed Zack for his wife's and dog's death. Had his shoes been on her feet, she might have blamed Zack, too. She remembered the newspaper clipping in Zack's office files.

"How long ago did all that happen?"

"It was last summer. Funny thing, though," he said, swiping the rag on the bar in front of her. "A guy with a Hummer like yours used to come in every once in a while for a beer and a burger."

Amy's attention snapped back.

"He came in here not long ago. Met some great big fellow in a suit, as I recall. Sat over at that table." He nodded in the direction of the lovers. "Single malt scotch. He sweated like a pig in a blanket. Hummer guy had a beer.

"Your Hummer . . . It wouldn't be the same one, would it? Can't say we get too many Hummers around here. Certainly not many pretty ladies in Hummers."

He smiled, and she knew where his mind was headed. If she had more time, she might have been more receptive to a date. It had been a long time. Casual sex wasn't in the rules of her playbook, but she was flattered all the same, and she knew it was time to leave before any kind of unwanted trouble found her and followed her home. The bartender looked up and then motioned to the window with the rim of his hat.

A group of men the size of tree trunks circled the Hummer, fists and jaws clenched. She couldn't see clearly through the greasy glass, but she saw enough to know they meant mean-spirited business. Terror gripped her as she watched one of them pull at the door handle of the Hummer. Another cupped his hands and peeked into the darkness of the window on the passenger side. Two of them pushed on the back bumper, rocking the car on its frame.

She held her breath as the posse punched its way into the bar, eyes steeled against the dark and searching. For Zack, she guessed. Still more people down here who knew Zack and his Hummer.

"Afternoon, Bubba," the bartender spoke up. "What's up?"

"None of your business," came the answer from the first man to walk through the door. His dirt-stained T-shirt stretched across a generous gut that rolled over jeans slung low on his hips. The others looked distinctly the same.

"Now that's a fine way to start a tab," the bartender replied.

Smart man. He was earning his tips.

"Where's the asshole driving that Hummer?" the man demanded.

The bartender and Amy exchanged glances. "Left with some babe about an hour ago," he lied. "Your old lady?"

Brave man. Maybe he was into earning a fat lip.

The leader snorted anger out of his flat, broad nose, and took a step forward. His companions snickered behind him. "What are you laughing at?" He yelled, turning to face them. The posse took a step back.

"We'll sit an' wait," he said finally, scraping a chair from a table and beaching his bulk. "He ain't gonna be gone too long, I bet."

"Uh-oh," she muttered. The bartender gave her a look that was full of warning. She could tell these guys were mean as snakes in summer when they were sober. Add some alcohol, and they could start a venomous war.

They piled in around the table in a clamor of chairs and grunts. "Beer," said the leader. He dug a sweat-soaked wallet out of his pocket, pulled out a fifty, and slapped it down on the table. The bartender filled a pitcher from the tap and brought five mugs to the table, picked up the bill, then laid it on the shelf outside the cash register.

The scene in front of her passed by as though she were seated in the front row of a horror film, trapped and intrigued, spellbound, and terrified all at the same time. Was there no one in the county who didn't have some feud with Zack?

What an idiot she was, driving off like a fool on vacation. She was in the backwoods, not some fancy villa by the sea.

Could she get to the car, unlock it, and back it out before they knew what was happening?

Possible.

If she stayed, she might hear something important. She needed to know how these men knew Zack and why they wanted to find him. But if they were looking for Zack, they didn't know he was dead. Which meant none of them was behind the wheel at the parking garage that day.

Amy smiled in spite of her circumstances. She couldn't picture any of them at the posh Bennfield, thundering like a herd of angry buffalo as they stomped the old wood floors, sending the crystal chandeliers jangling.

They may not know that Zack was dead, but they did know his Hummer. Their paths had crossed somehow.

"Keep 'em coming," the leader barked as they emptied the first round of beer.

"Asshole thinks he's gonna come down here and steal our gig, he's got another thing comin'," one of them said.

"Nobody's buying or selling here but us," another said as the beers were poured.

"Shut the fuck up."

Drugs. They had to be talking about drugs.

Zack must be planning on selling drugs on his cell tower runs. Maybe he was working with Rian.

But that didn't make sense. Maybe these men weren't even talking about weed. Maybe they were talking about meth. Rian would never touch that junk.

The conversation at the table turned to cars, women, and old rock and roll, with bodily sounds that came from one offensive end or the other. She'd had enough. It was time to get home. She hadn't found Zack's killer, but she was ready for a hot shower and a warm bed.

She drained her beer and shook her head at the bartender. She felt his disappointment. "I've got to go," she said. "I need to get out of here before they get ugly."

"Another time," he said quietly. "Another time."

How would she get out of there unnoticed? She could go to the bathroom and slip in through the kitchen and out the backdoor. If there was a backdoor. She still had to come around the front of the building to get in the car. She could wait until they left. But who knew how long that would be. Until Zack came for the Hummer, which would be never.

She nearly fell off her barstool when her cell phone rang.

"Where are you," Zelda yelled. "You've been gone all day."

"Yes, yes," Amy answered.

It was her chance. "Hold on a minute." She winked at the bartender. He winked back.

"Ready for another?" he yelled to the table.

"Hell yeah!" the men bellowed and burped.

The bartender refilled the pitcher.

"I'll call you back!"

"What?" Zelda yelled. "Why are you yelling?"

Walking alongside the bartender as he walked to the table, she let his frame camouflage her own, and then, slipping out the front door with her key in one hand, phone in the other, she was in the Hummer and backed out of the parking space before the round of beer was poured.

Back in the saddle again.

Would they follow her? She glanced in the rearview mirror as the miles flew by. She shook her head to clear what felt like cobwebs. She was more buzzed than she wanted to be. No driver's license, either. She'd be in trouble if she got stopped by the law.

Sitting forward in the seat, her hands gripping the wheel, she drove cautiously, her eyes alert. Her panic felt lighter as the road put more distance between her and Zack's dirty deeds. He seemed to have a lot of those going on in this part of the state. His dirty deeds. In fact, he seemed to have a whole other life going outside of Bluff Springs. She hadn't known that about him. Had Zelda known? Suddenly her stomach felt queasy from the beer and the excitement. Food would help, but there would be no drive-through options in this part of the state.

But she had gotten away.

She'd managed to flee from crazy Crawley and now that herd of bubbas. And what was the deal with that bumblebee? What a dirty look.

Zack had so many enemies. How could one person make so many people want to kill him?

Her heart sank, realizing with a pang in her ribs that the list of suspects wasn't growing in the right direction. There seemed to be a lot of people angry at Zack, maybe even a few angry enough to kill him, but none of them seemed to know Zack was dead. That realization didn't do anything to clear Zelda, Genna, or Rian from the list of suspects. Someone else had to be on that list. Someone else who was resting easy knowing Zack was dead.

She gripped the wheel with her decision. She knew she had to keep looking. She knew she had to keep digging. No matter how scary or dangerous or how far from home she was, she had to keep going until she found proof that would clear her friends. If one went to jail, they all went. That's just how it would be.

"Shoot!" she yelped, remembering she had forgotten to call Zelda. In the rush from the bar, she tossed the phone onto the seat for a two-handed escape. She reached now for the phone, patting the car seat to find it. There was no moon to light the sky, and no streetlights on this isolated stretch of road, so she couldn't see where the phone had landed. Fumbling with the canopy light above the rearview mirror, she turned it on. Both her and Zack's phone were on the floor of the passenger side, having fallen from the seat. When she reached to grab them, the car yanked dangerously toward the side of the road, where the hillside plunged hundreds of feet down the jagged rock.

Straightening in the seat, she flipped off the light and gripped the wheel. The phone would have to stay on the floor until she found a safe place to pull off.

As she scouted her position, hoping the now-familiar GPS voice would tell her she was closer to home than it felt, she saw that the GPS screen looked just like a video game, a race car on a blacktop with neon yellow lines. Through the windshield, there was nothing but black, but she was well aware there were trees and steep hills on either side. She drove as fast as she felt she could, given the curves that held tight to the hillside and switchbacks climbing through the mountains.

Her eyes played the side of the road, ever vigilant for the familiar flash of green that would tell her deer were present, their eyes glowing when the headlights shone into them. Deer crossing the road at night were hard to see and even harder to avoid, but she knew to look for the flash of green on the edge of the pavement.

She shivered. No doubt the Hummer would plow a deer down like a piñata, but she had heard stories of deer crashing through the windshield, hooves kicking the driver to death in its final thrust to escape.

Suddenly the brights of car headlights flashed in her eyes from behind. In that instant, she knew with certainty that the car had been following her with its headlamps off. Now light filled the cabin with such intensity that everything blurred white around her.

She flipped the rearview mirror up, although it didn't help. Gunning the Hummer for speed, she forced distance between the two cars. A yellow caution sign loomed ahead, warning of a triple S curve. She steered the Hummer to the center of the road and the vehicle behind her followed.

The Hummer's tires squealed, holding fast to the road as she careened from one tight curve to the next. Ahead of her, the highway was as dark as tar pitch, and behind her was nothing but blinding light. Hoping for a straight stretch, she pressed the gas pedal, and the Hummer shot forward, traveling the solid centerline like PAC-MAN chewing its way through the maze. This was no game. If she met a car coming from the other direction, that would be it. She would never be able to maneuver the Hummer back to her own lane in time.

How far could she travel this fast on these curves? How long before she missed a curve and sped down the hillside? Her foot instinctively lifted from the gas pedal and the Hummer dropped its speed.

Her head snapped back as she felt the impact, the headrest whacking the back of her head with a heavy thud. Light filled the cabin, and the roar of an engine filled her ears as the car rammed again into the Hummer with deliberate force. Again. And again. Each time a speck of time lapsed, as if the world stood still while the car behind caught up with its mark.

The two vehicles rode together, locked bumper to bumper, for what seemed like forever. Then the car behind her let go. Space filled the gap between them. She glanced in the rearview mirror just as one headlight winked out in the car behind.

Was she going to die right here and now?

Somehow the thought was strangely calming, like watching the credits roll in a movie that kept you tense in your seat, fingernails bitten to the quick. Was this how Zack felt as he lay bleeding to death?

Did he see the car coming at him from behind? Did he know in that instant that his lies were coming back to roost, like a pigeon with a message from Death?

Glancing in the side view mirror, she now saw the one headlight that was still intact shift to the center as the car moved farther into the left lane, a one-eyed creature intent on the kill. She gripped the wheel.

With a final blow that shattered the last headlamp, the car rammed the corner of the Hummer, the squeal of metal on metal filling her ears. She swerved, but she felt as if a giant magnet was pulling her off the edge of the road.

It seemed like a dream, then, a flash. Trees blurred in front of her as she sped down the mountainside. The Hummer bounced against the branches that grabbed at the windshield, cracking off like fingers on some wretched hand. Down. Hurling down toward the inevitable bottom, she sped. The impact snapped her hands against her chest and her head against the back of the seat as her seat belt held her tight. The dream faded, then there was the dark sea of nothing.

CHAPTER SIXTEEN

Rian felt the air kick up like it always did the moment before the sun set as if the earth needed to fill her sails to make the journey to the other side. From her dock, she watched the sun catch in the deep vee of the valley and then hang over the horizon like a brilliant red ship, the reflection in the water now turning copper-red.

She sat still until dusk took over and the whip-poor-wills took up their chant. The chimney swifts congregated over the old house ruins on the other side of the lake, whirling and fluttering their wings like bats in the evening air. Overhead, the birds hunted the sky for one last feast before disappearing into the remains of the crumbling chimney.

When dark closed in around her, she rose, reluctantly, and at the edge of the dock, she grabbed the shovel she had brought with her from the garden shed.

She had a task to do.

Jamming the shovel into the ground, she lifted out a spade of dirt, tipping it onto the mound piling up beside the hole.

The miner's lamp made a bull's-eye of light on the surface of the dirt at her feet, casting beams into the woods beyond when she lifted her head. She leaned forward on the shovel handle, took a deep breath, and blew it out sharply. Just a little deeper, she thought and plowed the spade into the dirt again.

She dug near the little pet cemetery that rested under a sour cherry tree about halfway between her cabin and the dock. The path between the two veered off to a bench where she could sit and look at the lake in the shade and talk to a whole generation of dead dogs and cats, even a dumb old chicken that fell off a Tyson truck. She had contemplated a meal out of that chicken—waste not, want not—but she brought her home in the trunk of her car and let the hen peck for ticks in the yard until she met her mortal demise sometime later.

There hadn't been a new hole dug for a pet death in quite some time, but last winter after a period of paranoia, she buried her coveted starter seeds. These were not just any seeds. These were the descendants from Bangladesh she had nearly risked her freedom to smuggle in. She flew over as part of a vacation tour with a group of Episcopalians, and while they were collecting trinkets at the local bazaar, she was buying seeds to start an undercover career in cannabis. Not just any cannabis, this *Cannabis sativa* seed was from a family who had been growing this particular strain for generations. She had made this connection in college, and their friendship held fast over the years even though there were many miles between them now.

The seed she brought back to her farm was perfect as it was, but with experimentation and her knowledge of botany, she created a hybrid strain for the North Arkansas climate that had become her signature crop. Her weed became known for its sweet, fruity taste and creative, euphoric high. Hers was not the skunky street weed that glued partakers to the couch. Hers was a wholesome, cerebral high and some of the best homegrown money could buy in Arkansas.

She was proud of that. It made delicious cookies, too. The kind of cookies that helped folks get beyond their pain and suffering.

Pride. It was a funny thing.

Proud of her crop. Proud of her freedom. Proud of her body, too. She was muscled and toned from hiking and hauling. Growing pot undetected meant hiking into the mountains with whatever she needed in a backpack. Once, but only once, after she twisted her ankle in the rock scree on a hill, she contemplated a pack mule for help. She had gone so far as to hunt down a livestock auction before paranoia took over. She was far less obvious headed to the woods with a heavy backpack and walking stick than with a braying mule. She'd never met a mule that worked without complaint.

The crop grew in the fertile soil of a valley between two gentle slopes of land her family had owned for generations. It was a strenuous hike, but it was discreet. The valley ran from east to west, so the sun shone on it all day in every season. When it rained, the water from the mountains brought all the right nutrients down to nurture the soil. She had carved a path with a heavy pick for the water to follow and irrigate the crop, lining the makeshift riverbed with rocks as it moved through the plants. She swung a pick for weeks, and her muscles had never ached like that before or since.

She ran a hose camouflaged with lichen and pieces of rock downhill from a deep spring to the patch so that if rain was scarce, she could still pull water from the spring. Bamboo potted from a nearby stand served as stakes to support the plants, but mostly it was for camouflage. By cutting away all but the leaf blades at the top of the bamboo culms, she hid the garden from spying eyes above.

It had been more than ten years.

Zack had ruined it in less than ten months.

He had surprised her in the woods that day, showing up at her secret camp. No one, absolutely no one, knew of its whereabouts—or so she thought. He stepped out from behind a tree with a smug smile on his handsome face. How long he had been following her, watching her, she didn't want to know. The very thought of him spying on her unaware made her skin crawl.

A month later, at the new moon, two men had shown up at her house. They were oily, and she knew in her gut they were the kind of men who lived without a dime of remorse. They claimed to have taken a wrong turn and gotten lost. She knew better. The black Lincoln was out of place on the country road. The mud-covered license plates were Pulaski County, and as she watched the car leave her ranch, she thought they had drug mafia written all over them. She didn't know who they were, and she didn't ask. But she knew they were there to send her a message.

We know who you are, and we know where you live.

Zack had ruined everything.

And now, Zack was out of the picture.

She had been thinking about this for days now, wavering between regaining the confidence to resume her trade once Zack's death blew over and the realization that it no longer felt safe or sacred. Zack muddied the water when he blackmailed her into making him part of her business. Now she felt soiled as if there was blood on her hands that had to be washed clean, purified by fire, and embedded in the ashes of time. She knew what she had to do.

She owed it to the ancestors who honored the sacredness of the herb, as they honored the Great Spirit. She owed it to the ancestors who taught their people how to accept the herb's gifts. If it were right for her to rebuild her business down the road, she would know it.

But for now, this was the right thing to do.

And Ben. This was for him, too. She could never have what she wanted with him as long as he was a cop and she grew weed. She knew he put himself in jeopardy to be with her.

Feeling a pang of regret, she stopped shoveling and wiped the sweat from her face and her tears along with it. Again, she heaved the shovel with determination and heard the clank of metal against metal. The old Nabisco tin had been part of her grandmother's kitchen for as long as Rian could remember. Now, as she pulled it free of its tomb, it was faded and dirty, spotted with rust. She laid the shovel down and pried the lid from the can, pulling out the burlap, then the jar. This seed was no longer viable, but it was a treasure just the same. The light from her lamp shone onto a piece of history that had changed the course of her life. For the better. Or not. That depended on one's perspective.

There was no way to understand what people had against cannabis. It was part of the history of the world, with a twelve thousand-year-old vita of medicinal use and healing. Cannabis was part of the spice trade some scholars claimed marked the very start of the modern age, an exploit that created vast empires and revealed entire continents to explorers. If they hadn't gone in search of cannabis, where would we all be now? Those explorations tipped the balance of world power from the merciless traders to the royals who wanted pepper on their meat, clove in their tea, and cannabis in their pipes. If marijuana was good enough for the Chinese Emperor 2,700 years before Christ, why wasn't it good enough for red-blooded Americans in the twenty-first century?

Sorrow filled her.

Caffeine, nicotine, and alcohol weren't illegal. That cannabis was, didn't make sense.

Here, on her home soil, Native American tribes that came to the healing waters of the Ozarks called it an herb of power that could heal people and places of whatever sickened them. She believed that and she believed in its power.

After striking a match to the brush she laid in the firepit, she watched the flame take hold and grow. She unscrewed the jar and then dragged the burlap bag out onto her lap. Pinching the seeds between her thumb and forefinger, she offered a prayer of thanks—to the herb, to the elders, to the belief that what she held was so much more than something white men called illegal and coveted all the same. With each pinch, she offered a prayer of gratitude—for her freedom, for her right to be free, for her right to be free of those who would tell her how to live.

Then she tossed each pinch into the fire, the seeds popping as they met the heat, her prayers rising to the heavens in the smoke, climbing to the Great Spirit, the maker of all.

And with each prayer, the tears flowed. She and the jar emptied at the same time.

She dug into the pockets of her jeans and pulled out a worn little black book. It was here, coded in a shorthand only she understood, that she kept track of her journey. The little pages held detailed notes of breeding and pollination techniques, annual weather and rainfall, crop yields, and of course, the names of her clientele. Her buyers weren't the average users on the street. They were movers and shakers with money. Hers was a small, discrete clientele of people who could afford the best.

The code discreetly detailed the habits of her buyers. She knew that 5R6 Green held a party every year at his cabin in the remote wilderness near the Buffalo River. His green brownies were legendary. She knew how much to set aside for his recipe each year. She kept track of who, what, when, and how much they consumed over the years. It was how she planned the crop and projected her earnings.

It was time to let it all go.

She tossed the book into the flames and watched the pages curl and wither.

The light from the fire reflected in her tears. The clouds in the sky accepted the clouds of smoke as if one of their own as the smoke curled and rose from the little valley she called home.

Patting the ground beside her, she stretched out beside the fire, now glowing with embers. The last of her smoke-filled prayers disappeared in a sky covered with stars even older than God. Then she closed her eyes and slept.

CHAPTER SEVENTEEN

Amy opened her eyes to deep darkness. The stench was overwhelming.

She swept a dry, swollen tongue over her lips and tasted rust. Her tongue touched a spot on her bottom lip, and she groaned. Tenderly, she licked at the place that felt split, making two plump bottom lips instead of one.

Turning her head to the left and then to the right, she saw nothing but darkness.

As she listened to the sounds around her, she hoped to get a sense of place and at the same time block out the smell. That gagging smell. She forced herself to listen in the silence—for the sound of an armadillo digging in the bush somewhere close, a nighthawk landing its prey, the wind rustling in the pines . . . anything that would help her know where she was.

There was nothing. No sound at all.

The stench filled her breath again, and she turned her head. Something soft was underneath her, not the hard ground.

She lifted her hand and then cried out as the pain shot up her right arm, her teeth clenching as she fell quiet again.

The crash came reeling back to her then: the light of the headlamps behind her, the hard thump against the Hummer, and the squeal of brakes and metal. She remembered the blur of the trees banging against the Hummer as she sped airborne down the hill.

She licked her lip again gently. How long ago was that? Minutes? Hours? Days?

The pain in her chest made her choke on the air as she inhaled. Was there something across her chest? It could be a dead animal. A tree. Another body? Fear raced through her and prickled the back of her hands. Was she still in the car? Maybe the roof had caved in on her.

Opening her eyes, she saw nothing but darkness. She raised her left hand and patted the space above her. There was nothing there. No car, no dead animal. She moved her hand to her chest. There was nothing there, either—just her shirt. Her fingers touched sore, bruised skin, from the seat belt that held as she tumbled down the hill. There was no seat belt against her now.

Again, using her left hand, she patted the air surrounding her, expecting to feel the rough edges of leaves and brush. The surface was hard. Scraping it with her fingernails, she knew it couldn't be a tree. It was smooth, solid. Sliding her hand against it, she let her fingers discover the surface and she found thin little grooves. Like paneling. Paneling?

She patted herself where she could reach, surveying her body inch by inch, pat by pat. She felt whole, at least, yet achy. Reaching across she tapped her right arm, and the pain shot through her again. A dull thud radiated from the tips of her fingers to her shoulder. She could sense that her arm was bound with something soft like a bandage or scrap torn from a sheet. Tenderly, she touched her arm again and discovered that the binding material was stiff. Blood. Her blood. She licked her lips again. There was blood there, too.

Directly beneath her felt soft. Again, she raked her fingernails across the surface. Flat, but not a car seat. Relief flooded her. She was definitely alive.

Fear filled her just as suddenly, bile rising in the back of her throat. Where was she?

She lifted her head slowly, her neck moving stiffly yet without pain. Slowly she willed herself upright, holding her right arm as still as possible as she strained to sit up.

When she moved, the air stirred and the stench rose around her. What was that smell?

It reminded her of ammonia. Or sulfur. Or an Easter egg left hidden way into June. Her eyes burned, her head ached, her throat was raw. She blinked and then swallowed.

She fought the panic trying to overtake her. Her heartbeat banged against her bruised chest, and she felt the beat all the way down her arm to her fingertips.

Suddenly, lights flooded over her. In that brief illumination, she saw where she was—on a bed in a room surrounded by paneled walls, a door at the end of the bed by her feet. The lights filled the room and then went out. Car lights. Again she was left in darkness.

Now dizzy, she lay back down and closed her eyes.

A car door slammed, then footfall ground on gravel. A door squeaked open and the shuffle of feet drew closer. Fear gripped her aching chest and flooded her veins with adrenaline as she felt the thud of the floor as the steps grew near. She felt a flashlight beam flood across her face, but she willed her eyes to stay closed. A heavy hand grabbed her ankle and shook.

She groaned but willed herself to remain still and silent.

"Waking up soon," a male voice muttered. "She'll be needing this."

Did she know him? Did she recognize that voice?

She fought the urge to open her eyes. If she did, she would only be looking into the beam of the flashlight, which would blind her, and still she would not know the stalker at the end of the bed. She held still.

The silence was interrupted by the slide of a zipper against its teeth. Her heart flooded again with fear, adrenaline banging against her bruised ribs. How could she defend herself with an injured arm? How could she push free?

The white heat of the flashlight beam moved across her face. With her ears trained on nothing else, she listened like prey for her hunter's next step, waiting for what would inevitably come next. She tensed, bracing herself against the struggle she was about to face, tightening her legs as she readied herself to kick out. Instead, she felt the prick of a needle near her ankle.

Instantly warmth rose from her ankle and spread up one leg. At first unwelcome, like an alien intruder taking over, then the feeling warmed her. The heat reached her arm, her neck, her head, and then she didn't care. Soft, warm velvet smoothed over her, and every molecule of every cell relaxed deeply against the bed. The pain in her chest disappeared first. The pain in her arm soon followed. With a smile on her bruised lips, she drifted again to sleep.

CHAPTER EIGHTEEN

"Amy is missing!" Zelda shouted to Rian and Genna. "She took off in the Hummer to run errands. That was yesterday morning, and she's not back yet. I can't reach her by phone. I've left a dozen messages."

Zelda jumped from her chair and paced the floor in the sunroom filled with early morning light. The sunshine streamed through the glass, the beams touching plants, furniture, and frightened faces. Dust motes danced eerily in the sunlight. She stepped in and out of the dust beams as she paced, the eerie illumination following her as she walked the floor in front of them.

"I had the strangest call with her." She told them about Amy's call. "It wasn't an SOS; it was just nonsense. I think she was in a bar. She said she would call me back, but she never did."

"That's not like Amy," Genna said and reached for a cigarette with trembling hands. "Where was she?"

"I don't know. Amy didn't tell me where she was going when she borrowed the Hummer. I assumed she was going garage sale-ing. I wish I'd asked what she thought she was doing . . ."

Zelda's voice trailed away to silence. She had been hurt and angry at Amy for breaking into Zack's office. It was hard to disguise the lingering scent of Amy's favorite strawberry papaya shampoo, but their conversation had confirmed it was her. Zelda hadn't had the courage to confront her then.

Amy had lied on the phone. She had lied to Amy. And that one lie proved one thing. She hadn't told Amy what was in the drawers when she called to complain that someone had broken into Zack's office. Amy knew there were files in the cabinet. Zelda had said only that the drawers were now empty. They weren't empty; not then.

Now they were charred pages of ash in the fireplace grate.

She had set fire to the newspapers from Zack's files, balling each page into a bundle that caught and fueled the flames. She had emptied the drawers of its manila folders and pages and fed them to the fire one by one, watching them curl and brown in the heat. She remembered how the sweat had curled the fine hairs on her bangs as the fire grew, taking with it every reminder of who Zack Carlisle was, really was, as it all went up in smoke.

The truth about Zack hadn't surprised her as much as it could have. And that surprised her even more.

She had done her own digging in Zack's files. It was the day he refused to pay for her birthday cruise. Fueled by anger, she had broken into Zack's desk and then into the file cabinet looking for a hidden stash of cash or a maturing CD she could cash without him knowing.

She found more hidden in that file cabinet than she could ever imagine, and far more than she wanted to know.

Amy had been in those files. No doubt she had read them. And now she was missing. What was Amy trying to do?

"She'll be home soon," Rian spoke up. "She's probably out having a good time. She probably had too much of a good time to drive home last night. Maybe she found a hot something-something she wanted to spend some time with."

Zelda paced the floor in front of them.

"Zelda," Rian said. "Sit down. Genna and I need to talk to you about something."

Zelda spun in mid-step and stopped.

"Uh-oh," Genna muttered. "This isn't going to be fun."

Rian took in a deep breath and exhaled as if steeling her mind against an unpleasant deed.

Zelda sat on the white wicker chair with its plump cushions covered in red poppies on white chintz. On any other morning, the chair would have been a soft little nest to curl up in and read while the geraniums bloomed around her. On any other day, the three friends would be laughing over someone's faux pas or funny turn of a phrase. Not today. Today the chair was as hard as the truth she had been denying herself for months.

"I guess you may know by now that we—Genna and I—each own a third of Carlisle Industries LLC. I'm guessing that if the police know, you know. The plan was for Genna and me to capitalize on the company as a cell tower lease provider. The goal was to buy land prime for a tower, bid for rights, and then lease to the highest bidders. We thought it was going to be a moneymaker."

"We each put in fifty thousand dollars," Genna added, picking up when Rian fell silent. "Zack had a plan for how we would triple our investment in less than five years. We were going to make a lot of money."

"And now that Zack's . . . gone?" Zelda asked.

"I assume if all your papers are in order, that legally you own Zack's third," Rian said quietly, "unless we buy you out. Or we dissolve the partnership. We have the right to choose. And Genna had the business sense to buy partnership insurance."

"We took out a policy in trust for each of the partners," Genna added. "On the death of any of us, the policy pays out while the company is intact." Genna leaned forward and touched Zelda lightly on her arm. "We didn't tell you because, well—honestly, sugar, Zack said not to. He thought it would be a fun surprise when we all started making a boatload of money. But your share isn't worth much because the company isn't worth much," she added.

"Anything," Rian corrected. "Your share isn't worth anything. We've just discovered the company is operating in the red. Genna and I may be liable for leases and agreements we don't even know about. It looks like the capital we invested has been spent. I'm not sure what we own and what we don't. Zack handled all of the real estate transactions."

Genna glanced at Rian for comfort.

"Maybe we can still make money on the leases if we can find someone who knows about that kind of business. Someone we can trust," Genna said. "But the money's gone, and I don't know where the deeds and leases are, or even if we have deeds and leases. Rian and I can walk away free and clear with the money from the insurance policy. We could also reinvest it. It's still a big blinking question mark in my mind."

"I see," said Zelda, her tone distant.

"I'm truly sorry," Rian added.

"Ditto," Genna agreed.

Rian grabbed a curled lock of hair and twisted it between her fingers. She glanced at Genna. "The devil is in the details," Rian said. "What you didn't know you can't testify to in court. What isn't shared out loud cannot be repeated to anyone," she said and stuffed her fingers in her pocket. "You know, dodging the truth is one of the things I do best."

Zelda and Genna nodded.

"Here's the devil," Rian added. She tugged a curl. "Zack was also going to use those sites to grow and dry weed."

Genna took in a sharp breath of surprise.

"He was purchasing FEMA trailers at auction and was going to turn them into growing houses, out of sight and downwind. He wanted me to get him started with a crop, and then he was going to take it over once he learned the trade. That's probably where the money went.

"I hated the idea of the FEMA trailers. They outgas formaldehyde that could leach into the crop. I wouldn't want my enemies ingesting that."

Rian chuckled. "But growing a cash crop on FCC-approved land, *that* made me smile. It's almost as good as my 'dealer' car tag I had to buy for delivering vintage cars." She sighed. "I'm sorry I didn't tell you, Zelda. I'm sorry I didn't tell you, either, Genna."

Zelda's jaw clenched. "Why are you telling me now?"

"Because it's been tumbling around in my head like laundry in the dryer. I can see the truth peeking through the glass every time I close my eyes. I can't sleep, and I don't think I can be your friend and keep these secrets any longer. I know it's bad luck to speak ill of the dead, and I had plenty bad to say about him, but he coerced me into that agreement. He badgered me and then threatened me until I gave in. He scared me, Zelda, and I was afraid for you, too."

She paused and looked from Zelda to Genna and then down at her feet. "I'm not proud of myself," Rian said finally. "I didn't do the right thing. He took fifty grand from me and Genna, and I thought maybe I could get it back in the end."

"I guess you will," Zelda said quietly.

The ceiling fan whirred above them, the only sound left cutting into the silence. Three friends suddenly felt like strangers in a room full of sunshine. Three women who thought they knew everything about each other were learning otherwise.

And Amy Sparks was still missing.

CHAPTER NINETEEN

"I know I don't have a favor to call in," Rian was saying on the phone. "But I need to call one in, anyway."

On the other end, Officer Ben Albright was listening.

"I have a friend I can't find," she said. "And I think she might be in danger."

"This has something to do with Granny?" he asked.

"No," Rian answered quickly. "But it might have something to do with Zack Carlisle."

"I heard about that," he said.

She told him about Amy borrowing Zack's Hummer, and about the strange phone call Zelda had from Amy, and the silence since.

"Something is not right."

"Why not call the police?" Ben asked. "You should file a missing person's report."

Rian was silent for a moment. If she was going to get Ben's help, she had to give him details. Just enough but not too much.

"That's the thing. I'm one of the persons of interest in Zack's death, along with Amy, Zelda, and Genna. We were interviewed—no, we were interrogated—by the Hot Springs detectives because they think we were involved in the accident in some way. They think we *were* the accident," she added with a bit of sarcasm. "We aren't guilty of anything more heinous than not wearing seat belts," Rian added quickly. "But we don't exactly have the clout to walk in and say that one of our own is missing. I'm not one to walk into a police station and say much of anything. You know me. I need your help to find her. She was driving Zack's Hummer, last we know."

Rian gave him a description of the Hummer.

"What's the license plate number?"

"I don't know. I can ask Zelda."

"Never mind. I can find it. Don't you have any idea where Amy went?" Ben asked.

"No."

"Come on, Rian. She's your friend. What is she up to? What are you not telling me?"

Rian fell quiet again.

"Rian," he said finally. "Was Amy involved with Zack Carlisle intimately? Were they having an affair?"

"Oh, no. No. No. No."

"What then? Tell me."

He listened to the silence.

"If you want my help, you have to talk to me," Ben said sharply. "If you want my help, you need to trust me."

"I trust you," Rian said. "It's—well, I was thinking about what you said." She lowered her voice as if hiding it from someone nearby. "What if Zelda thought Zack *was* having an affair? What if Zack was? Zelda said Amy borrowed the Hummer to run errands, but what if she sent Amy off to find out who Zack was having an affair with?"

"Would she do that? Why use the Hummer?"

"Maybe they thought it would draw this person out of hiding. Hummers are not a common sight—especially that one."

"Why would Amy do that?"

"Because Amy would do anything for Zelda."

"Do you think she is trying to cover up something? Something Zelda doesn't want the authorities to know?"

"Whoa, Ben, your imagination is getting way ahead of me."

"Amy could be in grave danger. If Zack Carlisle got himself involved with the wrong people down in Hot Springs, there's no telling what's happened if she got caught up in it. Hot Springs is a beautiful city with a crooked past, and it's still a hotbed for shady dealings. Trust me, I know. I gather Carlisle was that kind of a man. And I'm surprised you would have any business with a man like that, Rian."

"Why would you say that?" She felt her defenses rising, like fists in a fight. "I never said a word about Granny."

"No, you didn't," said Ben, "but I can hear it in your voice. The pitch changes when you talk about Granny. What do you think you are doing, Rian?"

"Are you finished scolding me?" she asked, her tone hard as flint.

"Maybe not."

"Maybe you need to focus on the important things."

"Maybe I should focus more attention on you. Special attention. *Really* special attention."

She caught his drift. "That could be arranged," she said, smiling into the phone. "But I need your help first."

"What can I do?"

"I don't know. Help me find Amy without raising red flags and shrieking sirens. Help me find her if she needs us to find her without any more questions from anyone who wears a uniform and carries a big stick."

Ben chuckled under his breath. "I carry a big stick."

"Stop!" she yelled, but she couldn't keep the smile from her voice.

"I'll see what I can do."

"I owe you."

"Yep," he said brightly. "And I will collect."

CHAPTER TWENTY

Officer Ben Albright glanced at the clock, then picked up the phone, then set it back in the cradle. He straightened the papers on his desk and blew at the crumbs on its surface. He dialed the first five digits of Rian's number and then hung up. Delaying the call he needed to make wouldn't change anything. No officer wanted to make that call, ever. He walked to the break room and poured a cup of coffee he didn't need or want, wincing at the bitter bite of the overheated brew on his tongue.

Arkansas State Police found the Hummer hung up in the trees off Highway 7 in Yell County not long after daybreak. The Hummer had already been identified as being owned by Zack Carlisle, deceased, his last known address in Bluff Springs, Arkansas. The report indicated the Hummer was headed north, left the road near Blind Bat Pass, and traveled 157 feet down the hillside until it stopped at a stand of pine and an outcropping of rock.

It had subsequently caught on fire.

Ben didn't see any mention in the report of what made the car leave the road, but a supposition was natural to make. A car going too fast on that stretch of highway was destined to crash. Ben found the forensics section of the report just as brief. The interior of the vehicle had burned with such intensity that the materials had fused, including two cell phones that had melted into the fibers of the floor. The origination of the fire was still to be determined, of course, and he knew it would be months before they had facts beyond these details.

"Rian," Ben said as the call connected, "the Hummer's been found. But no driver." He relayed the information he had to offer her. "Authorities are checking hospitals in the area, but there's no record of an emergency rescue called to this wreck. It looks like she left the road at high speed on a curve."

He waited silently for her response, his fingertips absently twirling the paper on the surface of his desk. Looking at a copy of the photograph of the Hummer, he paused as something caught his eye. He brought the fuzzy black-and-white picture closer and then pulled a magnifying glass from his desk drawer.

The driver's side door of the Hummer was open, and the photo was shot through the window from behind the door. It was an odd angle, but he could see part of the steering wheel and most of the driver's seat. The metal buckle was still engaged.

"Wait a minute," he said out loud as the idea took him.

"What?" Rian asked. "What is it?"

"I have a hunch I want to follow up on," he said cautiously. He didn't want to give Rian false hope or gruesome details, but something didn't fit. If the driver burned when the car burned, there would have been human remains. There were none, according to the report. That meant Amy left the vehicle before the car burned.

That was the theory, which made sense, and yet the buckle ends of the seat belt were still engaged. That didn't make sense. Ben looked over the grainy pixels under magnification. The belt itself was gone, burned in the fire most likely, but the buckle was still connected. How did she get out without unbuckling the belt?

"What is it?" Rian repeated. "Ben, tell me."

He explained the photo and his observations without the sordid details.

"If she survived the crash, where is she?"

"I can't imagine she walked away unharmed. More puzzling is how she got out of the car. And where is she now? Those are the questions that beg for answers."

"I have to go looking for her," Rian said with so much fervor that Ben knew nothing would stop her. "Come with me. You know where to start looking. You know what to look for."

"Yes," he agreed, and in that instant knew he would do whatever Rian asked him to do. Even if he had to cross a line to do it.

They agreed where to meet halfway, Ben driving from his side of the state, and Rian driving from her homestead near Bluff Springs. It had taken her more than two hours, and Ben was waiting for her when she arrived at their predetermined rendezvous.

"I think there is more to this story than you shared on the phone," Ben said, his hands light on the wheel. "Do you think Zack was having an affair? With someone in Hot Springs? You said as much on the phone."

Rian shifted uncomfortably in the seat. He knew she couldn't possibly enjoy riding in a police car, even if it was in the front seat.

"I don't know what to think," she said quietly. "We just need to find Amy."

"Tell me everything that led up to her disappearance."

Rian turned to face him. "Everything?"

"Well, the highlights anyway. As you see them."

Rian laid her head against the back of the seat and closed her eyes.

He saw dark shadows beneath her lashes and wondered how long she had tossed and turned before she made the call to him for help.

"So much of what I know puts you in jeopardy," she said finally, turning to look at him. He left his eyes on the road. "Zack was a dirty dealer. I didn't want to help him, but he just wouldn't take no for an answer."

"Why didn't you come to me for help?"

"I have come to you for help. I just waited too long."

Ben was silent. He knew to give her space. If she wanted to share, she would. If she didn't, no amount of harassment would change her mind.

He drove quickly, keeping his eyes on the road while the car sped along Highway 7's curvaceous lanes, tires squealing on the turns.

"We were playing dominoes like we do every week. Zelda mentioned she wanted Zack gone and that we should help her. Genna made a joke about it and, before we knew it, we were talking about killing a husband and getting rid of the body."

Rian glanced at Ben out of the corner of her eye. "I thought we were just joking around, but then he winds up dead, and then Genna's car gets a big dent right where a man's knees would be. I say to myself, 'Can this be a coincidence?'"

Ben glanced at Rian and then turned back to the road.

"I just couldn't take the chance. Genna was acting strange, indignant, like when you get caught red-handed and you won't admit it. She acts like that a lot, especially when she's cheating at dominoes. But I couldn't tell if she was covering for Zelda or herself, or if the situation just made her nervous for everyone. So we took the Mercedes to my detail guy. If there was any shred of evidence, it got fixed."

Ben frowned and shook his head. "So you've made yourself an accessory at the very least."

Rian shrugged her shoulders. "This is all my fault," she said stubbornly. "I know Amy thought the same thing, and I have to wonder if she found something in the hotel that might also have *gotten fixed*. I think she thought we *all* were in on it somehow, except we left her out of our plans. She's tender that way. Hates to be left out of anything—even if it's something horrendous like the flu."

"So what do you think Amy was trying to do?"

"She was looking for something or someone. I think she thought the Hummer would make a good magnet. The Hummer had to be well-known down here, even among those drug lords who drove up into my yard a few weeks ago."

Ben blew out stale air and shook his head. "You never told me about that."

"No, and I may not tell you about it now."

He couldn't help but grin.

From the Hot Springs detectives and the details they had shared with him briefly, Ben knew Zelda Carlisle was the primary suspect in her husband's death. They didn't have evidence to make an arrest, not for murder, but they were confident they soon would. They were following her every move, and they didn't believe Mrs. Carlisle was alone in that crime. They believed she had help from her friends.

Rian was one of those friends and the implication troubled him.

The detectives had yet to determine whether they were looking at a murder charge or involuntary manslaughter. Evidence would make that determination when they had more of it in their hands. Carlisle didn't die from impact; he bled to death from the glass shard in his neck. There was no way someone could premeditate that, so it could have been an accident—of sorts. It could have been an angry wife who ran him down and then realized later what she had done.

And that troubled him, too.

There was a possibility that Zelda and her friends were responsible for both Carlisle's death and Amy's disappearance. Was it possible that they had rigged the Hummer to go over the hill without a driver? Maybe the seat belt played a role in that. Possible. But probable? He couldn't quite picture any of it, knowing these four women. He didn't know all of them that well, but he knew Rian, and murder would never sit well with her.

Besides, it would take much more than daring to conspire such a dramatic series of events. Putting an end to the Hummer might put an end to any lingering evidence and confuse the investigation—if that's what they were trying to do—but it all carried such an untenable weight of danger and risk. Too much could go wrong.

Maybe that's why Rian was worried about finding Amy. Was there more to that than he realized?

Ben squared his jaw. He glanced again at Rian and saw that she was watching him closely.

"You look like you've got lockjaw."

Ben relaxed his mouth. "Just trying to figure this out."

"Don't try too hard. You'll fry your brains."

"Do you know who killed Zack Carlisle?"

"No," she said, shaking her head. "But I do know I wish our paths had never crossed."

Ben pulled the cruiser to the shoulder of the road. They stood on the hillside where the Hummer had been hauled topside. A wide swath of broken branches and tree trunks led down the hill, not all of it carnage from the Hummer's descent. Trees had been felled to make way for the wrecker crew, and the car had been wrenched up the hill and then towed into town. All that was left behind was a charred ring that looked like a spaceship had attempted a crop circle in the hard limestone of the Ouachita Mountains.

"Where do we start?" Rian asked. They were still standing on the shoulder of the road just above the wreck entry.

"I'm sure they already scoured this section of the woods," he answered, "but I want to look again. And then we need to widen our search."

Ben kicked the toe of his boot at the remnants of a shattered taillight on the edge of the pavement. It probably broke as the vehicle was towed to the top, but he made a mental note to check the report for that detail anyway, just in case it didn't belong to the Hummer.

He surveyed the woods that spanned out in front of them, a 360-degree view of dense forests and hard stone bluffs. It was a lot of acreage to search for someone alive, or dead. The hillside was far too treacherous for someone to travel in the dark, especially if that someone were injured. A climb uphill would be preferable, but difficult. A downhill climb would be easier but more dangerous. One wrong step in the dark and Amy could step off a cliff into nothing but air, or worse, take a rough tumble down the rocky hillside.

He thought to move down the slope to look, but he didn't want Rian to come with him. And he didn't want to leave her alone. He glanced over at her, where she was still scanning the expanse of woods surrounding them, her eyes dark with apprehension.

"Ready?" he asked and nodded to the rugged downslope. She nodded and followed.

Burnt brush crunched beneath their boots as they made their way down to the outcropping where the Hummer had come to a stop. The acrid smell of fire filled what little breeze rustled the hillside as they walked the site, slowly circling counterclockwise. The ground, charred black at the center, was blistered by the heat even as they searched farther out.

Ben considered that wild boar or a mountain cat could have pulled Amy from the car and dragged her off as prey, but an animal wouldn't come close to a raging fire. Even if an animal had pulled the body out from beneath the seat belt straps, which seemed unlikely, the force would cause some damage—as gruesome as that sounded—and leave evidence of some sort behind. He didn't see any such remains—no bones, hair, or shredded clothing.

While these were grisly thoughts he had no intention of sharing with Rian, the idea was hard to shake. How had Amy gotten out of the car without unbuckling the seat belt? And why hadn't this observation been included in the officer's report?

All the evidential findings might have been already bagged, but a crash site wasn't necessarily a crime scene, and the early responders were looking for injured, not evidence. To be fair, the crews were pulling an abandoned vehicle from over the ridge. They weren't looking for a missing person. And not all details got noticed in any investigation. It happened more than the public needed to know.

Logic told him there were many possibilities. Even more curious was how this was connected to Zack Carlisle. Rian had said as much. This question was like a fleabite he couldn't reach. An itch he couldn't scratch.

He glanced at Rian, who was following in his footsteps several paces behind.

"There's nothing here," she called out. "What are we looking for?"

"This," Ben said, bending down and reaching into a thicket. He pulled a glove from his pocket and gripped the steel of a blade before bringing the knife into full view.

Frowning, he examined the knife, a bowie with a sharp clip point that was honed only for the express purpose of killing. Etched into the wide blade was a name he recognized. *Hanby* was one of the finest knife makers in Arkansas, a White River Cherokee and buffalo rancher who lived in the Ozark Mountains not too far from Bluff Springs. He could feel the weight of the blade and heavy buffalo horn handle as he held it aloft. No doubt the buffalo hide sheath was still hanging from the owner's belt. Someone would be very sorry they lost this knife.

"Do you recognize this?"

"No," Rian said.

"This isn't Amy's? You're sure?"

"Of course, I'm sure. Amy doesn't carry a knife. And certainly not one like that!"

"Could it have been in the Hummer? Did it belong to Zack?"

Rian's forehead bunched over her brows. "I don't know. It could be, but I can't imagine why. He was no hunter."

Ben dropped it in a bag to preserve the fingerprints he knew would still be on it. "This is how Amy got out of the car," he said. "I had a hunch and here is the evidence that fits. Someone cut the seat belt straps to pull her out."

Rian's eyes widened. "But why?"

Ben shook his head. "I don't know. Maybe the buckle jammed. This could have been the only way she could get out. Maybe someone . . ."

He saw the fear flash across Rian's face. Amy really could be in danger, real danger, and the reality of it was coming home to roost. He saw that thought in her eyes. He felt the fear in her stance. While she usually stood against the world rough, tumble, and feisty, he knew her better. He knew the vulnerable place in her heart she hid from everyone. Even from those she loved. That place was laying bare now, and he saw it all.

"We will find her," he said softly and pulled her to him. He felt her shoulders relax against his chest. "I promise you, we will find Amy."

He hated the lie. There were miles of dense forest surrounding them, and within that, acres of bluffs with caves and outcroppings where someone could hide. Or be hidden. Or be attacked by wild game. He doubted they would find Amy unless whoever took her from the Hummer wanted her to be found. That troubled him more than Rian needed to know. If Amy's disappearance was connected to Zack Carlisle's murder, connected to a drug cartel, she was in more danger than any of them realized.

"It's too late to get a search for Amy underway, now," he said quietly, motioning to the sun heavy on the horizon between two mountain peaks. "We can get an early start if you want to stay over . . ." He smiled broadly at the thought. "There's a clean little motel not far from here . . . That is, if you want to stay the night."

"But I didn't bring my PJs," Rian said with a sexy smile, easing his mind just a little. He hoped that he would soon be able to ease hers, too.

CHAPTER TWENTY-ONE

She heard her name being called like a lullaby from far away. Standing on the beach in her childhood hometown, staring out at the sea, foamy waves flowing over her toes on the sand, she could hear them—her friends—calling for her to join them, but they were too far from shore to reach without a boat.

Overhead the shorebirds circled and dove, their wings beating the air like the blades of a fan on high speed. The beating wings grew louder and then moved away.

When she opened her eyes, it was daytime and the dream was gone. There was no ocean, no birds, no friends calling her name. Instead, she lay in a pool of sweat. Blinking in the light, she tried to focus her eyes. One small window letting in dirty daylight showed her the faded paneling that surrounded her. The room couldn't have been more than ten feet square.

She glanced at the mattress underneath her, naked of sheets, the black-and-white ticking old, threadbare, and stained. *Don't even think about those stains*. Her stomach grumbled and her throat ached with thirst. Her head felt too heavy to lift. She lay still, letting her senses awaken from a deep drugged sleep. The stench overtook her first. Gagging, she heaved, and her body rumbled with pain, like thunder bouncing through mountains. Her ears rang in her head and, beneath that, she heard the subtle beat of her heart pounding.

In a moment the nausea and pain passed, and then, wiggling until her feet hung off the end of the bed, she shifted until they touched the floor. Resting them there, she waited again for the pain to fade. Then, rising on unsteady legs, she steadied herself against the doorframe and then stepped through.

Ahead was a small kitchenette with a stove, sink, and fridge. Shuffling to the refrigerator she opened the door. Only stale air greeted her. Taking the few steps to the sink, she turned the tap. It didn't even hiss.

She rushed toward the door, hope flowing through her, but reaching for the handle, hope faded just as fast. The knob turned, but the door didn't open. She yanked at it, but something seemed to be holding it shut from the outside. Pressing her nose to the window, she drew in a breath, and foul air rushed at her. The stench came from outside.

She cupped her hand around her eyes and pressed against the window. Through the grimy grid of the window screen, she saw a campfire ring a few feet away. Five empty camp chairs circled the fire ring, with beer cans littering the ground at the base of each chair, cans piled as if the drinkers were claiming his trash as a trophy. The remnants of a leftover meal sat on the rocks by the fire. A metal grate balanced over the stones with a cast-iron skillet on top. Her stomach grumbled again at the thought of food.

Jiggling the doorknob again, she felt her strength wane, and although she heard something clang on the other side, the door held fast. She moaned again, and her shoulders dragged down with despair.

She was a prisoner in an old trailer, somewhere deep in the back-woods, injured, lost, and a long way from home.

The table with two wooden chairs and a bench against the wall caught her eye. At one time the cushions would have been festive orange-and-yellow stripes. Now they looked brown and dirty, the cloth showing the foam rubber pad underneath. Eyes widening with hope, she saw the bag on the table and stumbled to reach it. Inside was a six-pack of Mountain Dew, four cans of Vienna sausages, and an unopened box of saltines. Instinctively she raised her right hand, wincing at the pain. Then, after fumbling with the pull tab, she opened a can of soda and chugged down the warm liquid, bubbles burning the back of her throat like fire. She ripped the saltine package open with her teeth and slid a cracker over her split lip. The salt burned as she licked her lips. She guzzled another soda and ate half the sleeve of crackers like someone who hadn't eaten in days. Maybe it had been days.

Sated for the moment, she sat at the table and waited. Sooner or later he would return, she knew. And when he did, she would demand to be taken to a hospital. But what did she have to bargain with? What did he want with her? Where was she?

Somewhere in the boondocks.

Somewhere no closer to proving her friends' innocence. She had failed them, and she had failed herself.

She reached for the peridot charm at her throat.

It was gone!

An anguished cry escaped her lips. Shoulders sagging with sadness, her head dropped to the dirt-smudged table. Her tears flowed hot, salty, and full of regret, until finally she felt the last of her resolve run out of her as the tears pooled on the grimy surface.

She lifted her head when she heard them coming. Through the kitchen window, she saw three pickup trucks speeding single file in a cloud of dust down the road toward her before screeching to a stop on the other side of the fire ring. Fear swept through her. Who were they? What did they want?

When the trailer door flung open, she saw his face, and she recognized him. The man from the bar, the big one who led the pack. His bulk climbed the stairs, shirt taut against his belly, his frame filling the door.

His eyes swept the room quickly. "Oh, ho!" he said when he saw her at the table. He turned and spoke over his shoulder behind him. "The little vixen is up, boys. Whaddaya know about that?"

"What do you want with me?" she demanded, swallowing her fright, summoning as much ire as she could manage.

He chuckled. "Well, now," he said, eyeing her lewdly. "What any good ole redneck wants."

She wouldn't show her fear. Her chin jerked in defiance and the pain shattered through her. "Why did you run me off the road?"

"Run you off the road?" He turned to the other men outside the trailer. She saw their faces behind him. "She wants to know why we ran her off the road, boys!"

He turned back to face her, and the mirth faded from his bristled, sunburned face. "Stupid, ungrateful bitch," he muttered. "We saved your life."

"What? Why?" she stammered, surprised by his words.

"Why? That remains to be seen," he said coyly. "You got two strikes already for slipping out the door at old Garland Cooley's Bar. Had to beat the shit out of that bartender for telling such a lie. *You* were driving that Hummer. Wasn't Carlisle with you?" He wiped his huge hand against his forehead.

She shook her head weakly.

"You know where to find him, though. So here's what we want. We want him delivered to us right here. Don't we, boys?" He turned to look behind him and laughed. The others echoed his laughter.

She forced herself to stand and face him. "If you didn't run me off the road, who did? How did you find me?"

"That was a stroke of luck," he said, hitching up his jeans. He wiped at his forehead again and ran his hands over his thighs to dry them. "Lucky for you, darlin'," he added with a suggestive smile. "Fuck it's hot in here," he said and started to back down the steps.

"What do we do now, Beck?"

She knew that voice! It was much different than the leader's, much softer. It belonged to the man in the dark at the foot of the bed.

"How the hell do I know?" he shot back. "Get in there and find out where Carlisle is. He needs to show up for a showdown if he ever wants to see his woman again."

"You can't hold me hostage!" Amy spat, surprised by her venom. She hung on to the edge of the table to keep her balance.

He turned on the step, his red face scowling. "You're no hostage," he said, his lip curled into a sneer. "You're free to go. Highway's ten miles from here. You can make it. Might take a day or two, but you can make it."

He laughed with contempt and then slammed the door behind him.

She shuddered in defeat. Ten miles! She swallowed against a throat already parched and raw.

The door swung open, and a man as wide as the door entered on heavy footsteps. She saw the concern on his face even before he spoke. His cheeks were ruddy, his dark blond hair curled unkempt under a ball cap with a Peterbilt logo. He walked heavily toward her, but not aggressively, and when he wedged himself across from her at the table, the chair squeaked beneath his weight.

"You gonna be okay?" he asked. His voice was a near whisper. Did he not want the others to hear?

"I guess." She knew he saw the fear in her eyes. He would be looking for it. She wanted to keep it hidden.

He nodded at the bandage. "How's your arm?"

"It hurts a little. It hurts a lot."

"Need some more stuff?" Her eyes followed as he touched the fanny pack attached to his belt. The pouch had a zippered opening. "I'm diabetic. Need to carry insulin all the time. The boys poke fun at me about it, but they don't want me going comatose on them, either. You know?"

Amy nodded. She understood. Her cousin was diabetic. It was a terrible disease if you didn't take care. Terrible even if you did.

"I got some pain stuff from my sister," he volunteered again, patting the pouch. "She works in the hospital over at Garland Reg. . . ." His voice trailed away.

He drew a thick hand toward the chest pocket of his charcoal gray uniform. *Clay* was embroidered in red cursive above the pocket. The other side said *Murphy Oil.* "Clayton. My name's Clayton," he said and smiled wide. "My friends call me Two Ton. Seeing how I'm wide like a truck."

Amy eyed him carefully. She wasn't sure if he was friend or foe. Could she trust him? She didn't think she had a choice. She swept a dry tongue over her swollen lip. "Who found me? Why am I here?"

"I found you." His face lit up with a prideful smile, pushing his cheeks under his eyes. He was cherubic in a redneck kind of way, with dark blond curls and blue eyes and chubby cheeks that went along with his stature head to toe.

"Me and Charley stopped to take a piss and get another beer right around Blind Bat Pass. Saw a deer carcass on the road and thought we'd bag it. That's when I saw headlights down the hill. The Hummer was hung up in the trees. Your engine was still running." He shrugged. "I guess you missed that curve. It's a sharp one."

"Somebody ran me off the road!"

"Nah," he said in a consoling voice and pushed at the bill of his cap.

"I saw you at the bar, drinking. You were drunk and you missed that curve. That's how come I brung you here. It's right near. Right down the road from the dump. We woulda all gotten popped for drunk driving if I had taken you anywhere else. We couldn't just drop you off at the hospital curb and run like dogs, seeing who you was and all. I couldn't leave you there in the trees, now could I? This was as good a place as I could think of. We come out here all the time. Me and Beck and the boys."

She motioned to her right arm with the other hand. "You did this?"

He nodded. "I had first aid. Thought to be a paramedic. Didn't work out."

"Thank you," she said. The words sounded lame, but she meant them. Even under these circumstances, she was better off than on the side of the road. She couldn't have walked up the steep mountain in the dark.

Clayton smiled at her and rubbed his gut. "I bet you're hungry. I'll bring you a hot dog in a few minutes. You like mustard?"

"Can't I come out there with you?" She smiled, knowing she had to look pathetic with a split bottom lip. No doubt she had bruises everywhere, too.

"Nah. Boy talk," he said. "You don't want none of that."

"Could you leave the door open? It's so hot in here."

Clayton rose and backed down the stairs, but he left the door open as she asked. The breeze was heavenly even if it did smell like rotten eggs.

At the table, listening to the little circle not far from the door, she couldn't imagine how they sat so casually in the stench, but then, she was starting to get used to it herself. The smell was the nearby landfill, as Clayton said, with its refuse left to rot in the sun.

Somewhere in the backwoods off Highway 7, the road she had been traveling on her way home, must be where they were.

Beck had said it was ten miles to the highway. Even if she did make it that far, who would pick up someone who looked like a fugitive on the run?

She glanced down at her torn jeans, covering her bruised and scratched legs. Her favorite lavender T-shirt, which had started fresh and bejeweled when she left home, was ripped and crusted with sweat and plastered to her chest. The bruising from the seat belt had turned an angry mauve-edged blue and was still sore to the touch. Her wrist was swollen against the makeshift bandages, and when she tried to move it, the pain overwhelmed her. She needed a hospital. That was clear.

What was the real reason Clayton had brought her here? Was she brave enough to ask? He should have taken her to the hospital when he found her hanging from the trees, but he hadn't. Was it really because he thought she had drunkenly driven off the road?

Chills broke out on the back of her neck as she thought of the Stephen King novel, where the woman kept the novelist hostage until he wrote the story she wanted to read. She shuddered. The woman pulled him from a car wreck, too.

This was no book. This was real.

Still sitting at the table, she leaned her head against the wall at the window, cranked open as far as the glass would go, and listened to the conversation at the campfire. When she moved her head around the obstacles in her view, she saw which voice belonged to whom. The conversation was loud and getting louder as the beer cans popped open one after another. She heard the empty cans pinging to the ground. After a few minutes, she recognized the individual voices.

"Whatta we goin' do, Beck?" That was Clayton.

"Don't sweat it, bro. I got a plan." That was Beck.

"You ain't got shit." His name was Charley.

"I got one biggerun yours."

They all laughed. Amy heard five distinct laughs.

"When you gonna call that azzhole?" Charley.

"Not callin' on my phone." Clayton.

"Me either." They called him Root.

"What's going on?" Amy didn't know his name yet. He never said much.

"You bin asleep, boy?" Charley asked.

"No."

"Lyin' sack a shit." Root.

"I already called 'im. Ain't no answer," Beck said.

"You left a message?" Clayton.

"Of course, I left a message. I told him I want them trailers he stole from me at auction. And when I get 'em, I'm gonna build my trailer park like just like I want. That's what I told him. Give 'em back, or else."

"What if he don't call back, Beck?" Clayton said.

"*What if he don't call back?*" Beck mimicked in a singsong voice.

"Well, what then?"

"Then I guess we'll keep her for ourselves!"

The others laughed.

She couldn't help the groan that escaped her.

The posse fell silent around the fire.

"Listenin' to ever' word," Beck said with venom.

"Maybe she should call him. Ain't he more apt to do what she says?"

Amy sighed. Zack wasn't going to answer a call from anyone.

Zack is dead!

Why couldn't she say it? What was wrong with her? If they knew Zack was dead, wouldn't they just let her go? Wouldn't they take her to the nearest store, drop her off, and be done with her? Maybe they would. Or maybe they would leave her here to rot like trash.

"You know what we done is kidnapping," Clayton said. He still sounded sober.

"You didn' kidnap nobody, Two Ton!" Charley said. "We rescued her."

"Yeah. But there's a line between rescue and, whatever. We got a hostage."

"What's this *we* bidness, bro? Ain't nobody asked you to do nothing. And she's free to leave if she wants to walk out of here."

Clayton and Beck fell quiet.

The chairs shuffled around the fire, and she heard grunts and groans as big men rose on heavy legs. She heard the crunch of branches and rocks underfoot.

What were they doing? Were they leaving, and leaving her behind? She needed to get out of this desperate little box. If they were leaving, she didn't have much time to act. Rising again from the chair, her body suddenly sagged as if she were a bag of wet cement. Her strength was gone. Still gripping the edge of the table with her good arm, she hung on, looking up as Clayton appeared in the doorway, a hot dog and bun in each hand.

He watched as she devoured them both.

"Is Beck your big brother?" she asked, wiping gently at her lips with the neck of her dirty collar.

Clayton nodded.

"I don't have any siblings. I wish I did." If she could get him talking, maybe she could figure out what was going on. "Did I overhear him say he was going to build a trailer park?"

"Aw, Beck's been talking about that since we was kids," he said and chuckled. "He wants to build a rock and roll trailer park. Gonna use those FEMA trailers got used after Hurricane Katrina down in New Orleans. They've been coming in at auctions up here."

"What is he going to do with them?"

"Beck thinks he's going to make his fortune that way. I don't know about *that*, but I guess it does sound like fun. He wants to circle a bunch of trailers on a spread out here so bikers and their babes can cruise in for the weekend. Thinks they'll spend money at his outdoor rock and roll bar, and then spend the night at his 'don't come knocking if you see it rocking' trailer hotel."

His cheeks grew red as if the thought embarrassed him.

"Like I said, I don't know how it's going to happen, but Beck's hellbent."

The idea wasn't too far-fetched, seeing how Highway 7 was a beautiful ride for motorcyclists, and there weren't many bike-friendly stops between the interstate and Hot Springs. None, she knew of, that allowed bikers to party in a private setting surrounded by woods.

So Zack fit into this picture, not because he was stepping on drug territory toes, but because he was buying up all the trailer inventory. How many did he have? If Zack was growing in L91, maybe all the carboard tab keys fit trailers just like it.

"What does Beck want with Zack?" she asked.

Clayton eyed her carefully, his eyes darkening. "I think you better call and tell him it's time to come fetch you."

"Who?"

"Your old man, that's who."

"Wait, you said, 'Seeing who I was,' earlier. Who do you think I am?"

"Ah, you ain't got no amnesia, do you? Beck ain't gonna like that a bit."

"Who do you think I am?"

His face hardened like a trap snapping shut. "I ain't stupid," he said sharply. "You're Carlisle's old lady. And once he shows up to give Beck what he wants, Carlisle can have what he wants. That'd be you."

"No! I'm not Carlisle's old lady. Or his wife. I'm not Zelda. Or . . ."

"What! You mean I dragged some stranger out here?

The Hummer looked just like his. Oh sweet Jesus, save me now!" He took off his ball cap, ruffled his greasy blond curls, and settled the cap back on his head. "So what is your name anyway?"

"Amy," she squeaked.

"Amy," he said and chuckled. "If you ain't Carlisle's woman, we're not going to get nowhere. But I can't take you back to the Hummer. It's not just wrecked, Beck set that bad boy on fire."

She gasped. "What? He set it on fire?"

"Yep, Beck slit the tires. Slashed the seats. Set it on fire. It ain't a pretty Hummer for a pretty boy playing on the wrong side of Arkansas no more."

There was malice in his words, but he sounded like he was quoting someone else. Like a bully of a big brother.

"Why were you driving that thing?" His eyes grew wide. "Did you steal it? Are you a carjacker?"

The idea struck her funny, and she cracked a smile, which made her lips hurt, and her body ached, and there was nothing funny at all about how smelly things were. These men didn't know Zack was dead, and if they didn't know that, they didn't kill him. The thought was as painful as her ribs. How was she going to find Zack's killer sitting in an old trailer in the woods?

"That was Zack's Hummer, but I didn't steal it. And somebody did run me off the road. Was it your brother?"

Clayton shook his head. "That ain't nice. I been good to you. You'd still be sitting in the weeds with that busted up wrist if I hadn't come along."

"Why didn't you take me to the hospital?"

Clayton hung his head and spoke to his lap. "I told you already. We thought you'd be in trouble."

"You thought you could help Beck, didn't you?" She spoke softly. "You thought you could help him get what he wanted from Zack."

Clayton lifted his eyes to hers.

She knew how that felt. She had gone out on a limb for Zelda. She was still out on that limb, and nowhere close to any truth.

Her eyes suddenly filled with tears. They came before she could drown them out with bravado she didn't feel. Her chin trembled, and she hated herself for it.

"Aww," he said softly. "Don't cry none." He reached out and touched her shoulder. His hand was heavy and lighthearted. "You can trust me. You really can."

She nodded. It was now or never.

"Zack Carlisle is dead."

Clayton's eyes opened so wide she wondered if he might pop. "Dead?"

She nodded again.

He cocked his head and looked at her sideways from under his cap. "Nah, you're pulling my leg."

"He's dead. He was killed in a parking garage in Hot Springs. He was run over by a car, a hit-and-run."

"Well I'll be," he said quietly, whistling under his breath. "Things just keep getting wilder. Beck's gonna want to hear about this." He scraped back the chair and gathered himself to rise, squeezing from the table like a roll of biscuits pushed against the counter.

She raised her eyes to meet his. "Wait," she begged. "Wait just a minute. Please."

If Clayton told Beck that Zack was dead, that would be that. With Zack gone, what did Beck need with her? He might let her go, but he might not. She was being held hostage, even if Beck said she wasn't. She was a witness of sorts now, too, wasn't she? He might panic and do something far worse than leave her to walk ten miles to the road. It was a crapshoot, a roll of the dice. She had to take the chance.

"I need your help," she said finally. "I know you don't have any reason to help me, except I can tell you're a good guy. A nice guy. A gentleman even."

She watched him relax, but his eyes were still wary.

"My best friend, Zelda, who really is Zack's old lady—his wife," she corrected, "is getting blamed by the police for his death. They think she's the one who ran him down. But I know she didn't. She just couldn't have. And neither did Genna. And I need to prove that. I have to keep moving through his last day until I find out who killed him. It's the only way I can keep us out of jail."

"How do you know she didn't do it—run him down."

Amy stared at Clayton for a long moment, culling the tidbits that would allow her to answer that question. Whatever evidence was stacked against Zelda, she knew her friend's character. Even the shoes she threw in the trash couldn't overshadow her belief that Zelda was no husband-killer. That none of her friends were killers of any kind. But if she did find evidence to the contrary, she wouldn't think twice about tossing it in the trash, too. There had to be something on the trail that led to the one person who ran Zack over, and she was determined to find it.

"Well?" he said after several seconds of silence. "How do you know?"

"I don't. I don't know. But I have to believe she's innocent because she's my best friend. I need to go to the garage and see for myself. Maybe we will find something the police missed."

"We?"

"Will you help me? Please."

Clayton sat back against the chair's thin frame. Beads of sweat dripped from his brow and his cheeks were red. His blue eyes felt piercing.

She reached into her jeans pocket and pulled out the mangled cardboard tab and key that opened the door to L91, then dropped it on the table in front of him. "I think Beck might want this." She looked at the key and then back at Clayton. "If you will help me, I'll tell you what that opens and where it is. I think it's something Beck would want."

Clayton shook his head. "You ain't playing me, are ya?"

Amy smiled. She *was* a player. A good one. But her games were played on cardboard with plastic pieces, not on rowdy men in the backroads of Arkansas. She could only hope her plan would work well enough to convince Clayton to help her. If he couldn't get her to Hot Springs, he could at least get her to the highway, away from Beck and this horrid trailer full of stench.

Her head pounded and her arm ached. What Clayton had in his pouch would make the pain go away, but she wanted a clear head. How else was she going to keep looking for what she had to find?

"It's a FEMA trailer," she said. "And it's full of pot."

CHAPTER TWENTY-TWO

Rian stuck her head out the car window and watched the helicopter turn wide circles in the air. She listened as the dispatcher radioed Ben with the location of another encampment that had been sighted from the air. The words were hard to decipher over the static, but she heard enough to know there was another clearing to investigate not far from the Hummer crash site. It had to be *not far* as the crow flies because she and Ben had been driving dusty dirt roads near the crash site on Highway 7 all day.

"Copy that," Ben said into the radio mic.

Shortly after daylight, she had filed a missing person's report, with Ben's urging, and had given a full description of Amy and her particulars, including the assumption that she was probably injured. Ben had tagged Amy's disappearance as part of the Zack Carlisle investigation, and that along with the torched Hummer brought the hunt into full focus. The rugged terrain was reason enough to bring in a search-and-rescue chopper. With a helicopter, they could cover a lot of ground quickly. She felt bittersweet about dragging in the police, but the crash site had brought her to reality. This was no longer just a game of hide-and-seek.

Ben believed that Amy had been taken from the crash site by someone who had cut her out of the seat belt. She was inclined to agree. Whether Amy had been rescued from the burning car or dragged out against her will was still up for grabs, but either way, Amy hadn't shown up at any of the nearby hospitals for emergency care.

Was Amy being held hostage? The thought had been in her mind all night long. She thought of the black Lincoln that had shown up at her homestead, the message loud and clear: *We know who you are, and we know where you live.*

She thought then they were Little Rock drug mafia, but maybe they were Hot Springs goons, instead. Maybe they had gotten wind of Zack's little pot-in-the-trailer scheme. Maybe they *were* Zack's pot-in-the-trailer scheme.

None of it made her feel any better.

If they had been following the Hummer, if they had seen the Hummer on the highway, they would have thought Zack was driving it. They would be surprised when they saw who was behind the wheel.

Had they taken Amy with them? And for what reason?

The thought made her want to scream. Amy wasn't safe with the likes of that.

Ben turned the car in the direction given by the dispatcher. This latest location would be the fourth one they had scouted so far—without finding Amy.

She sat sullenly in the seat beside Ben, her faith beginning to fade. She wasn't about to turn sissy and panic, but she couldn't set her mind at ease.

"What are you thinking?" Ben asked, a glance in her direction.

"That this is my fault," she said sharply.

"Not again."

"I knew Amy had something up her sleeve. I could just tell. I should have talked to her about it. I should have—"

"Should have," Ben interrupted. "You're not a should-have kind of person. And it's not in your nature to poke your nose in other people's business. It's not your style to tell people what to do."

"Yep. That's Genna's MO."

"So why is Amy's disappearance your fault?"

"Because I'm the connection between Zack and those drug thugs. I'm the one they should have kidnapped."

"Do you think she was kidnapped? Isn't that a big leap?"

Rian turned to look at him—at his dark hair cut short above his ears, at the dimple on his chin. He really was Dudley Do-Right. "I hope we find her in time."

"We will," he said brightly, a genuine smile on his lips, his green eyes kind.

She wanted to believe him, though she sensed even his confidence was slipping. It would be dark again in another few hours, and there were still miles of forest to search.

They turned off the highway at an open gate marked *Private* and followed the long winding dirt road to a campsite with an old trailer parked in a flat spot at the center of a copse of pines. It looked as if it had activity around it recently but now appeared to be abandoned.

Ben motioned to the pilot out the window of the car, and the helicopter turned to the north, continuing its search mission, but still nearby should help be needed. He stopped the cruiser near a campfire ring with its chairs set around it in a haphazard circle. A thin gray wisp of smoke rose from a darkened log, and beer cans and food wrappers littered the ground.

They eyed the trailer, the door still standing open.

"Stay here," he said, and Rian did. She watched him leave the car, his fingers ready on his gun. He circled the trailer, then disappeared inside, his gun drawn.

He reappeared quickly, climbed down the steps, and squatted, peering at the ground under the trailer, then he motioned for Rian to join him.

"Someone has been here recently," he said as Rian walked up beside him. "There's food trash inside. But not much else."

"Oh no!" Rian cried when something winked from the dirt. With trembling fingers, she picked up a gold chain with a peridot stone. Tears welled in her eyes, the chain dangling from her fingers. "This is Amy's necklace." Her voice trembled. "She never takes it off."

"Bring the chopper back," Ben said into the radio mic. "We're in the right spot." Ben reached for Rian and helped her to her feet, meeting her eyes with his. "Amy has to be nearby. We're going to scour every inch of this place. Today we find her . . ." He knew better than to fill in the unspoken—dead or alive.

CHAPTER TWENTY-THREE

Leaning against the concrete piling of the Bennfield Hotel parking garage, Amy stared at the dark spot on the pavement. Chills ran up her spine. In her mind, she saw the lifeless figure from the police photos. Lodged in her memory were the sirens from her dream, a dream that seemed so long ago now in an almost forgotten time when she was snuggled up with her lavender-scented sheets and fluffy cat.

Poor Victor! She'd almost forgotten about Victor. Thank goodness she had filled his cat food feeder and water fountain before driving off in the Hummer. If he wasn't missing his meals, she hoped he was at least missing his mistress and her warm lap. She missed him. She missed her shop. She missed the lively camaraderie of her friends, but she was determined not to return to Bluff Springs until she had answers and the truth.

Clayton stood beside her, and she fought the impulse to grab his hand. Had she known him a little longer, a little better, she wouldn't have resisted the urge to put her hand in his for support. She swayed on unsteady legs.

"This is where it happened?" he asked.

She nodded and then looked away. "I think so."

In her mind, she saw the blood pooled in the photo the detective had shown her. The red stain was now dark grit at her feet, evidence that a cleaning crew had attempted to remove the stain.

It was silly to think the tire tracks that led to Zack's dead body would still be prominent in the busy parking garage. She now felt foolish about this errand she had finally talked Clayton into. Although, it hadn't taken all that much. She had told Beck where he could find the growing house, and while she knew it was the trailer he was after, not the pot, neither would go to waste, she was sure. She had put the ace in her hand when she told Beck about Genna and sung her praises as a promoter. Then, promising Beck that Genna would help launch his rock and roll motel when he was ready, he not only had let her go, he let Clayton go with her.

"I didn't realize there would be so many tire tracks here," she said quietly, scanning the garage floor.

"Well, heck, it's a car garage," he answered with a chuckle. "That's all there should be. What are we looking for?"

"The detective said they determined the intent of the force because of the tire tracks. But how do we know which tracks belong to which car? There are so many."

Clayton pointed to a set of tracks. "Shoot," he said, "that's easy. These tracks belong to a sedan like a Toyota or a Honda. And these fit a truck. Probably a Ram. These, well these go to a tinker toy car, like one of those little BMWs."

"How do you know all that?"

"My daddy taught us about tracking. And not just about animals. You can track a thief by his tires just as well as you can track a deer by his hooves. Besides, that's what I do all day. Change tires and fix flats."

"So what kind of tire track does a Mercedes make?"

Clayton surveyed the floor, walked a few feet, and stopped. "These are on a Mercedes, I betcha. And these, too," he said, pointing to tracks leading out of another space. "What are we looking for? You're shopping for a car or a set of tires?"

Amy stood next to him, her good arm on her hip. She had brushed her hair with her fingers and, fumbling with one hand, tied her hair back with a rubber band Clayton had on the stick shift in his truck. She'd tenderly wiped away the grime from her face with a wet wipe from the cab glove compartment, finding every single bruise on her face and lips as she did. He had given her one of his work shirts to pull over her battered and torn top, and now she and Clayton stood like twinkies in the garage, except his shirt fit her like a dress three sizes too wide.

"The detective showed me a picture of the tire tracks that led them to realize that whoever ran over Zack went from idling to fast. I'm looking for those tracks. I need to know what kind of car that would be."

"Did they look like this?" Clayton stood at the bottom of a set of black tracks. She couldn't tell if they were the same as in the picture, but she couldn't say they weren't.

She searched her memory. She had no reason to study the treads in the photo when they were shoved in front of her with an accusatory explanation. She wouldn't call her memory photographic by any stretch, and the memories of her dream were getting in the way, too.

"What made those?" she asked, pointing to the first set of tracks they noticed that had scorched the pavement.

"I'd say it was a pickup truck. An older model. I'd say the owner buys a set of high-quality Goodyear tires and drives on 'em until they're about run through. See this," he said, pointing to a place in the track. "This is a wear imperfection. I could spot that truck in a line-up."

"You can tell all that from this?"

"Well, no, but like I said, we learned about tracking and I know about tires. Tracking is about using what you know matched up with what you can guess. Sure wish you had that picture," he added. "I could tell you a lot more then."

"And what about these," she called, pointing to a set of marks just outside the dark stain on the floor.

He walked to where she stood, his gait faster than she would guess, given his girth. He was beside her in seconds. "That's the same truck. Leads from the top of the ramp all the way here. See this," he said, pointing with the toe of his work boot. "There's that same wear pattern."

She saw what he was pointing at. The tracks were indeed the same. No dark tire tracks led away from the stain, but the authorities said that Zack hadn't died on impact. He bled to death. Whoever hit him was long gone by then.

Amy sighed and shifted her weight from one leg to the other. It was impossible to reconcile these tracks with the ones made weeks ago. Even if the garage had been closed to process the evidence, there would have been many vehicles tracking through the scene since reopening. The police would have their photos from the scene of the hit-and-run, and they would have their suspicions, too. But looking at the tracks made her realize that what she was looking for was a set of footprints tracking blood away from the scene of the crime.

They weren't there. Of course they were not there. Her heart lifted in her chest.

She looked up at Clayton and beamed.

"What are you smiling at?"

"I don't see any Jimmy Choo footprints."

"Huh?"

"Take me back to Cooley's Bar, would you? I need to talk to the bartender."

"I need to get to work sometime today," Clayton said, looking at his watch. "I had a vacation day coming, but I got a car on the rack. Ain't your friends looking for you?"

"I don't think so. I bet they don't even know I'm gone." It was a bittersweet revelation. They wouldn't know she was missing. She was off on one of her estate sale shopping excursions. That's what they would think, even if they weren't already sitting in jail.

All the more reason to push ahead.

She swung herself back into Clayton's truck with its king-size off-road tires and rumble NASCAR sound. She held her arm in her lap. Having again refused Clayton's shot, she could feel the pain deepening. Her face felt hot and flushed. She glanced in the visor mirror, shocked to see the person looking back. Her skin was gray, her eyes dull, her lip still swollen, and dark bruises shaded her forehead and chin.

Clayton was watching her. She shut the visor and settled back against the seat.

"Why do you want to go back to Cooley's?"

"There was a truck following me the other day. I didn't think too much about it then, but I wonder if it was following me because it was following Zack. Maybe he thought I was Zack. Just like that old guy with the shotgun. I know he thought I was Zack pulling into his driveway."

"What old guy?"

"I think his name is Crawley. He's got a cell tower in his front yard."

"Yep. I know him. Crazy as crazy does. He used to drink at Cooley's Bar a lot, but I haven't seen him much lately. Except, now that I think about it, he must have been at Cooley's that day. You know, the other day when we saw the Hummer. I don't remember seeing him in the bar, but I remember seeing his beat-up old truck in the parking lot. Honey Bee Queen was there, too," he said and smiled, his eyes glazing over with admiration. "She sure is pretty."

Amy smiled with a side glance at the driver. "Honey Bee Queen. I remember her. She had bitter eyes on me and the Hummer. What's her name?"

"Shannon. Shannon Gregory. We were in the same grade. Her granddaddy owns that bar, and her family owns this county. The next one over, too. Apple moonshine from way back when."

"Do you think she knew Zack?"

Clayton chuckled and looked at her sideways from under his cap. "She knows everybody," he said, his eyes twinkling. "Especially all the pretty boys. And most of them in the biblical sense."

Amy laughed. She hadn't heard that expression in a while. "Do you know everybody at that bar?"

He blushed. "Not in that way."

"I didn't mean in the biblical sense." It was her turn to blush. "Do you know Jetson Gregory?"

"Yeah," he said. "Big dude with a big ranch and a big pile of money. It's his truck I got on my rack. Needs tires and a tune-up."

"So is she dangerous?"

"Who?"

"The Queen. Shannon Gregory?"

Clayton burst out laughing and banged his hand on the steering wheel. His cheeks rolled up into pink balls of mirth. "Dangerous? She's a dangerous little heartbreaker. I don't know a guy in my high school who didn't get his heart broke by Miss Shannon Gregory. She takes what she wants and leaves the rest to the buzzards."

"Or the bees."

"Or the bees," he agreed with a smile. "Her daddy started that competition so his princess could have a title."

How *did* Shannon know Zack? What could she possibly want

with him? Other than something obvious, like a good time in the sack. He was a very handsome man. But he was married. He was at least two decades older if not more, and he wasn't rich. He wasn't powerful. Not that either of those things mattered because it sounded like her family was both. Amy remembered the mean curl of the lip sent her way when she and the Honey Bee Queen first locked eyes at Cooley's Bar. There was no doubt in her mind. Zack's and Shannon's paths had crossed. She needed to cross Shannon's path herself and ask a few pointed questions she hoped she would have the courage to ask.

Laying her head against the headrest, she closed her eyes and cradled her arm in her lap. It was starting to hurt worse. Behind the ever-constant dull thud, a new sharp pain ran up her arm. She tried to flex her fingers and gasped in pain. Clayton glanced over at her, his eyebrows raised with concern.

"Why was Beck so mad at Zack that day at the bar? What was he going to do?"

"Aw, Beck's more bark than bite. You saw that yourself. He gets that from our daddy. He acts tough because he thinks he has to, but he's an old softy on the inside."

She doubted that. "Why was he looking for Zack?"

"He saw the Hummer in the parking lot and saw his chance." Clayton shifted gears through the stoplight and the engine roared. "He was mad because he had his eye on a fleet of trailers at an auction, but Carlisle beat him to the bid. Beck had his whole idea based on those trailers, and then Carlisle just swooped in and stole 'em out from underneath him."

"That happened *that day?*"

"Nah. Weeks ago. Maybe even two, three months back. Beck was as mad as a wet rooster. I don't know what he thought he was going to do when they came face-to-face. Kick his ass and make him give 'em up, I reckon. Most of 'em are still sitting on the auction lot waiting to be moved."

She opened her eyes as the truck stopped at a light, and then Clayton made a right-hand turn.

"Hey, this isn't the way to Cooley's Bar."

"Nah," he said. "I'm taking you to the hospital. Should have done that from the get-go. You don't look so good."

"Wait! Clayton! I need to get back to Cooley's Bar. I have to find Zack's killer."

"You need to get some anty-biotics in you, that's what you need."

Aunty Biotics! She grinned at his country accent, and before she could stop herself, she was howling with laughter and pain.

CHAPTER TWENTY-FOUR

The voice over the police radio overpowered the silence. Ben had the radio turned loud enough for them to hear outside of the car.

"Probable missing person, white, female. Late forties. Admitted Garland Regional. No identification. Injured. Not critical."

Ben and Rian exchanged glances.

"It's Amy!" Rian exclaimed. "It has to be!"

Ben nodded, and they both scrambled into the cruiser. Driving quickly even through the steep curves, an expert behind the wheel, Ben was focused. He squared his jaw as he rounded a curve at high speed. It was easy to see how someone could drive off these slopes. He gripped the wheel a little tighter and then glanced at Rian, relief flooding her face.

"I can't wait to hear Amy's story," he said.

"Hail Mary. *Nach a Mool.*"

CHAPTER TWENTY-FIVE

Amy's eyes lit up when Rian entered the room with Ben at her heels.

"Rian! Ben!" She struggled to sit up, winced, and let her head fall back to the pillow.

Rian pressed her cheek to Amy's. "I've never been so glad to see you in my whole effing life. Honest to God."

"Honest to God," Amy said breathlessly. Tears that had welled in her eyes were now falling freely. She knew just how Rian felt.

"I can't believe we found you," Rian said softly. "We thought you were dead."

"I thought I was dying."

"You're so hot," Rian said, pressing her hand against Amy's cheek.

"I'm too sexy for this gown!"

"A cast for *a crown*," Rian agreed. She touched Amy's cast lightly. "I get to be the first to sign it."

"I'd rather keep score on it. Or play tic-tac-toe."

"Does it hurt?"

"Not anymore. They have really good drugs in this place."

Ben smiled and shook his head.

"But I'm so very tired." Her eyes drooped closed, but she forced them to open again. "They won't leave me alone for a minute."

The cast from thumb to elbow weighted her arm to her side.

"It's been a constant flurry of nurses. They poke me. They prod me. Then they do it again. I've even had to talk to the police. You'd think I was Patty Hearst or something."

"You might want this," Rian said, the necklace dangling from her fingers.

Amy's eyes filled again with tears.

"It was at that trailer, on the ground," Rian added, letting the chain fall into Amy's outstretched hand. "I can't tell you how frightened I was when I saw it."

Amy held the necklace to her chest. "I thought it was gone forever."

A nurse hustled in and shooed Ben and Rian out.

"See what I mean?"

It took several tries, bits and pieces, and a few slurred words to get the story told without interruption.

Rian sat on the edge of the bed, with Ben standing a few feet behind her. "Take me through it one more time, because it still doesn't make sense to me. You said you were at a bar, and somebody named Beck Beer kidnapped you and held you hostage to make Zack give him a femur. But that was after you were pulled from the Hummer by a two-ton truck. And that was after somebody ran you off the road. Why would anybody run you off the road? Why would Zack have a femur—isn't that a bone? Are you sure you aren't delirious?"

Amy giggled. Leave it to Rian to hear another angle. "Beck is a guy, not a beer. Clayton is his brother and Two Ton is his nickname.

They wanted the FEMA trailers that Zack has been buying up. Someone *did* run me off the road, and I think it's because they thought it was Zack driving the Hummer. Someone was trying to run him off the road."

"FEMA! Femur. Now I get it!" Rian exclaimed.

"I wasn't kidnapped, but I thought I was, and I thought I was being held hostage. But it was all a big misunderstanding. And that's how I got here."

"What were you trying to do in the first place?" Ben asked.

Amy looked at Rian and back at Ben.

"Ben is one of us," Rian said sharply. "Whatever you can say to me, you can say to both us."

"Was it something to do with Zack's murder?" he asked.

Rian sighed. "Murder. What a rap."

"I think you both need to tell me what you know," he said.

"Why don't you tell us what you know, first," Rian said.

Ben smiled then looked from Rian to Amy and back to Rian. "You know I'd be out of line to share details of an investigation. But, if I give you a tidbit, will you give me one in return?

"I'll take that as a yes," he said after a moment of silence. "After analyzing the scene at the parking garage, investigators believe the vehicle that struck Zack went from zero to about thirty miles per hour in a span of fewer than fifty feet. People don't go that fast in a small parking garage unless they intend to do some damage. The tire tracks show that the deceased was directly in front of the driver's side of the windshield. There's no evidence the driver made any effort to veer away or avoid hitting him. Nor does it appear the car veered after hitting him."

"That feels like *déjà vu*," Amy said. "The car that hit me didn't try to avoid me, either. It rammed me right off the mountain."

Rian twisted a curl in her fingers. "Zack was buying up FEMA trailers to grow weed at the cell tower lease sites. He coerced me into helping him get his business started."

"I saw the grow room in L91. I guess that's what you meant when you said Zack was pressuring you for a share of Granny's business," Amy said.

Rian nodded. Ben looked uncomfortable.

Amy wrinkled her nose. "Oh, and Rian, I gave that key to Beck. He wanted the trailer, and I guess what's inside was just icing on the cake."

Rian laughed and glanced at Ben. "Good riddance."

"And," Amy continued, "I broke into Zack's office to see if I could find any clues. I broke into his file cabinet and read all of his papers."

"Why would you do that?" Ben asked.

"Because she thought Zelda and Genna hit him."

Amy didn't respond. She was struggling with her self-control. If she was going to tell Rian and Ben about Zelda's Jimmy Choos, now would be the time.

"You know, I thought so, too, at first," Rian added. "I didn't believe Genna hit a deer. But that was folly."

"What did you find in the file cabinet?" Ben asked.

Amy shut her eyes for a moment as if trying to remember, but that day was clear in her mind. "I discovered that Zack was an even more horrible husband than we thought. I also discovered that I am a terrible person to think my best friend killed him." Her chin quivered.

"Then the police came to the door while I was there. I just knew they were going to arrest Zelda. And then later Zelda told me that someone broke in and took all the files and papers. I had to do something."

Ben shuffled his feet. "What do you mean?"

"I decided that if I followed in Zack's footsteps that day, I would come across someone who could take the blame and guilt off us."

"Did you?" Ben asked.

"I ran across a lot of people who knew Zack and a fat handful who didn't like him."

"I think you ran across one of them who hated him enough to kill him," Ben said.

"But who ran me off the road? And why?"

"I think whoever saw you in the Hummer thought it was Zack. They were trying to run him off the road, not you."

They looked up just as the doorway filled with perfume and the clack of high heels. Genna entered the room first, her Dior mules tapping at the floor like Morse code. Even through her drug-hazy glow, Amy recognized the periwinkle raw silk jumpsuit tailored to fit Genna's curves in all the right places. She glanced down at legs that seemed to go on forever. A Hermes silk scarf highlighted the shades of silver in her hair.

"Dang. Are you meeting the queen for cocktails?"

Zelda rushed in on Genna's heels, her fashionably faded jeans hanging from her hip, embellishments and bling fitting over well-filled back pockets. She tugged a Mylar balloon behind her. *It's a Girl!* glittered on the surface.

Amy looked down at her own sheet-covered body. She'd never felt so out of fashion in her life.

"You're alive!" Zelda said.

Amy beamed at her. "You're not in jail!"

"Miracle of miracles!" Genna exclaimed. "You scared us crazy."

Ben slipped out the door and left the ladies to their own.

Slightly embarrassed by the way they gushed over her injuries, she let them gush anyway. She didn't mind being the center of their attention. They demanded a blow by blow of every mile, so she told them about driving up to the old geezer's trailer and how he chased her off his driveway with a shotgun. She told them about the bartender who helped her get away but really wanted to help her into her bed. She told them about the bubbas—Beck, Clayton, Charley, Root, and No-Name—and their plans to open a rock and roll trailer park in a place that smelled like rotten eggs. The four of them laughed until tears ran down their faces and Genna snorted coffee out of her nose.

"Some things never change," she said, smiling at Genna.

She told them about the hot little trailer and her diet of Mountain Dew and crackers. She told him about Clayton and his kindness in spite of everything else he had done. "I think Clayton's sister works at this hospital. Maybe we should find her."

Her story finally told, and told again, Amy looked from face to face at the women perched on the corners of her hospital bed. She had defied the odds stacked against her, and now, as they gathered around her, she felt the connection of their friendship once again. She felt it stronger than ever. She hadn't proven anything, except that she was loved by these women. And that she felt the same about them. She would never doubt them again.

"I'm sorry about the Hummer," she said to Zelda. "I wrecked it."

"You did more than wreck it," Genna said. "You torched it like barbeque."

"No, Beck did that."

"Water under the bridge," Zelda said, touching Amy's cheek with a cool hand. "I don't want to drive a Hummer anyway, and it was fully insured."

"Which means I get my money off the top," Rian piped up.

Genna poked her with an elbow.

Satisfied and empty of angst, Amy's eyelids grew heavy, their voices ushering her to sleep.

"Things are going to be just fine," she heard Zelda whisper as the nurse entered the room.

"Yes," the nurse said sweetly. "Everything is going to be fine. And it's time for you ladies to leave."

CHAPTER TWENTY-SIX

Ben drove toward the Bennfield Hotel, his mind hopping like a hungry rabbit.

Some of the facts were finally falling into place. He had learned that Carlisle purchased champagne at a liquor store right inside the Garland County line at a place called Garland Cooley's Bar and Package. The same bar that Amy claimed she visited before her mishap on the hillside.

He learned from a friend of the force, who shared more than a few details of the case, the receipt from the ruined bottle of champagne led them to the store, where they were indeed able to confirm from the surveillance video that Carlisle was in and out of the package store before 7 p.m. It would have taken him a few minutes to drive into Hot Springs proper. He went to a lingerie store at the mall, and receipts from the store showed his purchase—$127.19—was made at 7:48 p.m. Assuming he went straight to the hotel from there, this would have put Zack Carlisle in the parking garage just past eight.

The report also claimed the time stamp on the garage surveillance video showed a Hummer entering the garage at 8:11.

Cooley's Bar was at the center of this. Someone saw Zack there that day and followed him to the Bennfield Hotel. Someone who hated him enough to run him down.

There was malice in the way Zack Carlisle had been run down and left to die on the cold cement floor. An unhappy wife could have that kind of rage, but Zelda didn't strike him as that angry. And four women planning such a crime didn't fit. He didn't think they were guilty of anything more than a few bold lies and a lot of DUI.

Zack was alive at 8:11 p.m. and dead thirty minutes later when a hotel guest exiting the parking garage found his body.

Ben pulled up to the curb at the Bennfield Hotel and parked.

"Like I told the other cop," the bartender at the lobby bar said, "these two women drank at the lobby bar way after happy hour. One was tall and thin and a great tipper. The other one was shorter and dark-haired and pissed off at someone. They went to the bar balcony to smoke, but the floor had just been painted, so they stood right outside the door. I could see them from here," he said. "The tall one left about ten or fifteen minutes before the other one. I don't know where they went from here."

Ben nodded. It was possible, even probable, that Genna Gregory left the garage minutes before Zack arrived. In her statement, Gregory claimed she was on the road home by eight. Unfortunately, the surveillance video only recorded cars entering the garage. One way in, another way out. That was a foolish mistake on the hotel's part, Ben thought, but unless some other evidence surfaced, it was impossible to know for sure when Genna Gregory left Hot Springs.

In her statement, Zelda Carlisle claimed she had fallen asleep in her room only to be awakened by those "horrible sirens."

No one had yet corroborated her story about her whereabouts at the time of Carlisle's accident.

But that didn't mean she was guilty.

If he wanted to make sure Rian and her friends didn't get hauled in for a murder rap they didn't commit, he had to come up with something more than a hunch.

CHAPTER TWENTY-SEVEN

"No offense, Amy, but your story makes my head hurt," Genna said. "This Beck dude was in a buying war with Zack over FEMA trailers? Can you imagine that?"

"I don't think Zack knew about Beck's plan or vice versa," Amy said. "I think Zack and Beck shared bad timing."

Genna, Rian, and Zelda were back and crowded around the little table in the hospital room. She was trying to track their conversation, but, as usual, it was bouncing around the circle. What she needed was Mitch Miller's bouncing ball to follow along.

Good drugs. Did she say that out loud? No one seemed to notice.

Genna poured lukewarm beer she had smuggled in via her purse into three Styrofoam cups. "You don't get one, Amy. You're already juiced," she said with a swift smile.

Rian ripped open a bag of Fritos from the vending machine, stuffing several in her mouth at once. "Maybe Zack overheard a conversation at the bar when he was there," she mumbled. "Maybe that's where he got the idea of using the trailers at the tower sites in the first place."

Genna burped.

"Excuse you," Zelda said.

"Yes, ma'am," Genna responded and burped again.

Zelda rolled her eyes.

Amy lay against her pillow and watched the circus in front of her. It was a familiar three-ring performance. Something special happened when they got together, no matter where. It was a fabulous feeling of belonging, even when it got heated. She drifted in and out of their conversation, her attention holding just enough to know they were still talking about Zack. It didn't seem right, somehow, with Zelda present. She was, after all, a new widow.

"Zack wasn't exactly the person we all knew him to be," Rian was saying.

Zelda raised an eyebrow.

"I'm just saying that there was more to Zack than any of us knew—obviously—because, because he's . . . gone. And we're not."

"Criminy," Genna said. "Just lay it out there, Rian."

"I guess I shouldn't mention that you're both now two hundred fifty thousand dollars richer," Zelda spat.

"And you're five hundred thousand dollars richer," Genna barked back. "This was all your idea anyway. We thought you were kidding when you asked us to help you get rid of Zack. We didn't know you were going to hire a hitman and set us up for the fall!"

"A hitman! Is that what you think I did? Is that who you think I am?"

"If the shoe fits . . ."

"Hold on, hold on," Rian interrupted. "We're just short on facts and tempers. It's been an exhausting week. 'What we've got here is . . . failure to communicate,'" she said in her best Cool Hand Luke imitation.

Amy giggled. The humor broke the tension.

"She's out to lunch," Genna said with a nod at Amy. "I'm jealous."

"We all know that no one here killed Zack, firsthand or second," Rian continued. "But Ben said the police still don't believe that. Amy's accident may have thrown a wrench in their thinking, but they'll be back asking questions before too long. We may not *be* guilty, but we *look* guilty. We've passed off quite a few lies for the truth, and they know it."

They had lots of white lies in their mouths. Amy giggled again as if they tickled her tongue.

"Really out of it," Genna repeated, nodding toward her.

Rian poured another foamy cup of beer for herself, emptying the last warm can. "The person who was behind that wheel is still out there. I think the person who ran Amy off the road is the same person who tried to kill Zack. Ben thinks so, too. When they saw the Hummer again, they thought it was Zack behind the wheel. A Zack who didn't stay dead the first time."

"Zombie Zack."

Zelda cast a dirty look at Genna.

"Dudley Do-Right said that?" Amy giggled.

"Right," Rian agreed. "Amy ran into Zack's killer somewhere on her path that day—somebody she called, spoke to, or saw. It could have been someone she had a beer with at the bar and got a little too chatty. You know how you are, Amy."

She nodded, but she wasn't sure what she was agreeing to or with.

"What if we try to lure him out into the open, just like Amy tried to do?" Genna asked. "What if we set a trap to catch him hot-handed? Or her."

"How would we do that?" Zelda asked. "The Hummer is toast."

Rian pointed her cup at Zelda. "With you. With the lovely Zelda."

"Yes!" Genna said, her enthusiasm showing. "We're going to bait the killer's hook with Zelda. Dangle her out there like a fat ole worm."

"I am not fat," Zelda shot back. "I'm not."

"You are not," Rian agreed. "But we have to figure this out or we're going to land in jail just like Amy thought we might. We have to find out why. Were they after money? Pot? Power? Property? What? What was he after?"

"Or her. It could have been an evil vixen," Genna added. "Or a jilted lover."

Zelda poked her in the arm. "Jilted lover? Thanks a lot! You're no comfort. You're a pain in the rear."

"Look in the mirror, sweetie. This is *your* rear end that's showing," Genna shot back, but she was smiling, affection filling her eyes. "We wouldn't be in this fix if you would stop getting married."

"Oh, so this is all my fault?" Zelda complained.

Genna nodded. Zelda stomped her foot.

Amy turned her attention to the hypnotic drip of the IV and her eyes grew heavy. Her head was full of chatter. Too full. "I love you all. So just be quiet and be nice," she said dreamily as she drifted off in spite of the noise they made.

CHAPTER TWENTY-EIGHT

When Amy heard a rustle near her hospital bed, she opened her eyes. Ben was standing at her feet, a broad smile on his handsome face and a file folder clutched in his hands. Her friends were gone. She shifted her arm and noticed a note on her cast. *Be back soon. XXOO.*

"Amy," he said quietly. "How are you feeling?"

"Dudley Do-Right," she answered, her voice still thick.

Ben chuckled. "If you feel up to it, I have some photos I want to show you." He reached inside the folder and pulled out a stack of pictures.

Her eyes widened with terror.

"No, no," he said quickly. "These aren't gory. Just pictures of cars."

She nodded, and he handed her the photos.

"These are stills from the video surveillance camera at the hotel garage," he said. "These are cars that entered the garage just before Zack Carlisle's Hummer entered between eight and eight thirty. I was hoping you might recognize something from the vehicle that ran you off the road. Maybe you'll recognize the manufacturer's logo on the grill or a hood ornament. Anything."

Setting the photos on the bedsheet, she said quietly, "I can't. I don't want to know."

"I can understand how you feel. I can understand why you thought your friends were involved. But you know they weren't. I don't believe that either. But the police are not out looking for new suspects. They are looking for proof of how an angry wife premeditates her husband's death and gets a little help from her friends.

"The police know the Carlisles were having marital difficulties. Divorce would probably have been financially devastating. Death was much more lucrative for everyone. At least, that's how it looks. And you—you're the one who wasn't near the scene of the crime that night. That's convenient in and of itself. You're the one who didn't need an alibi—the only one who gets run off the road to divert attention.

"The way the detectives might see it, a group of friends plan to murder the husband, and they make sure the one person who is guilty looks the most innocent, staging an accident and throwing suspicion somewhere else. Did you know the police suspect you were closely involved?"

"I . . . I . . ." Amy stammered. "I didn't . . ." Her lips trembled, and she gripped the bedsheets at her side. Why was he saying this? Wasn't he on their side? Wasn't he going to help them?

"I don't mean to upset you," he said quietly. "Personally, I don't think any of you were involved, but I do know you've done an excellent job of scrambling evidence. Even if you are not guilty of murder, you've all made a mess of an investigation that was pretty messy from the start. And then you went off on a wild goose chase to find someone to blame. Tell me again what happened. Tell me everything from the time you left Bluff Springs until we found you here."

Amy looked at Ben with relief. He believed her. He was trying to help!

Getting started felt awkward, a bit too private, but before long she had told Ben about faking the return calls to the voice messages on Zack's cell phone, about the apple trees, the board meeting with the church lady that Zack never made it to, about the man who had money to offer Zack to get the job done, whatever that meant. She had never figured that out. She told him about the GPS in the Hummer, about L91, about the man and his shotgun. She shared what she had learned at Cooley's Bar, and how the Hummer seemed to be recognized by so many. The bartender, the woman with the bee tattoo and a mean smile, the bubbas who were looking for Zack and his trailers. She recounted the chase on the curves of Highway 7, the lights that had blinded her, the horrible crunch of metal, and then waking up in the stench of the old trailer. She told him about Beck and his trailer trash motel, which they all knew now was about the FEMA trailers Zack had bought at auction. About how Beck had set the Hummer on fire as revenge. She replayed her conversations with Clayton, who worked at a Murphy Oil garage and gas station.

"Yes," Ben said finally. "It's beginning to make sense."

"Not to me," Amy said.

"I have a theory. Want to hear it?"

Amy nodded.

"I do believe it was full-on rage that ran Carlisle down, most likely with murderous intent, but then the Hummer shows back up in this part of town, and this person thinks Zack isn't dead after all. They follow you, looking for their chance. You were not the target, Amy. They didn't know you were driving the Hummer. No one could see you behind the glass in the dark. The killer saw the Hummer and thought Zack was driving. I think the killer was trying to finish what he or she thought was already done."

Amy shivered. "We thought of that, too."

"You were lucky."

Amy sighed deeply, his words hitting home with the truth. She *had* been lucky.

He picked up the photos from the stack she had set down on the bedsheet and handed them to her again. She looked at them quietly, her eyes brimming with tears.

"This is important," he said.

The photos were black and white, but the cars were clear enough. Looking from one picture to the next, she strained her memory for recognition. She lingered on photos of a Mercedes, a sports car, and a pickup truck. She and Clayton had identified tracks to all three of these types of cars in the parking garage. Focusing on the faces behind the windshield in each photo, she looked for recognition of the person driving, even though the photos were grainy and dark. She saw a man and a woman behind the wheel of the Mercedes. The sports car was too new to be Rian's, and the woman behind the wheel was blonde.

"This," she said finally, holding up the photo of a truck with a man behind the wheel. A ball cap shadowed his face. "This is familiar. I've seen this truck, but I don't remember where."

Ben took the photo and glanced at the old truck. "You don't remember where you saw it? Amy, there are a thousand of trucks like this in Arkansas. Every man with a 'honey-do' list either has a work truck like it or wishes he did. Can you identify this as the one that ran you off the road?"

She shook her head. "No," she said and closed her eyes again. "I can't . . . I didn't see it. I only saw its headlights. But . . ."

"But?"

"There is something familiar about him."

"Think, Amy," he encouraged. "Clear your mind of everything but the faces you've seen in the past few days. Scan through them like a video on fast-forward. Block out everything else and focus only on that."

She shut her eyes and let the scenes and faces of the last few weeks flood past in her memory. Seeing her dream first, the lights flashing blue and red over Zack's dead body, then she remembered the face of the rider on the horse in the other dream, too, but she didn't recognize him, either. She pictured the thin man in her shop, the bartender and his sad blue eyes, the lovers at the bar, the man with stringy hair. She put herself behind the wheel of the Hummer, tentatively at first, afraid to relive the crash.

"Wait!" she said, opening her eyes and snatching the photo from his fingers. "The hat. I remember seeing that hat." Amy poked the photograph with her finger and then pulled the picture in for a closer look. "Isn't that a John Deere hat?"

She saw his disappointment before he spoke. "Unfortunately, there are as many John Deere hats in Arkansas as there are Ford trucks. We might as well hunt a needle in a haystack."

"I remember this angry look," Amy said with excitement. "An old man in an old truck was right behind me for miles on Highway 7. He was right on my bumper. I pulled off on the shoulder so he could pass, and he did. But that's it," she said. "Nothing else happened. But I swear, this looks a lot like him."

"You did well. I think we're looking for an older man in a John Deere hat, and there can't be too many of those in Arkansas."

His sarcasm didn't go unnoticed.

CHAPTER TWENTY-NINE

With a list of auto body shops in hand, Ben drew a circle on the map with Cooley's Bar at the center. Any car or truck that ran down a person and then ran a Hummer off the road would have severe damage to repair. That person probably saw the Hummer at Cooley's Bar and waited to follow. Ben was 99.9 percent certain the driver thought Zack was behind the wheel.

Each dot he added represented one of the auto body shops. He added all the Murphy Oil stations, too. Most of the dots clustered around the outskirts of Hot Springs, but a clutch of fewer than a dozen made sense based on the geography and the timing between the bar and the hotel.

Ben looked up from the table where he was sitting, watching as Cooley's Bar began to fill up with the after-work crowd. It was a mix-and-match jumble of ranch hands and construction workers, women in nursing scrubs, and men in worn suits. He looked at them carefully without being too obvious, sizing up each one as a potential killer. Most of these people were regulars, he thought, judging by the way they entered the bar and moved swiftly to a specific place in the room. People were habitual beings, especially in the pursuit of alcohol and social interaction.

The man at the bar with a long black ponytail seemed to know everyone. He made a point of nodding to those who walked up to the bar as if he were giving them his permission to buy a drink.

He found himself drawn to the social happy hour. He sipped his beer and watched. He recognized the honeybee babe, as Amy called her, when she bounced through the door. The energy she brought into the room was noticeable. She seemed delighted that so many eyes turned her way as she sauntered across the floor. Long blonde curls bounced against her breasts as she walked, and her skirt barely covered her bottom as she passed him. When she sat at a table of men, he wondered which of the four would catch her attention.

She must have felt his eyes on her because she looked up at him and smiled.

Ben smiled back and tilted his head.

Bars were marvelous places to watch humanity, he thought, returning his gaze to the room. The hometown bar was a perfect dumping ground. He believed people sought the familiarity of their local hang to liberate whatever they wore on their sleeves. He imagined some of them came to cheat on their spouses, smoke cigars, or listen to music. Some of them came to eat in a crowd and not feel alone. Some might come to meet a friend or make a friend. Or borrow money. Or start a fight. Everyone came for something.

Somebody came here to kill Zack Carlisle.

Whoever ran Amy off the road could have been in this bar that day. Any of them could be guilty. Any one of them could have rammed into the Hummer thinking they were ramming into Carlisle.

He made his way to the bar with the picture from the surveillance video in his hand.

"Sure, I know that truck," the bartender answered. Ben laid the picture on the bar in front of him. "That's a Ford F-150 pick-'em-up truck. I had one just like it a few years ago. Hated to see her go. What's that? Is it 1985? Eighty-six? Don't make 'em like that anymore."

"Have any idea who owns that truck?"

The bartender popped the top off a bottle of Busch and handed it to the person standing next to Ben. "That depends," he said, "on whether it's blue or red. Can't tell from that photo. That's black and white."

Ben swallowed his impatience. "Let's say it's red."

"I can't say I know who owns it."

"Then let's say it's blue."

The bartender smiled. "What's wrong with it?"

"This truck was left alongside the road with ten thousand dollars in a bag beneath the seat. We're worried about the owner."

"A bank robbery?"

Ben shrugged.

The bartender shook his head. "For real? There's ten grand under the seat?"

Ben nodded. He wasn't sure why he invented the lie, though one smart-ass comment deserved another, but money made people talk. "Don't know what we're going to do if we can't find the owner."

"Heavy." The bartender picked up a dirty rag and wiped a mug.

"How long have you been working here?"

"A few days. The last bartender just up and quit. Some redneck tried to put his head through the wall." He pointed to the busted place in the wall just beside the door to the kitchen. The indention was about the size of a grown man's head.

"Where is he now?" Ben asked.

"Still licking his wounds, I guess," the bartender answered.

Ben showed the photo to a couple of others at the bar who

claimed they didn't know the truck or its owner, but he didn't believe them. Then he caught the honeybee's attention and motioned her over.

"Hey," she said in a sultry vibrato. "Do I know you?"

Ben shook his head.

She flashed her smile. "Do I want to know you?"

The top of her head came just level with his chest, so he had to look down—look way down, right down into the top of her blouse and the cleavage made by two perfectly round, perfectly sized breasts. He smiled almost without realizing it. He was almost tongue-tied.

"I hear you're the Honey Bee Queen," he said, wishing he could pull the words right back into his mouth.

"Arkansas's one and only," she purred. "Honey being the sweetest thing on earth." She batted her eyelashes and smiled. "Did you know that honey is the only food that includes everything we need to sustain life? A couple of tablespoons a day, and you could have enough energy to do whatever you want for as long as you want. Maybe that's why honeybees never sleep."

Smiling at the innuendo, he said, "What do you do? As the Honey Bee Queen? What is the job that goes with the title?"

She giggled into his bicep, leaving her hand to rest on his arm. "My job is to make sure we keep our bees healthy so we can keep making honey. I go around to events—I like to think of it as visiting flowers—helping people understand why bees are so important to our economy here in Arkansas. Did you know bees are responsible for pollinating all our crops? From apples to alfalfa. Without them, our farmers would have to spend billions to pollinate their crops artificially.

"Honeybees in a hive visit more than two hundred thousand flowers every day." She giggled again, her hand stroking his arm.

He knew it was a speech she had given before.

"I don't get around to that many flowers, but I do my best to visit as many as I can. I'm available for any engagement anywhere, anytime. Do you have something you need me to attend?"

Pulling the picture of the truck from his pocket, he handed it to her. "I was wondering if you recognize this truck and the owner?"

She took it and frowned. He couldn't tell whether the frown was because she recognized the truck in the photo or she was disappointed that their conversation had taken a different turn. She was probably not used to being denied.

"I never kiss and tell," she said, the lust fading from her eyes. "You a cop or something?"

"I am."

"You're not dressed like a cop."

"I'm off duty. I'm down here looking for someone."

"Oh? And who would that be?"

"This man in this picture for one," he said and regretted the shortness of his tone. "And . . . also anyone who knew Zack Carlisle. Did you know him? I think he came in here every once in a while."

Her eyes flashed, and the blue of her irises turned dark. "That redhead can have him all to herself if that's the way he wants it. He's a mean old bee killer anyway."

"Do you know him?"

She smiled, showing all her perfect teeth, but he could tell there was more sting behind the smile than seduction. "Like I said. I never kiss and tell," she said and moved away.

Ben watched her walk across the room, her bottom swaying in her little black skirt. That was a dangerous little bee, he thought as he left the bar.

Heading for the first dot on the map that marked the closest auto body shop, he received a wary-eyed response, and then the same from the owners at the next two shops on the map. Now about a half-hour away from the bar, he headed north when he saw the County Road sign. The number pinged in his memory. Amy had mentioned this road, he remembered as he turned off the highway and bounced onto the dirt.

He took the road slowly to hold the dust to a minimum, but behind the car was a thick powder cloud. The road turned sharply to the left, and a driveway turned right. The cell tower looming overhead didn't escape his notice.

Ben pulled in and parked about halfway up the drive, and a man who looked to be in his late sixties met him at the door before he could knock.

"What do you want?" he asked gruffly.

"I'm Officer Ben Albright from up in Crawford County. I'm sorry to trouble you, sir, but we're looking for the owner of a Ford F-150 pickup truck seen around these parts recently. About a 1985 model. Know anyone around here who owns one?" Glancing at the carport adjacent to the trailer, he noted a shiny John Deere tractor parked but nothing else. "You out here by your lonesome without nothing but a tractor?"

The man didn't respond. His rummy eyes narrowed, and Ben smelled old liquor leaching from his skin.

"How do you get to town?" Ben asked.

"I don't need to get to town." His tone was terse. "I got everything I need right here." He glanced at his feet, and Ben's eyes followed. The shotgun leaned against the doorframe.

Ben pulled the picture from his shirt pocket and held it out. "The truck I'm looking for looks something like this."

The man looked at it briefly. "Where'd that come from?"

"Police business."

"What kind of police business?"

"We think the driver of this truck may have been a witness to a crime. We're hoping to corroborate another witness's account of what happened."

The man's eyebrows furrowed in his silence. "I had one like that years ago," he said finally. "I sold it. Didn't need it no more."

"You got a bill of sale?"

"What do I need that for?"

"It would provide me with the name of the person who bought it."

He shook his head. "I don't recall the name. He gave me money and I gave him the key. I never witnessed no hit-and-run, and I ain't been down to Hot Springs in ages. If you got no other business with me, I need to get back to my chores." He moved to shut the door.

Ben put his foot into the doorway.

The man's eyes narrowed again. "I said I can't help you none. Now, you need to get off my land."

Ben moved his foot and stepped back toward the rusty steps. He turned back quickly. "Sir, do you know a Zack Carlisle?"

Silence crackled between them.

"Never heard of him," he barked as he slammed the door.

Ben idled in the driveway, his mind thick with thought. The bill of the John Deere hat was pulled low over the man's forehead in the picture, shadowing eyes that Ben figured had seen either too much liquor or too much pain. Probably both. The man looking at him from behind the curtain of the trailer looked like the same unhappy man behind the wheel of the truck in the picture, sans the hat. The likeness was undeniable. The time stamp put the truck there exactly two minutes after Carlisle's Hummer had passed through the garage entrance.

But where was the truck now? Were they the same? Or was this as he thought when Amy mentioned it—that Arkansas was as full of John Deere caps as it was old Ford trucks. Could he make that leap?

The old man had made that leap.

Ben had not mentioned a hit-and-run. He had not mentioned Hot Springs.

Backing out of the driveway, Ben made a note of the address

and name from the faded stickers on the mailbox at the end of the drive, where a little cemetery with a homemade cross stuck out of the ground.

He had no evidence and he had no truck. If there was a truck, it could be anywhere by now. He didn't believe the story that it had been sold months ago, but he had no evidence otherwise. A truck of that age in ruined condition would barely make the salvage yard let alone the auction block. It could be in pieces or set in motion and rolled off the mountain, left to join other junk cars that sat rusting at the bottom. The hill folk considered a deep holler as good a dumping place as any, especially for something they wanted to hide.

Was he hunting for a truck in a holler? That really would be a needle in a haystack.

CHAPTER THIRTY

"What is this?" Amy screeched as Zelda held up a shopping bag.

"You certainly couldn't go out in those rags you were wearing when you came in," Genna said, the twinkle of mischief in her eyes.

"We did the very best we could under the circumstances," Zelda said sweetly. "Our very best. There's not a Macy's for miles!"

Zelda pulled the underwear and bra from the bag and held it up. Amy snatched it from her hands. "This is the best you could do? Hello Kitty thong underwear? A purple polka-dotted bra?"

"They're adorable. Sexy, even." Genna snickered. "Rian picked them out."

"Don't blame this on me. I only pushed the cart."

Amy winced as Zelda reached for the next item. A jumble of bright red material unfolded to a pair of sweatpants. Zelda held them up for her to see. The design splayed across the butt looked like a dragon pooping bowling balls, its forked tongue placed obscenely up the seam.

"That's the real deal," Rian said. "It's the local high school mascot, believe it or not."

"A pooping dragon?"

"It's a sand lizard. And their baseball team is in first place in this region."

"Isn't that nice for them?" Amy said acidly.

"Oh, no, not even."

Zelda pulled the next item from the bag. "But it's so you." Zelda flashed her a giddy grin as she held the sweater up to her chest. It was a pale pink cardigan with a matching shell. Bright green-and-pink Easter eggs and a fuzzy rabbit were appliquéd to the front, one paw raised in a permanent high-five.

"It was a bargain," Genna said. "It was in the Easter clearance bin."

"For good reason," Rian agreed.

"I'm not wearing this. No way."

"Oh, and these," Zelda added, pulling a pair of bunny slippers from another bag. "Look, the ears flop up and down when you walk!"

Genna giggled. "You'll be perfectly dressed for a Looney Tunes convention!"

Tears came to Amy's eyes. Were they making fun of her or showing their horrible, sweet, irreverent love? She touched the bunny on the sweater, and the tears fell harder.

"Hey," Zelda said and touched her shoulder tenderly. "We just wanted to make a lousy situation more fun. We wanted to make you laugh."

"No, you just wanted to make me look silly. Is this my penance for wrecking the Hummer?"

"And for going off without telling us where you were going."

"And for winning the domino game three times in a row," Genna added. "I told you I would get you back in due time."

Amy sighed with resignation. What was she going to do otherwise? She couldn't put on the filthy clothes she came in wearing. Genna pulled out a pair of scissors and a box of safety pins, and between her and Zelda, they managed to cut the material to accommodate the cast and then pinned it back together. They draped the sweater over her shoulders and buttoned the top button to keep it in place. Genna pulled a barrette from her purse and worked at smoothing Amy's curls into submission with her fingers.

"I look ridiculous. Absolutely ridiculous."

"Yes," Rian agreed. "You do."

"You can be captain of the ugly sweater club," Genna said.

"I'll be captain of the revenge club, thank you very much, and you'll all get yours. When you least expect it, you wicked women," she threatened with a growl, but she couldn't help but smile.

Zelda touched her arm. "We love you, too. We do."

They walked down the hall, strained faces hiding their amusement, with Zelda pushing Amy the Easter clown in the wheelchair out the hospital door, out to the curb, and into a bright white sunny day.

"We need a plan," Genna said to Amy in the rearview mirror as she pouted in the back seat of the Mercedes. They were still sitting in the car in the hospital parking lot. "We are still suspects, you know. We still need to find the rightful owner of this crime before they try to put us behind bars. We'll go back over your day and work backward until we make our way home."

Amy was sullen. "I don't want to. I don't want to go back over that day. I just want to go home."

Rian turned around from the front seat. "Don't be scared. I'll be with you every step of the way."

"Oh, that's a real comfort. You're the one who picked out pooping lizard pants!"

Rian turned away so Amy wouldn't see her smile.

"And where do I fit in?" Zelda asked. "Where does the fat worm dangle?" She glared at Genna in the rearview mirror.

Genna glared back. "I'm just trying to be helpful in case you haven't noticed. I don't hear you coming up with any brilliant epiphanies about who killed your husband."

"Oh like you really hit a deer?" Zelda spat. Her eyes didn't stop piercing Genna's in the rearview mirror.

Genna turned in the seat. The expression in her eyes was alarming. A vein on her neck pulsed with anger. Amy found herself drawing back against the seat as if seeking protection from a storm. "All this time you thought I was the one who ran Zack down? After all this time, you thought I killed him?"

Zelda leaned forward, her face inches from Genna's. "You expected me to believe that stupid deer story? And then you had Amy break into Zack's office. What were you after? Your business agreement? Your insurance papers?"

"What? Amy broke into the office? I thought you made that whole thing up to take the suspicion off yourself!"

Amy groaned. "You knew it was me? You knew I broke into the office?"

She hadn't realized their guilty suspicions were still alive and well, and kicking their friendship's butt. She had come to an understanding herself. Maybe she had a little help with some painkiller meds, but she had reconciled their innocence in her mind. *Almost.* Some pieces niggled her, questions that provoked her peace about the friends she loved like family. There were still remnants of reality that didn't fit comfortably enough to let slide, and now she could see they had them, too.

Zelda turned to face her. "I knew it was you. But why? Because you thought I killed him?"

"You had blood on your shoes!" Amy cried. "You had Zack's blood all over your Jimmy Choos. They were in the bathtub in the hotel where you tried to wash it off! I threw them away!"

"You took my favorite Jimmy Choos?"

"I had to! They had blood on them!"

"Blood? It was paint! I stepped in wet paint outside the lobby bar when Genna went out for a smoke."

"It wasn't blood?"

"That's why you thought I killed Zack?"

"I thought you were there when it happened!"

Zelda exhaled and sat back against the leather seat. Her chin trembled as she tried to keep back the tears. "I can't believe this. I can't believe I was so naïve, so gullible, so trusting, so stupid!"

The tears loosened and they began trailing down Zelda's face. It was the first sad tears Amy had seen since Zack's death. There had been many a tear since then, but to Amy, they had been trauma tears, shocked tears, frustrated tears, even angry tears. But not grief, and because of this, she held on to the shoes as evidence even when she wanted to put them away. Even though she had thrown them away. Out of sight. But never far out of mind.

Zelda put her head in her manicured hands and wept. Amy pulled her close and held her. Silence filled the car.

"I didn't want him dead. I wanted him gone. I wanted him out of my life because he wasn't the man I married. At least, he wasn't the man I thought I married. He wasn't the man I wanted him to be. He wasn't. He was a con man, and I was his mark."

She looked up, tears rimming her dark lashes. "I didn't want him dead," she said again. "I just wanted him to go away. When I asked for your help in getting rid of him, I was talking about helping me through another divorce. But then we started talking about dead bodies, and I thought it was a joke. It was a fantasy that made everything seem easier."

"And then you thought we killed him to help you," Amy said. "Because we love you. And because we would do anything to make you happy again. To keep you safe."

"Then we need to find the rightful owner of this crime," Genna said quietly and turned back to the steering wheel. She cranked the engine, put the Mercedes in gear, and maneuvered out of the parking lot and into the Hot Springs traffic flow.

"Where are we going?" Rian asked.

Genna shrugged. "I'm driving. I'm thinking. I'm plotting, all at the same time. I'm an excellent multitasker."

"I know where we need to start," Amy said. "I've been dreaming about that truck for days."

"Another psycho vision?" Genna asked as she glanced in the rearview mirror.

Amy ignored her. "We need to go to that cell tower site at County Road 214. There's something I need to see for myself."

"I know that road," Rian said. "That's where I met Zack."

"Yes," Amy said. "There's a mobile home site there, too. That's where I drove up in the driveway and the guy came out with a shotgun. I think he's the one who was riding my bumper off Highway 7 on this side of L91. I didn't think anything about it then, but it can't be a coincidence that I showed up in his driveway a few minutes later. It was one of the frequent destinations on Zack's GPS."

"That's why Zack wanted to meet me there that day. He was making his tower site rounds."

Amy leaned forward and put her hand on Rian's shoulder. "Ben showed me a picture of a truck from the hotel garage. I want to see if I recognize it. I want to see if it was the one that followed me. Followed Zack," she corrected. "Or so he probably thought."

Genna sped along the highway a few miles over the speed limit, as was her norm. Amy watched the familiar sights zoom past.

The redbud and dogwood blooms that filled the woods with splashes of white and pink were giving way to the bright green of summer leaves. The sky was a brilliant blue overhead, dotted by clouds that looked like popcorn had been scattered in the sky. The air was fresh, and she rolled down the window to take in a breath of crisp air. She'd never forget the stench of that dump. She'd never take a sweet, clean breath of air for granted again.

They soon passed Cooley's Bar & Package, and she glanced at the cars scattered in the parking lot in the middle of the day. They drove on and then passed the county line.

"It's right up here," Amy said. "I recognize all of this."

Genna turned off the highway at the blue-and-yellow County Road sign.

"Drive on down, Genna," Rian said as they bumped along on the dusty dirt road. "I know where we are, too. Here. Turn here."

Genna turned into the driveway and stopped the car.

Amy peered out the car window and her heart thudded. Last time she was here, she had been blasted at with a shotgun. She had fled for her life only to be forced off the high mountain road later. She been held hostage for those silly FEMA trailers. She glanced at her cast, the surface now scribbled with messages, tic-tac-toe grids, and a sketch of Victor in a heart that Zelda had drawn with a Sharpie. The chain of events seemed like so long ago, and yet, only a few days had passed.

The home now looked as if it had been abandoned. The windows were dark, although yellowed lace curtains hung in the windows. The outside of the trailer was dirty with mold, just as she remembered it, but the weeds seemed taller now and bending softly in the wind coming across the mountaintop. She glanced at the metal carport that stood about fifty feet from the trailer. A bright green-and-yellow tractor was parked in one of the stalls, but there was no other vehicle parked beside it.

"I don't think anyone is home," Rian said. "Let's get out and look around."

"Not on your life," Amy said. "He has a shotgun and he's not shy about using it!" She wasn't eager to get out of the car, nor was she willing to come face-to-face with a shotgun. She wasn't sure, now, what had made her so certain that she would find an old pickup truck in the carport, one just like the picture in the photo from the hotel garage. Just like the pictures that ran through her mind in the dream she kept having since Ben showed her that photo from the garage. The dream seemed to loop through her head every time she fell asleep.

"He's not going to use a gun on us," Genna said as she opened the car door and stepped out. "We're just a bunch of women lost on a back road. What kind of a man would shoot a carload of confused women?" She tugged the silk scarf in place around her head and then patted the wrinkles from her jumpsuit.

The others followed until they were side by side in the yard facing the front door of the trailer. Amy's heart was racing. She grabbed Zelda's hand.

"*Eeek!*" she squeaked as the front door rattled opened and the man stepped out on the stoop. The shotgun was down at his side, but his stance wasn't friendly. Amy took a slight step behind Zelda but kept her hand clasped tight.

"What do you want?" he hollered. His voice was deep and thick.

"We're looking for the owner of this place," Genna hollered back.

"What fer?"

"We're looking to buy a cell tower site."

He took a step onto the porch.

"I might be interested," he barked. "What do you want with a tower site?"

"You got an asking price in mind?" Genna asked. She smiled her Genna Gregory smile.

His eyes narrowed as if contemplating the question and his answer. He moved down the steps and walked toward them, the shotgun still gripped in his hand.

As he walked closer, she saw that he looked the same as she remembered him the day she rolled up in the Hummer. Except she didn't remember him wearing a hat, but he did now. It was a John Deere cap, pulled low over his brow. His face was wrinkled with age and what she could only imagine was a hard-knock life of hard work and poverty. Maybe too much drink. Maybe too much sorrow. She noticed the white stubble of a day-old unshaven face. His eyes hid beneath the bill of the cap, but she sensed something more than anger in them.

Clad in faded denim overalls, he had the bib buckled at his chest, a checkered shirt underneath with its sleeves rolled halfway up his arms. One arm rested against his knee, the barrel touching the ground and the stock end still gripped in his gnarled fingers.

The newspaper clippings she'd read in Zack's office came to her mind in a flash. There was a picture of him standing next to a grave marker, and she realized the picture was taken at the end of the drive, where the lonely cemetery stood with its faded plastic flowers and white wooden cross. She had almost run over it that day as she peeled from his driveway to escape his bullets. He had blamed the cell tower for his wife's death. No wonder he had shot at the Hummer.

"Who'd you say you were?"

Genna walked forward as if to shake his hand. "Genna Gregory," she said, her smile even brighter. "We represent Carlisle Enterprises."

His face clouded over. His lip curled into a snarl. "Get the hell off my property," he bellowed, stepping toward Genna aggressively. "You just get in that high-falutin' car of yours and drive on out of here. I don't have time for you foolish women."

"We can pay in cash."

His jaw tightened, and his eyes darkened beneath his brow. "I don't want your rotten cash," he spat between clenched teeth. "You and your kind can rot. Git!" he yelled as if he were kicking a cur dog. "Get out!"

In that instant, she knew the face. She saw the impatient scowl behind her on Highway 7 when she had pulled off to let him pass. She saw the rage on the face behind the wheel as it entered the Bennfield Hotel parking garage, mere minutes before Zack had been run down like a cur dog himself.

Her anger flared. "Where is your truck?" she yelled. "What did you do with it?"

Turning his eyes from Genna to look at her, she wondered if he recognized her at all. Had he seen behind the dark windows of the Hummer at who was driving? Did it even matter? She glanced at her bunny slippers and winced at how she would appear to any stranger, let alone someone who had mistaken her for someone else.

"What are you talking about? You crazy or something?" he said hoarsely, taking in her attire with a nod. He motioned to the carport with another nod. "I ain't got no truck. You see a truck?"

"You ran me off the road at Blind Bat Pass!" The words were out of her mouth before she knew it. "You almost killed me!"

The look on his face told her everything. His eyes widened and he stumbled slightly as if he'd been struck with the recoil of his gun. He caught his step and steadied himself against the gun that now seemed rooted to the ground.

Anger rose in her again.

"You thought it was Zack driving that Hummer, but it was me! You ran me off the road! You left me for dead! You followed me from Cooley's Bar. You tried to . . ." Anger choked her words.

He raised the gun slowly, and she saw sanity fade from his eyes like a cloud that passes over the sun.

"I'll give you to the count of three to get in your car and go," he said, his voice deep and gnarled by pain and rage. She saw all of it in his eyes, in the sag of his jowls. He'd been carrying that load for a long time, and he was ready to lay that down, but not the gun. He sighted the barrel.

Amy tugged Zelda's hand and took a few steps back. She glanced at Genna and Rian, who were also stepping back toward the car. She felt as if the world had slowed down, like time-lapse photography in reverse. Her legs were moving, her steps pulling her ever closer to the car, but the sensation was one of standing still. The shotgun was pointed at her, or no one—she couldn't quite tell. She could only tell that it was time for them to leave.

"We have to get out of here," Amy yelled when the car door shut, her eyes never leaving his face. "Hurry!" she said as Genna fishtailed the heavy car.

Without warning, Zelda rolled down the window and yelled, "You killed my husband you crazy son of a bitch! You're not going to get away with that!"

The ping of buckshot followed them as Genna gunned the motor in the dust.

Her breath was ragged in her chest. Her heart pounded. In her mind, the headlights were behind her, and suddenly she was back on the road in the Hummer, racing to get away from Beck and the bubbas in the bar, and the bright lights that were too close behind her. There was no truck in the carport, but the face was the same. She wasn't sure how they would connect all the pieces, but she was sure that Crawley had killed Zack. Whether he meant to or not, the deed had been done.

"It was his truck I saw in my dreams," she said. "It was his truck I saw behind me on Highway 7 the first time. I know it had to be the one that ran me off the road. And I know it had to be that truck that ran Zack down. I know it, but we have to find proof!"

"But he doesn't have a truck," Genna said. "There wasn't a truck there. Just a John Deere tractor."

"But I've seen his truck," Rian said. "I noticed it the day I met Zack out here. I turned around in the driveway, and I saw it then. An eighties Ford-150. Blue and white. It was backed into the carport next to the tractor with the cab pointed out. I noticed that. It's an old-timer's way of parking."

Amy gasped. "When I was here it was parked with the cab pointed in first. I can see it in my head."

"Because it had damage," Rian said. "Because it had an indentation where it hit a man in a parking garage."

"We have to call the police right now," Amy said. "We have to let them know who killed Zack. Hurry, Genna. Drive faster!"

Genna jammed the gas pedal, and the Mercedes lurched forward on the dusty road. The tires caught in the deep sand at the edge of the dusty road, and the back end swerved. Genna grabbed the wheel and twisted, but the car spun out of control, off the road, and straight for a copse of trees.

"Look out!" Rian yelled.

Genna stomped on the brake but the tires spun, and the red Mercedes plowed into a tree.

The horn blew, then silence overtook her.

Déjà vu.

Her head throbbed and her casted arm was twisted beneath her. The pain was searing. Head suddenly flooding with memories, she felt as if every dream she'd ever had was flashing through her mind, mingled with reality, memories, and fantasies, too. She felt is as if she were spiraling through the rabbit hole of her life, every one of her senses engaged.

She tasted chocolate truffles melting on her tongue. She saw her favorite childhood bike and felt the power of the wind in her hair.

She felt the soft fur of all the kittens she had cuddled, heard their purrs, and felt the tickle of their whispers on her cheek. She smelled the starched heat rising from the iron and Grandmother's crocheted doilies. She heard the choir sing at church. She felt the touch of the men she had loved, felt their kisses warm and wet on her lips. And then she became weightless as if swimming in the ocean's warm, watery womb.

She felt comforted, peaceful, safe.

The images went on and on. Like a movie that never ended.

Was this death? Was this heaven?

She opened her eyes and raised her head. She was on the floorboard of the Mercedes. Zelda was beside her. Something warm was running across her arm, and she glanced down at a rivet of blood. She nudged Zelda gently with her elbow, and Zelda's head fell back, a thin line of blood running from her forehead before dropping onto Amy's arm.

"Shit," she said under her breath.

"Shit, shit, shit," came an answer from the front seat.

"Rian, is that you?"

"Ouch. Yes."

"Is Genna okay?"

"Her eyes are open," Rian answered thinly, reaching across to touch Genna's head, which lay against the steering wheel, a small gash in her cheek.

Genna blinked.

"She blinked," Rian said. "So she's not dead. Where's Zelda?"

"Her forehead is bleeding," Amy answered.

"You okay?"

"I'm pissed. And I've had it up to here with car crashes in the woods. And my arm hurts."

"But you're okay."

"Well, I'm not quite dead yet."

"I can hear that."

"We can *all* hear that," Genna said, raising her head from the steering wheel. "What are we doing in this predicament?"

Amy let out a soft giggle, unsure why. And then another. Her giggles turned into chuckling, and before she could gain control, she was hysterical with laughter.

"Shut up!" Genna called, breaking into a smile and then into laughter. "You're making my head hurt."

Amy touched Zelda's cheek, and her friend opened her eyes and frowned.

"Whoops," Zelda said. "We fell—went boom!"

Amy howled. Her ribs ached, her tears stung, and she was glad to be alive.

"Genna," she said between happy sobs, "you drive like crap."

Genna put her hand to her cheek and then glanced at Rian. "I'm beginning to think this car you sold me is jinxed. I don't guess I can get my money back anytime soon."

"Not a chance."

Amy helped Zelda from the floorboard. "You're okay. Just a scratch, but it's still bleeding." She handed Zelda a glove that was sticking out of the pocket in the seat. "Here, hold this against it."

"We're not going to drive out of this one," Rian said, opening the door and then letting it slam shut.

Amy opened the heavy car door, finding it difficult because of the angle the car had come to rest. She pushed a foot against it to hold it open while she clambered out, hindered by the cast and the uneven ground. Rian did the same, and together they stood with shaky knees.

Rian touched her forehead lightly, a goose egg already beginning to show. "That's not going to be pretty."

Making her way to the rear door, Rian helped Zelda from the back seat, then Genna from the front. They were up to the floorboard in Arkansas brush.

"You've got to be kidding me," Genna said as she stumbled around for footing in her mules. "Is this poison ivy?" She stomped around in a circle. "Oh, this is a superb circumstance," she said, bumping the door shut with her butt. "The path to our freedom is lined with poison ivy. What is next, I ask you? What is next?"

They looked at the ruined Mercedes, which was stopped by an ancient oak about thirty feet from the road. The radiator was still hissing, and the hood was crumpled around the tree. Genna reached in the front seat, grabbed her purse, and left the keys in the ignition.

"Good riddance," she said as she brought up the rear of the troop stomping its way through the brush and poison ivy. "Maybe someone will steal it!"

They reached the road in a single file, Rian leading. "Do you hear that?" she said.

A tractor engine revved in the distance.

It was an unmistakable sound. There was only one house near the road, and that house had a tractor, and that tractor belonged to Crawley.

Amy turned just in time to see the John Deere turn out of the driveway and mow toward them. Crawley's hat was down low on his brow, and she couldn't see his eyes—just the stern set to his jaw. His hands gripped the tractor's steering wheel, and the dust blew up behind it like a giant grasshopper chewing up the dirt.

What was he doing? Was he chasing them? Or was he just on his way to town for milk and eggs? They weren't going to wait to find out.

Zelda clutched Amy's sleeve. "He's coming after us. He's going to run us over, too!"

"Ease up on the panic," Genna said. "We can outrun that Deere."

Rian laughed. "You run like a girl."

"I am a girl. How else would I run?"

"I can't run," Zelda said. "I'm wearing heels!"

"You can," Amy answered and cradled her cast. "Now go!"

They sprinted to the highway. Rian was the first to hit the pavement, a short sprint by her standards, with everyone else behind, coughing and covered with road soot. Amy stopped to catch her breath, watching as the tractor moved at full speed. Crawley's face was dark.

What was he doing?

They stood on the side of the blacktop, the two-lane highway near nothing but woods and a crazy man on a tractor. She didn't think she couldn't run any farther. They could walk, but it wouldn't be long before the tractor caught up with them. And then what? She just couldn't go there.

"Help!" Amy yelled as a truck approached them on the highway and then passed them without stopping.

Another car passed slowly, and Amy watched as the driver gawked at the sight of three women and a clown standing near the road before speeding on. She knew they looked ridiculous, desperate even—not something you'd want to pick up.

"Help us!" they yelled in chorus as yet another car approached on the highway. The driver hit the brakes and then sped on. Amy watched the car drive out of sight. She glanced back at the dirt road. Crawley and the tractor were getting closer. Was no one going to help them?

"We're going to die!" Zelda yelled, her hands beating the air like wings.

"Not if we don't stand here like bowling pins," Genna yelled back.

Genna grabbed Amy's elbow and pulled her into the highway, stepping in the middle of the road where she straddled the double yellow line.

"What are you doing?" she yelled. "Are you trying to kill me?"

"They're either going to stop, or they're going to kill us both," Genna said, flagging down the car now headed toward them at highway speed.

Amy flinched, but the car slowed and stopped right before them.

"We've had an accident!" Genna yelled to the closed window. "We need your help."

"Please!" Amy yelled. "Help us!"

Amy noticed the woman behind the steering wheel hesitate briefly before she rolled down the window. She had a kind face and a pile of black hair. "Why are you standing in the middle of the road? What's the matter?"

"We need your help," she said to the woman, pointing to the tractor, which now mowed down the weeds between them and the highway. Crawley's face was dark with rage.

Zelda and Rian rushed to the car.

"He's trying to kill us," Zelda said. "He's going to kill us all!"

The driver's eyes widened. "Get in!" she said quickly and popped the lock on the doors.

CHAPTER THIRTY-ONE

"What are you still doing down here?" Ben's friend asked. "Don't you have bigger fish to fry in your part of the world?"

Ben laughed it off without answering. He was leaning against his fellow officer's squad car in the Hot Springs precinct parking lot. He was still in plain clothes and on his own time, and he didn't need any interference.

He had given the information about John Jacob Crawley to the precinct captain, making it clear that he had gathered it unofficially, but it was a reliable lead in the Zack Carlisle investigation all the same. He knew they would take it from there. The case was far from closed, and he'd never see any glory for it, but he was confident he had shifted the investigation away from Rian and her friends. That was all he could ask for.

He had taken time for a bite to eat, and then he planned to go back to the hospital and talk with Amy and Rian about what he had found.

He heard the familiar static of the police radio in the background, the chatter always in one ear. The bulletin caught his attention: Reckless driver off CR 214. Reported by a passing motorist. White male on a tractor. John Deere. In pursuit of four mature females on foot.

Ben heard amusement in the dispatcher's voice.

He would have found it amusing, too, if he didn't know better.

As he listened to the field report their positions, the dispatcher working through their locations, he had no doubt in his mind that the four mature females were named Rian, Amy, Genna, and Zelda. There was no doubt they had sprung Amy from the hospital and went looking for trouble. *Again.*

Crawley was driving the tractor in pursuit, and he did not doubt that, either. Crawley had gone over the edge, and he felt he had something to do with that. He had seen the madness in the man's eyes when he mentioned Zack Carlisle. There was a fine line between reality and insanity, and he had witnessed that line snap in two. Whatever disturbing rage had caused him to run over Zack Carlisle, that same rage was chasing four women with the same murderous intent.

Amy must have come to the same conclusion and led her friends right to his doorstep. Hadn't he led her to the discovery by showing her the photos? There wasn't anything more he needed to hear from the radio.

Wheeling his car out of the parking lot, his tires squealed against the pavement.

CHAPTER THIRTY-TWO

Amy twisted around in the back seat so she could look out the rear window.

When Crawley reached the highway, he drove the tractor right up onto the highway lane. Now he was driving as any traveler might, only at caterpillar speed. The tractor was several hundred yards behind them. Stacking up behind the bright green tractor, a line of cars was stymied by the no-passing, double yellow line down the middle, with no room to pass even if they dared.

Crawley's back was straight as a board, his hands tight on the wheel, dark eyes focused on the road ahead. To the other cars, he would appear to be a farmer headed to the field on his tractor, nothing more than an annoying inconvenience taking up space. She knew better. She doubted he even saw the road ahead of him. He probably didn't even hear the cars honking behind him. She couldn't imagine that he heard anything but the thoughts in his head.

Their car sped on and the tractor fell farther in their past.

"You won't believe what happened to us," Rian said to Ben on the phone. "We'll be at Cooley's Bar when you get around to us. We're leaving the bar tab for you."

The five of them were sitting at a table near the bar, cold beers in front of them. The courageous woman who picked them up was rapt as she listened to their story. The conversation bounced from one to the other while they scrambled to share their part in the mystery, punctuating their stories with laughter, squeals, and giggles as they eagerly told their tale. It felt like familiar times around the domino table on Genna's back deck, only they were many miles away from home.

Excited to be part of such drama, the woman was as engaged as if she were watching her favorite soap opera live on stage. Her name was Candy, and not coincidently, she owned a fudge shop with her mother, who made the "best chocolate and praline fudge this side of Georgia, USA." These were the only facts she managed to get in edgewise. By the time they drank a pitcher of beer, they had shared all the details of the last few weeks, minus Rian's private matters, all the way up until Candy rolled down her window, rescuing four women standing in the road.

There was finally a brief lull as they sipped their beers and, eyeing Amy's clothes, Candy said, "So that's why you're dressed that way?"

Amy beamed at her. Their heroine! And they were her heroines, too. They would be the topic of her story to tell for quite some time to come, all the way down to the bunny slippers with its flopping ears and the cardigan and shell with a rabbit's paw in a permanent high-five. Women rescuing women was irresistible news for the gossip mill, and no one had a story dressed like this.

"Do you think I should hold a grudge?" Amy asked.

Candy smiled and shook her head. "I've seen much worse at Walmart. Besides, you gals are rock-solid."

Rock-solid. She liked the way that sounded. Friends that were so loyal they would go to the ends of the earth for each other. Friends who were willing to chase down killers, chase down facts and fibbery, chase down anything that needed chasing down in the dusty back-woods of Arkansas. Despite the rigors of what they had just endured and the bruises that were starting to pop up, she felt safe inside the bar. Even if Crawley could make it that far on his tractor, he would be no match for this crowd. Unless he came in shooting.

Would he barge into the bar shooting?

No reason to go there. The four of them might be strangers to this part of Arkansas, but they were the topic *du jour* in the bar, and there was no way Crawley could enter without resistance, shotgun or not.

Amy looked up when she heard the sirens. Jumping up from the table, she limped outside, her legs stiff. The others followed. Zelda, Candy, and Rian were side by side. Genna had lost one of her Dior mules in the poison ivy and had its mate stuffed in the top of her bag. Now bringing up the rear, limping over and scowling at the sharp rocks under her tender bare feet, she joined them just as two patrol cars blasted past them on the highway. Not far down the road, the sirens stopped with a final whimpering whoop, like a bagpipe giving up its last bit of air.

"He got pretty far on that Deere," Rian said.

"Too far," Zelda said.

"What happens now?" Amy asked.

"Crazy sucker's going straight to jail."

"Genna, it's a tractor, not an 18-wheeler," Rian said.

"What?"

"You said, 'crazy trucker's going straight to hell.'"

"Rian, you need a hearing aid."

"You need to stop mumbling."

"I need another beer," Zelda said. "Y'all make so much noise, I can't think."

"*Nach a Mool!*" Amy pulled Zelda close. "I sure have missed you, my friend."

CHAPTER THIRTY-THREE

Watching as he was walked to the squad car with his hands cuffed behind him, Amy realized that the angry scowl was gone. Now his body sagged with misery and resignation, head hanging forward from his shoulders, heavy jowls slack.

Even though he had been the reason she crashed the Hummer, broke her wrist, and suffered the stink in the woods, she felt sorry for Crawley. She felt sorry for the way his life had turned out. Everyone had obstacles to face, with some bigger than others. Some were full of sorrow. Crawley's had been a lot of both. It was written in the lines of his face.

Forgiveness? Sure, she could forgive him all that. The Hummer was insured, her body would heal, and the stink was a fading memory.

But she couldn't forgive him for killing Zack. Whether it had been premeditated rage or an accident with a tragic twist, they might never know. She wasn't sure it mattered.

Zack was gone.

She glanced at Zelda out of the corner of her eye. How did Zelda feel about Zack's death? She didn't know, and she wasn't ready to ask. On the outside, Zelda appeared so composed it was unnerving. Appearances weren't everything, or maybe they *were* everything. Maybe putting on a calm front was the only way Zelda could face the past. Maybe it was the only way she could face her future. Under the calm, coiffed façade that Zelda showed to the world, there might be a fiery fissure channeling all those emotions buried under the surface.

Like the lava flows under the Hawaiian sea, with its molten magma hidden from view. Except for a plume of smoke escaping now and again, you would never know the lava was there. Maybe Zelda didn't know what was under the surface, either—wouldn't know until it erupted.

She vowed to be there for Zelda when that happened. If it happened. She vowed to be a death-do-us-part kind of friend.

Zack's death seemed so long ago now. Only a few weeks had passed, and yet the memory of the man was already fading.

Even so, Zelda had loved him, once.

Had he loved her? Or had he used her? They would never know that, either.

Glancing around the table at Genna and Rian, she vowed to be a loyal friend to them in the same way. Their friendship had been stretched to its boundaries, but instead of ruining their closeness, they had strengthened their bonds. Even though each of them had suspected the other in being part of a horrible crime, they had stayed true to those bonds. By trying to cover up whatever they thought they had to, they had put their safety on the line.

Loyal. Courageous. Sweet. Stupid. Stupid, but sweet. They had experienced all of that, and their friendship had endured, persisted, and prevailed. Now the tough part was over, and the best was yet to come. She hoped that was true.

The ride to Hot Springs was a quiet one. No one seemed eager to replace the silence, even Ben. As Rian shared the details with him of their encounter with Crawley, she realized they were all tired of telling the story, as if the wind in the sails had sagged, a lot like Crawley's care-worn face.

The four of them had refused medical care after the Mercedes collision, and Ben had dropped them off at a coffee shop across from the Hot Springs police station, which was where they were waiting now. The café's large window front looked out onto the bustling downtown street.

Absently, Amy listened as Genna grumbled about the absence of a Bloody Mary on the menu. The barista was losing her perky demeanor until Rian pulled a flask from her backpack and covertly poured a thimble of bourbon into each of their coffees.

"Shut up and drink," she demanded, and they consented while the barista pretended not to notice.

They waited and they watched. They waited. And they watched.

Admittedly, she didn't know what they were waiting for, except they were out of cars to take them home. The Hummer was a torched-out shell in the police compound, and Genna's Mercedes was getting towed to a body shop in town. They needed Ben's help to get home.

She needed Ben's help to set her mind at ease. What *had* happened in the parking garage at the Bennfield Hotel? Why *had* John Jacob Crawley run Zack down?

She had come so far to uncover the truth, and hadn't she succeeded? Hadn't she done everything she set out to do when she took off in the Hummer and drove south?

It wasn't enough.

Why niggled her, nudged her imagination, nagged at her curiosity. She had to know.

Curiosity killed the cat.

Cats have nine lives.

They waited and drank their coffee.

She looked up when Ben appeared in the window across the street, exiting the police station and skirting the traffic before crossing the street to the café.

Joining them at the table, he said, "What a sad story." He nodded as Rian handed him her cup of coffee, then smiled at the fumes. "There are no rules you women won't break, are there?"

"Tell us what we don't know," Genna urged. "We don't make the rules. We just break them."

"So I've come to know," he said with a smile.

"So what can you tell us?" Rian asked, taking her cup from his outstretched hands.

"I can tell you that Crawley lost his wife to cancer, and a few months later, he lost his dog."

"I knew that!" Amy exclaimed.

Ben held up his hand for silence. He slipped a tape recorder out of his pocket and grinned.

"Is that what I think it is?" Rian asked.

"And you're harassing us about rules?" Genna added.

Ben glanced at Zelda, his face full of compassion. "Are you sure you want to hear this? It's pretty raw."

She nodded, and Amy grabbed Zelda's hand as Ben pushed play.

A thin, weak voice came across the recorder then, sounding as if it were the last lonely sound left in the world. She felt Zelda shiver.

"It was that cell tower that killed her," the voice intoned. "All those invisible rays shooting cancer at her every day. Like a beacon of death, 'cept I didn't know all that at first. Saw a flyer at the bar on the corkboard. It was all about those death ray beams.

"It was my fault. I'm the one who got greedy. I wanted more money than I could make in an honest day of work. I wanted to buy my Penny a new washing machine and maybe something pretty for her to wear to church. She was so beautiful, my Penny. The most beautiful girl I ever saw.

"My greed. And then that devil came with his flashy smile and fancy car and cash in his pocket. The devil knows what you want. The devil knows what you're willing to give to get it. I took his money. I cashed his check every month. I did, and I watched my Penny get sick. The doctors said it was brain cancer. They said there was nothing that could be done but make her comfortable until the end. They didn't see the end. They didn't understand what happened to my Penny.

"Rascal died three months after Penny left this world. He was the best dog a man could ever have. Doc said he had cancer, too. I think he died of a broken heart. Guess it don't matter. I buried him under the tree Penny's daddy planted the day she was born. He gave us that land when we married."

There was a long silence on the tape, then, as if he had gotten lost in his tale, or lost in the past. Nothing but white noise rolled through the recorder. Amy shuddered, her hand still in Zelda's. The white noise was like a cold fog that seeped in under the door and into her bones. The same cold fog and feeling she had after a dream woke her from a sound sleep. One of *those* dreams. The kind that left her aching for more insight than they gave. The kind of dreams that ran through her mind like a clip from a movie snipped from the reel. Jagged pieces of imagery, like grainy movies from childhood, flashing past without rhyme or reason. Without a reason for what she was supposed to do once she saw them.

She wasn't clairvoyant. Not psychic. She didn't channel wisdom or speak to spirits. She didn't find things that were lost, nor could she move anything without touching it. She didn't stop bad things from happening to people she loved.

Tele*pathetic.*

Hadn't she learned from her mistakes?

Like when she joined Dial-A-Psychic on a dare from Genna. She had helped a caller find a lottery ticket that had won a little money. It was in the pocket of his jeans. But that had been a lucky guess, right? Not lucky enough. The Dial-A-Psychic company turned out to be phone-in fraud that shut down overnight, still owing her money.

Pathetic. Tele*pathetic*. She hadn't seen that coming.

But then . . .

But then the county had been looking for a lost child in the middle of an ice storm. The jagged dream that woke her then was of a dog barking and bell clock chiming three. Goosebumps had risen on her arms at the stroke of every hour, the same cold fog in her bones as she felt now.

Police had found the little boy curled up and sleeping with a stray dog at the base of the old church tower. She wasn't responsible for how they found him because she had told no one. And yet, how could she explain what she dreamed?

She couldn't.

She couldn't explain the pale image of Zack Carlisle and the screaming sirens.

And yet, that had come true, too.

She slipped her hand from Zelda's and touched the burn scar on her forehead.

Sparkplug was what the school bullies called her because her hair was frizzy. Making fun of the new girl in town. Making fun of her name. *Zzzt, zzzt.* Fingers forked into an imaginary electric socket.

She had hated them for that. Hated how it made her feel—like an outsider, not one of the cool kids, or the rich kids, or the pretty girls with straight blonde hair.

The accident happened on the Fourth of July. They were dancing around the campfire at summer camp, sparklers swinging in the warm night air. Girls were flirting with the boys and their summer camp appeal, the thought of kissing behind the boathouse making them silly with desire.

A stray spark landed in her hair, and in seconds her hair lit up like a halo, and she was spinning and screaming until a counselor tackled her to the ground. She could still taste the grit in her mouth. She could almost smell the stench of burnt hair and skin. She could hear the screams that were her own.

Sparkplug had new meaning.

Hadn't she dreamed that?

She touched the peridot necklace at her throat.

Everyone had obstacles in their life. No one escaped that. Some hurdles were higher than others, some deeper and more sorrowful, and some that could not be explained away. Luck, superstition, dreams, and wishes that seemed to come true—they all had their place in the unexplained. Those chapters in everyone's lives compelled belief in the unseen, the unknowable, the divine. Like the love of family and friends. Like faith in a higher power. Like the courage that comes when you need it most.

She had done her best. She had made a difference. She had found the missing piece to the puzzle and couldn't ask more of herself than that. Not today.

The voice on the tape recorder sighed heavily. A male voice in the background urged him on.

"I spent every dollar that devil gave me on doctors, on medicines, on preachers who swore they could heal. I spent ten months watching her die. Life ain't worth living when your girl's gone. I couldn't drink myself dead. I tried. I sure tried."

He fell silent again. The white noise on the tape whirred on.

"He was handing me the check like he always done, and I told him it was his fault—Zack Carlisle of Carlisle Industries. I told him it was his cell tower that killed Penny and my dog. I told him he needed to pay me more or get that tower off my land. He grabbed the check from my hands, ripped it up, and laughed. When he threw it on the ground, I scrambled after it like a hungry dog. He shouldn'ta done that. He was stooped over at the tower when I walked up right behind him. I shoved my shotgun in his back before he even knew I was there. I pushed it hard so he would know I meant business.

"It should have ended right there." He paused again and exhaled a rattling breath. "I couldn't shoot a man in the back. Coward wouldn't turn to face me. 'Get out of my way old man,' he said and laughed. 'I get what I want and you can't stop me. Shoot me or get out of my way.'

"When he left, I followed him. I rode his tail all the way to Hot Springs. I followed him to the liquor store, and the shopping mall, and then to that hotel. I don't even remember driving. I do remember watching the back of his neck. I wanted to choke the life from him like he choked the life from me and mine. He knew I was following him. He got out of that truck and flipped me the bird. Dirty bird. *Foul devil*," he said, his voice rising in anger. "That's the last thing I remember before I woke up in my bed. The empty bottle was still in my hand."

Again he paused. "He didn't stay dead long, did he? He rose from his grave like the devil that he was. He drove up in my yard, drove up to taunt me because he knew I couldn't get shed of him no matter what I did—haunting me like a *haint*.

"I followed him then, too. I followed him when he left the bar . . . up Highway 7. I kept my lights off, driving the road with his taillights leading the way. Then I blinded him with my brights at Blind Bat Pass. I hit him again and again, and then I watched that truck go down the hillside for good. It's done now . . . He's going to stay dead this time."

Ben stopped the tape, and the table stayed silent. All that flowed were tears.

CHAPTER THIRTY-FOUR

Victor was yowling when she reached the door to her apartment, key tumbling in the lock, then the fat, fluffy cat leaped into her arms when she opened the door. He nudged her cheek and purred, bit her gently on the chin, and then purred some more. Her penance for leaving him behind these last few days. She stroked his soft fur and rubbed noses while his purring grew louder.

His food and water bowls were dangerously close to empty, but he had not gone hungry or thirsty. Lonely, perhaps, his habit of lying in the sunshine at Tiddlywinks put on hold while his mistress saved the world.

She felt that way. As if a giant weight had been lifted from her shoulders. Like the famed Atlas and his burden of the weight of the world, she had carried more than she thought was possible. And yet, the weight had been of her own making, her punishment for what she thought her friends had done. She thought of Hercules, the demigod son of Zeus, and how he had conquered monsters to prove his worth.

Hadn't she, too, performed amazing feats and wrestled with monsters? She even felt like she had traveled to the underworld and back again.

Hercules was the hero in the mythological realm who proved that life is never perfect, that no one is free of flaws, that suffering falls on every life at one time or another. There was comfort in knowing all of that could be moved aside with one simple emotion.

Love.

Love was a powerful force. She was beginning to see that. Whether in friendship, marriage, family, or a cat, love could conquer anything. Emotions that looked like love could be duped, but the real thing—the real thing was powerful.

She hugged Victor tightly now, feeling that love, even as he squirmed in her arms. She had hugged Zelda, Genna, Rian, and Ben in turn, with the same feeling expanding in her heart as they parted ways. Ben had brought them back to Bluff Springs where they belonged, and the fact that she *did* belong never felt stronger than now. Nor had she ever felt so homesick as she had these past few days.

You don't know what you have until it's gone.

She wasn't any Cinderella, but she knew to thank her lucky stars. She had been foolish, and she had been lucky. And that's all there was to that.

The Cardboard Cottage & Company would reopen tomorrow. The doors to all of its shops would swing open for the first time in weeks. The smell of cinnamon and yeast would once again drift up the stairs to her apartment in the early morning, and all would be right with the world.

CHAPTER THIRTY-FIVE

Amy looked up as the man entered Tiddlywinks Players Club at the Cardboard Cottage & Company. She recognized him immediately. Apprehension rose in her mind.

"Hello," she said warmly even though her heart was racing. "Can I help you?"

He approached her timidly, glancing around the room, which was empty of customers at the moment.

"I came to give you these," he said quietly, his hand diving into his pants pocket to retrieve a fist full of a handkerchief.

He opened it slowly. Her eyes widened. "It was you!" she cried.

In the folds of the cotton handkerchief were the four Sulphide marbles that had been stolen from the locked case the night of the break-in. She looked at the marbles and then at the man. Her eyes were full of questions. He motioned for her to take them.

She looked at him and then again at what was in his hand.

The marbles, transparent except for their soft amber glow, were made in Germany in the 1800s. They were not as rare as the striped marbles made in China during those times, but they were more valuable than the vintage marbles made by machines in the US. These were collected because they had little figures embedded inside, mostly barnyard animals and household pets, each inserted by hand by the maker. They were treasured because of the way they made their way to America in the pockets of men looking to start a new life for their family, the German immigrants who flooded American soil long before World War I.

Embedded in this set were a wolf, a bird, a sheep, and a squirrel.

"Here, take them," he said. "I can't live with myself for stealing them."

"Why did you take them?"

His eyes were gray behind the wire-rimmed glasses balanced on his thin nose. "These have been in my family for generations," he answered after a long pause. "I used to play with them. My uncle Karl taught me how. He was the first of the brothers to come to America. These were his and they were always in his pocket."

He rubbed them lightly with his fingers.

"My sister sold them in an estate sale, along with everything else our family left to us." His tone suddenly turned bitter. "She had no right to do that."

"Why did you break in?" Amy asked.

"I didn't. Well, yes, I broke into the case, but the outside doors had already been destroyed. I saw him break the glass in the doors. I watched him from across the street. He tried to destroy your shop."

"What? You were watching? Why didn't you call the police?"

He hung his head, shaking it slowly. He glanced up once again, and she saw the regret in his eyes.

"I was wrong. It's as simple as that. I was trying to get up enough courage to ask you to sell them for less because I didn't have the price you were asking."

"And you saw who broke in?"

He nodded again. "A man. He was here that day, too. I saw him storm outside."

Zack Carlisle. She had known all along, hadn't she? She took a deep breath and exhaled.

They were both silent for a long moment, standing in the quiet of the shop with no customers, just a bright ray of sunshine making a path and pattern across the ancient wood plank floors.

"You keep them," she said finally. "They belong to you."

"But . . ."

She shook her head. "No buts. The insurance company has paid me their value, so I am out nothing. And they belong to you. Rightfully, they do."

"Thank you," he said, a smile stretching his thin lips. "Thank you," he said again. "This is unexpectedly generous."

She could tell he was near tears as he turned to leave.

"Hey," she called after him. "Did your nephew like his chemistry set?"

He turned and smiled at her, a crooked little smile on his face.

"I did," he said and was gone.

CHAPTER THIRTY-SIX

Amy reached for a nibble from the tapas plate. She'd made dates stuffed with goat cheese wrapped with maple bacon and had eaten half of them right out of the oven.

"Back to the boneyard!" she complained, her mouth full, her pile of tiles growing on the table in front of her. "Who has all the twos?"

"My lips are sealed," Genna said.

"That's a first," Rian countered.

"But probably the last," Zelda added. "A freight train couldn't stop Genna and her big words."

"Don't blame me because I'm smart."

"Smart, fart," Zelda said. "You and Noah Webster go way back."

"Speaking of getting old, where are we going on your birthday cruise?" Amy asked, wiping the corners of her mouth with a freshly manicured fingernail.

"So many choices!" Zelda exclaimed. "My dining room table is cluttered with travel brochures and cruise lines booklets. I have a dozen color-coded flags marking destinations and excursions that look like fun. What do you think? Should we sip champagne on the Seine or drink Ouzo on the Aegean between Athens and Istanbul?"

"We will go wherever you want to go," Rian replied. "It's your birthday cruise."

"It *is* my birthday cruise," Zelda said, the delight bright in her voice.

"The big five-oh," Amy said. "You're ancient history in the making. Maybe we should pilgrimage to some ancient ruin. You know—see if we can find your long-lost twin."

"Don't push your luck, Sparks. You're not but a wrinkle or two behind me, and I'm a much better liar."

"Fifteen!" Amy yelled, slapping the domino on the table.

"If you win again, I'm not playing anymore," Genna complained. "I think you cheat."

"You cheat," Rian added.

Genna defended herself with a smirk. "I don't believe you said that. I never cheat. Ever."

"Always," Zelda returned. "You always cheat, Genna."

Amy smiled at her friends, her best friends, her sisters of the hood. Some things never changed, and she didn't want them to. She wanted this little clutch of friends to go on forever, just as they were, bickering over nothing, defending blood against whatever they faced, whenever it mattered most.

If you want to belong, you have to believe you belong. If you want others to trust you, you have to trust them first. With your life. With all the vulnerable soft spots you hide from everyone else. No matter what happens, the game of life goes on. And wherever there was a game in play, there would be one winner and three sore losers.

"Cheaters," Genna said. "All of us. We're going to cheat old age if we die trying."

"To forty-nine and holding," Zelda said, raising her glass.

"To friendship at any age," Rian added.

Amy smiled and raised her glass. "To Zelda!"

"To us!" Zelda replied.

"To us!" they all agreed.

She tipped her glass and drank.

The Cardboard Cottage & Company was back and booming with customers after its makeover and a perfectly timed spread in *Belles & Bloom* magazine. Sammie was cranking out crumpets and cones as fast as she could bake. All the plants in the Pot Shed were in full bloom and fragrant, and Zsa Zsa Galore Décor was overflowing with fun junk and household treasures. Tiddlywinks Players Club was again stocked full of games, with the Lock, Stock, and Barrel escape room close to a grand opening.

And Bonaparte was a contender in the Kentucky Derby.

THE END

ACKNOWLEDGEMENTS

The list of encouraging souls who have helped make this dream come true would fill a good old-fashioned phone book. Those who have gone above and beyond the duty of friendship know who you are because you have listened to me crow ad nauseam about what I want to be when I grow up. I am grateful to Carolyn Keene whose Nancy Drew had me hunting for clues in the old clock tower, thus planting the seed in my imagination. I cherish the friendships that led to the creation of this book, the adventure in Zihuantanejo that launched it all, and the undying embers of passion that kept me puffing along in a dream that felt too big to reach. Thank you to the Writers' Colony at Dairy Hollow in enchanted Eureka Springs, Arkansas, for giving me the space to be the writer I wanted to become and the opportunity to connect with others who truly appreciate the craft of wordsmithing. Thank you to the members of the Very Important Players Club for your trust in me. And finally, on the cusp of this new chapter of life, I must appreciate cozy author Tricia Sanders for being a sideline cheerleader and walking encyclopedia of all things cozy, my editor Cayce Berryman for being real, and Bailey McGinn, whose graphic design prowess turned an idea into art. I am endeared to you all.

ABOUT THE AUTHOR

Jane Elzey is a mischief-maker, story-teller, and bender of the facts. A career journalist, she now writes modern-day, not-so-cozy mysteries without much regard for the truth. Born and raised a wild child on Florida's sandy beaches, Jane now lives in the Ozark Mountains of Arkansas, happily trading sand spurs for sharp rocks underfoot and concrete for trees overhead. An insatiable world traveler, Jane turns her bucket list travels into backdrop settings for her books, sharing destinations with armchair readers on the hunt for whodunnit.

Jane Elzey writes about four mature women who love to play games ... while the husbands die trying. The husband always dies. To connect with the author or to join the Very Important Players Club, visit JaneElzey.com.